Monster
in the Dark

by

Loretta C. Rogers

A Doc Holliday Mystery, Book 4

Monster in the Dark

Cover Art by *Diana Carlile*

The Wild Rose Press, Inc.
PO Box 708
Adams Basin, NY 14410-0708
Visit us at www.thewildrosepress.com

Publishing History
First Edition, 2023
Trade Paperback ISBN 978-1-5092-5047-9
Digital ISBN 978-1-5092-5048-6

A Doc Holliday Mystery, Book 4
Published in the United States of America

At first, I thought it was a mannequin. You know, like the ones used in store windows. There was no blood. She was sitting in a chair with her back toward us. The room reminded me of a scene from a horror movie.

Dad said, "Mrs. Gardner?"

I thought about the time I'd been on the movie set of *Lights...Camera...Murder* where the stunt man was killed, but in this act, there were no supporting actors. In the distance, a dog barked, and there was no movie director to call, "Cut!"

I swallowed the bile rising in my throat. The beats of my heart echoed inside my ears. I eased around the table. Oh, God! She was real. She was once...like flesh and blood and bone...just...oh, God! The woman I had thought was a mannequin was a corpse.

It was only the extreme brutality of her death that made her appear as if she were not, as if she was some creation of the most brilliant and lurid mind working in a Hollywood special effects studio.

A heavyset woman, clad in an old-fashioned granny dress, her wrists and ankles wrapped with silver duct tape, securely bound to the chair's arms and legs, and with a double strip of tape that sealed her mouth shut, stared vacant-eyed at an empty soup bowl.

She appeared to be in her early sixties. Fleshy jowls, perfectly manicured fingernails painted ruby red, and a faint floral scent of perfume mingled with the putrid odor of rotting flesh.

Dad gasped against the offensive smell. "How long do you thinks she's been dead?"

Praise for *MONSTER IN THE DARK*

"A dark mystery that grabs you from the beginning and doesn't let go."

~D. Royalty

~*~

"An ingenious plot and a sufficient flow of suspense and occasional terror to keep the reader engrossed."

~Lynn Fuller

**Look for these titles also by Loretta C. Rogers
at The Wild Rose Press**

Contemporary Romance
Forbidden Son
Christmas at Hope Ranch

Historical Romance
Bannon's Brides
The Witching Moon
Lady Adel's Captain
Cloud Woman's Spirit
Taming the Lyon
When Comes Forever
A Little Kringle Magic (novella)
Isabelle and the Outlaw (novella)
McKenna's Woman (novella)
Fate Comes Softly (Anthology)

Mystery and Suspense
Murder in the Mist
Shadowed Reunion
Fatal Passion (Book #1-Doc Holliday Mystery Series)
The Boneyard (Book #2)
Lights…Camera…Murder! (Book #3)

Audio Books
Murder in the Mist
Shadowed Reunion
Isabelle and the Outlaw
Taming the Lyon
McKenna's Woman

Ladybird, ladybird,
Fly away home,
Your house is on fire
And your children all gone;
All except one
And that's little Ann,
And she has crept under
The warming pan.

A Mother Goose rhyme (1744)

~Author Unknown

Prologue

She clapped her hands over her ears to shut out the voices. Ritual, they told her, was important. This was her first kill. Three, they said, was the magic number. Use a jigsaw, they said. Her hand trembled as she made the first cut. Blood splattered. She wiped the plastic face shield as best she could and kept at it. There was no stopping now.

She was sick of being told what to do. Sick of other people's expectations of her. Sick of the punishment. She mopped up the blood, leaving the room spotless. There was one little spot of red, on the cuff, that she had trouble getting out. Fearful of being punished, she worried at the spot for a moment.

The voices scolded her. *You're late; you're late, for a very important date!*

She hissed, "Stop pestering me."

She finished dressing the corpse. And wouldn't all those people dressed in their Halloween costumes be surprised.

Her laughter was loud and brittle. "Because mine are the best costumes of all!"

Chapter One

Mornings are normally my favorite time of day. There is a magic in the first moments of wakefulness, but not this morning.

The cold wet nose of River, my black Lab, nudged me from a restless sleep. I awoke groggy and filled with a sense of dread. Although the morning's pale yellow light spilled through the window and across the foot of my bed, filling the room with an ethereal presence, I sensed something terrible was going to happen. I know this because when I awoke the metallic odor of blood assaulted my nostrils. I glanced around the room, trying to orient myself, and I let out a long, silent breath. Sliding out of bed and stumbling to the bathroom, I eyed myself in the mirror. The image that stared back at me wasn't mine. Instead, she had short hair the color of snow—a contrast to my long, dark black tresses—and she wore a mask. Her eyes were clear blue, direct, and filled with malice.

I leaned closer. "Who are you? What do you want?"

The image faded. I glanced around and even pinched myself to make sure I was truly awake and not locked inside a weird dream. Was this a warning? When something out of the ordinary is about to happen, I'm usually contacted by a spirit animal. Never has a human essence communicated with me. An eeriness chilled my insides.

But I'm getting ahead of myself. Perhaps I'd better explain.

My name is Tullah Crow Holliday. Most everyone calls me Doc Holliday. I am a veterinarian and on occasion assist the sheriff with complicated cases. By the way, the sheriff is my father, John Henry Holliday, and before you ask, yes, our ancestor is the infamous outlaw better known as Doc Holliday.

If you're wondering why I, an animal doctor, assist my dad, it's because I was born with a special gift. It's not really a gift but rather a curse, a nuisance, that quite often interferes with my life. I sense and feel and sometimes see things that are not perceptible to other people.

I also have a special connection with spirit animals. My mother and my grandmother were born in the *A-ni-wa-ya* (Wolf) clan. Tanti says it is because of my Cherokee heritage that I have these special abilities.

My hometown of Enigma, Kentucky was a dying town until my grandmother, Mayor Tanti Crow, and her best friend, Vice Mayor Patty Sweet, persuaded a soft drink company to build their newest bottling plant in Enigma.

Sometimes growth of a rural town isn't good. Personally, I liked Enigma when it was a quaint community where everyone knew everyone else. Growth brings change, and most often that change includes not only more people but some unsavory ones and increased crime.

On this crisp October Friday evening, the town's people gathered to celebrate our annual Shocktober Fest. Revelers turned out to enjoy the Monster Mash costume barn dance. Tonight was the perfect setting to kick off the three days of Halloween festivities. There was a chill in the air, a brisk breeze, and a full moon.

This evening, the main barn at the 4-H fairgrounds was decorated with pumpkins, scarecrows, and massive cottony spider webs. The sounds of rattling chains and eerie moans and cackles were piped through a sound system. A large black syrup pot, containing dry ice that sent steam into the air, served as a witch's caldron. People sat on bales of hay enjoying a variety of homemade goodies. Others milled about or stood in small clusters waiting for the band to begin playing.

I made my way to the refreshment table and helped myself to tiny marzipan witches and pumpkins, white chocolate ghosts, and a cup of hot apple cider. As much as I wanted to leave, it would have been impolite, and though Grandmother rarely gets angry with me, it would have hurt her feelings if I left. She and Patty and the garden club ladies had gone all out this year to create a plethora of spooktacular fun.

The costumes ran the gamut from mundane to creative. The most prevalent, of course, were black-clad witches wearing pointy hats. Normally, I'd rather eat sawdust than dress up, especially in costume. To appease my grandmother, I had dressed as a jockey, wearing red, white, and blue silks; after all, we do live in the great state known for horse racing.

My gaze lingered on the crowd. Patty Sweet was dressed as a giant donut complete with pink frosting and multi-colored sprinkles. Maybe that's because she owns Sweet's 'n' Eats, the town's café and pastry shop. Grandmother and our favorite curmudgeon, Dr. Paul Ritter, were dressed as Alice in Wonderland and Prince Charming. Even my ever-so-serious father had finally relented and dressed as his famous ancestor, John Henry "Doc" Holliday, complete with a fake handlebar mustache and dual pearl-handled pistols.

An eerie feeling had again crept over me. I shifted to my right, where a tall figure dressed as the Grim Reaper, complete with a scythe, stood gazing at the crowd, face obscured by his black hood. Although he was a considerable distance from me, I could tell he was looking for someone, and suddenly he threw back his hood and grinned at one of the several people approaching him. He didn't seem to be a threat. Farther away, almost behind the arrangement of cornstalks and pumpkins by the door, my gaze caught on a smaller figure in costume as Little Red Riding Hood. I couldn't see her face, again because of the hood, but I knew I hadn't seen her earlier. She must have just come in, and from the stiff stance and fisted gloves she appeared angry.

"What bothers you, Little Sister? You have a troubled look in your eyes."

I had been so lost in thought the voice startled me and I let out a little squeak but smiled up at my godfather, Charlie Whitehorse—who, by the way, was dressed as Paul Bunyan, which was quite appropriate since Charlie is a giant of a man. "I'm not sure, Uncle Charlie."

His eyes narrowed. "Did you have one of your *special* feelings?"

I worked to rein in my emotions. "Maybe. I'm not sure."

He wrapped my hand in his. "The band is playing a slow song. How 'bout a turn around the floor with an old man? A little fun will take your mind off what ails you."

I forgot about the apparition in my mirror that

morning and laughed. I placed my hand in his giant paw and allowed him to lead me onto the dance floor. Charlie is a graceful dancer and never complains when I step on his toes. Midway through the waltz, icy chills slithered over my body, and I shivered.

"There is a definite chill in the air. Are you cold?"

The sun had set and the air had definitely grown downright cold. By morning there would be frost on the ground. I craned my neck to look into Charlie's ebony eyes and shook my head. "Not really."

He pulled back, holding me at arm's length. "Little Sister, you cannot fool me. Might as well 'fess up."

I lowered my voice. "If you insist. When I awoke this morning, I smelled blood."

His smile puddled into a frown. "That is a bad omen, Little Sister. What do you think it means?"

He twirled me around the floor. I stopped and stood still. Listening.

"Tullah?"

"Do you hear it, Uncle Charlie?"

He cocked his head sideways. "Hear what?"

"Horse's hooves. The horse is frightened. He's running."

Charlie made light of my unease. "Aho, probably some rancher's thoroughbred jumped a fence and decided to join the party."

I didn't want to seem dramatic and decided not to say anything more. Still, I couldn't help the dread that filled me.

In the middle of our dance, a gust of cold wind blew through the wide-open barn doors. A rider, his black cape flapping in the breeze, raced in from the darkness astride a Thoroughbred black stallion. The horse whinnied and reared. It reared again and again. The rider on its back listed sideways, unable to control the frightened animal.

The band stopped playing. People scattered to avoid the frantic horse's dangerous hooves. Parents gathered their screaming children and sought safety.

I raced forward and held out my hand, speaking to the frightened horse in the language of my mother's ancestors The stallion tossed its magnificent head and pawed the floor. I could almost see my reflection in the large brown eyes. I inched forward and continued to speak until I got close enough to grab the dangling reins.

Someone from the crowd shouted, "Look, it's the headless horseman! He definitely wins the contest for most authentic costume."

Nervous laughter filtered around the room. One of the band members blew his bugle. The blast caused the mighty horse to rear again, lifting me off my feet. I grabbed the bridle's cheek straps and held on.

Uncle Charlie rushed to my aid. The frightened animal fought against the restraint, and then the unspeakable happened. The rider tumbled from the saddle and crashed to the floor.

Folks twittered and pointed, like a joke had just happened. I've always wondered why people laugh when they witness someone getting hurt. By this time, Dad was at my side. My stomach roiled. Don't get me wrong—as veterinarian, I'm used to seeing blood and guts and gore, though it's not exactly an image I want rattling around inside my brain. This, however, was an exception. Just like when I awoke this morning, the metallic odor of blood fouled my nose.

Feeling disoriented, I drew in a deep breath. "Dad,

someone has chopped off his head." The extreme brutality of the victim's death, combined with the costume, made it appear as if the killer had carefully and perhaps deliberately created an appalling sensation.

Dad grimaced as he leaned in for a closer look. "Who is the victim supposed to be?"

"Brom Bones Van Brunt, a character from the fairy tale 'The Legend of Sleepy Hollow.' " I noticed the only thing missing from the costume was a carved jack-o-lantern.

A note was pinned to the dead person's jacket. I say "person" because at this point we weren't sure if the corpse was a man or a woman.

I reached for the piece of paper. Dad stopped me.

Dressed as Johnny Appleseed, Deputy Tiny Goodbody knelt beside us. "Figured you could use these." He pulled a pair of evidence gloves from the pocket of his breeches and handed them over.

Dad thanked him. "Tiny, clear the room. I'm afraid the party's over."

Uncle Charlie led the quivering horse outside. I stood to follow, but Dad said, "Tullah, I need you here." Only under dire or professional circumstances does Dad use my given name. This situation was about as dire as it gets.

I nodded and remained next to the body. There was something about this scenario that didn't sit right with me.

Dad unpinned the note and read aloud, "I am death, and I make all people equal." Furrows lined his forehead when he said, "It's signed 'Godfather of Death.' "

I exhaled deeply. "That's a quote from the Brothers Grimm fairy tales."

"You're frowning. What's bothering you, Tullah?"

"Nothing."

"That's not your *nothing* face."

"Okay, two things." I pointed. "Except for that small speck on the cuff, there's no blood."

"Yeah, and what's number two?"

Dad's expression flattened when I looked at him and said, "Where's the head?"

He stared at me for a moment, his blue eyes growing dark and tension suddenly lining his face. "Tullah, I'm going to need you on this one. It appears we have a real sicko running loose."

Dr. Ritter's voice drew my attention to where he stood with my grandmother. "Come, Tanti, we're not needed here."

She cajoled, "But Paul, I want to see. How bad can it be?"

I rushed forward and helped the aged doctor gently steer my grandmother toward the barn's gaping doors. "Believe me, Grandmother, it's worse than horrible. Some fiend cut off the victim's head."

The color drained from her cheeks. Her knees wobbled. I said, "C'mon, Grandmother, you and Dr. Ritter must be tired from all that dancing. Would you like me to drive you home?"

She placed her hand on my arm and gave me an endearing smile. "It's a short distance. We can make it."

I leaned down and kissed her cheek. Trouble filled her eyes when she looked at my dad and said, "Henry, should we cancel the other festivities? I don't mean to sound insensitive, but we'd have to refund money for the haunted graveyard tour. It involves a lot of bookkeeping."

He offered an empathetic smile. "There's no need to spoil everyone's fun. This is probably an isolated incident. My guess is we have a looney who wants to see his name in headlines and decided to capitalize on Halloween."

I knew by the way his jaw worked that Dad was really trying to set Grandmother's mind at ease. He escorted her and Dr. Ritter outside and waited until she turned on the car's headlights and headed toward town.

I stood next to him in the yard. "Dad, I'm going to check the stallion for tattoos and anything else that might be an important clue." Often breeders tattooed registration numbers inside a horse's lip or inside the ear. If such a number was found, it would lead us to the Thoroughbred's owner, and hopefully to the killer.

Dad's brow scrunched into a deeper frown. "What's that on your hands?"

In all the excitement I hadn't noticed that my hands were coated with a waxy black substance. I lifted the palms to my nose and sniffed. "It smells like boot polish."

I followed his gaze as Dad glanced at my black jockey boots. I knew what he was thinking and said, "Not from my boots. They're new."

"Then where?"

I lifted a palm and sniffed again. "I detect a faint odor of horse sweat."

"What you're implying is that whoever committed this heinous crime smeared boot black all over the horse?"

"It appears that way."

"Why?"

I felt a headache beginning to form and heaved a

deep sigh. "My best guess is it has to do with the reason the corpse was dressed like a fairytale character."

Chapter Two

Almost shoulder-to-shoulder, Charlie and Tiny marched toward us. Addressing no one in particular, Charlie said, "I've stabled the stallion in Barn B, the first stall, and unsaddled him. And here's the strange thing. When I removed the saddle blanket, the horse wasn't black, it was gray."

I lifted my blackened palms and held them forward. "I guess that explains these."

My vet tech, Ella Sanders, had scrounged a tablecloth for Dad to cover the corpse. She quickly averted her eyes. Pushing himself to stand, he offered a weak smile. "Thanks, Ella."

Her voice trembled when she said, "I feel just terrible because, like everyone else, I thought it was a joke, and I laughed." She swiped a tear that dribbled down her cheek.

Dad placed an arm around her shoulders and gave her a gentle hug. "Don't beat yourself up, Ella. You're only human."

My heart melted a little. Dad is a tough lawman and capable of taking down dangerous criminals, but he also has a tender heart.

"Oh, my gosh!"

"What's the matter, Tullah?" Dad released Ella.

I drew a deep breath, closed my eyes, then opened them. I looked away from where the victim's black riding boots protruded from beneath the orange tablecloth. "I had a horrible thought. What if he, or maybe she, is someone we know?"

Ella shivered and verbally expressed the chill I suddenly felt.

A siren sounded in the distance. Dad's mouth formed a grim line. "I guess that means Bubba and Rita are on their way."

Bubba Dawson and Rita Graham are Enigma's resident EMTs. For years, two emergency medical techs were all we needed. Unfortunately, as the town grows, Bubba and Rita have more business than they can handle.

Tiny said, "The saddle and blanket are in the trunk of my patrol car. I'll brush them for prints as soon as I get back to the office."

Dad nodded at his deputy. "Find anything outside, Tiny?"

"Nope. Even with a full moon it's too dark. I'll give the grounds a thorough going-over once it breaks dawn."

"Do you mind if I tag along, Tiny? I'll bring coffee."

The burly deputy winked at me. "I'll bring donuts. Meet me here around six-thirty. Another pair of eyes is always welcome, Tullah."

A thought occurred to me about the horse. "Uncle Charlie, other than the black paint, were there any identifiable markings on the stallion?"

He cocked a busy eyebrow. "Tell you the truth, goddaughter, I didn't think to look."

Bubba and Rita entered with a gurney. Bubba glanced at the blanket-covered corpse. "Heart attack?"

Before I could blurt out a warning, Rita squatted and pulled back the tablecloth. "Holy mother of…" She made the sign of the cross. "Guys, if this is some kind of sick Halloween joke, I'm not laughing."

Bubba expelled an anguished rush of breath. "What kind of crazed monster did that?"

A worried look furrowed Dad's brow. "A person with no soul."

Ella glanced toward the open barn doors. "Bubba, where's my mom?"

The spare tire around his waist attested to his love of Patty Sweet's donuts, and he huffed to stand. Before he could answer, Dr. Sunny Sanders entered, chief surgeon at the hospital and Enigma's medical examiner, as well as a no-nonsense woman with an easy smile. Ella ran to her mother. "Mom, it's absolutely horrible. You'd better brace yourself."

Dr. Sanders nodded a greeting toward my dad. I didn't miss the subtle blush on her cheeks when he smiled. I might be prejudiced because he's my father, but he is ruggedly handsome. She said, "That bad?"

Dad's smile shifted to a frown. "Like Ella said, you'd better brace yourself."

Dr. Sanders squatted next to the corpse and opened her medical bag to pull out a pair of rubber gloves. She snapped them on her hands with practiced ease. It felt like everyone in the barn was holding their breath until she slowly pulled back the tablecloth.

For a second, she said nothing. She looked up at me, then at my dad, her face a mixture of puzzlement and revulsion. When she tried to speak, she had to clear the rasp from her voice. "There's no head."

Dad snatched the fake mustache from his top lip as if it were an annoyance. "Yep! Whatever your exam can tell us will help us with the identity."

Dr. Sunny Sanders looked at me. "Tullah, did you

examine the body?"

I squatted next to her. "Briefly. In my opinion, an autopsy might be difficult."

She cocked an eyebrow. "Oh, and why is that?"

I pointed to the headless shoulders. "There's no blood. It appears the body has been embalmed."

Dr. Sanders and Dad spoke in unison as they nearly shouted, "Embalmed?"

"Of course, that's just my opinion."

Dr. Sanders knelt closer to the cadaver. She traced a gloved finger around the decapitated neck. "I believe you're right, Tullah. The ghoul that did this knows their stuff."

Dad asked, "What do you mean?"

She pointed to the exposed area above the clavicle. "The head wasn't hacked off. It was removed with the precision of a skilled surgeon."

Dad simply shook his head. "There's only one funeral home in Enigma. Once embalming has been officially confirmed, that'll make finding our killer easier. I've known Arnold Lewis and his grandson my entire life. They'll cooperate."

"Dad, surely you don't suspect old Mr. Lewis or Arnie of doing this?"

"I guess that came out wrong. What I meant is that hopefully they can give us some insight to who might have the skill and equipment to perform this type of crime."

Like Dad, I'd known the Lewises my entire life. I couldn't fathom either of them committing such an atrocity, especially the meek and mild grandson.

Dr. Sanders huffed a breath. "With or without the head, we can still identify the victim, although it'll be more difficult to set the time of death." She replaced the tablecloth and motioned for Bubba. "I'm finished here."

Bubba helped Rita roll the body onto the gurney. They lifted the conveyance into the ambulance. Bubba said, "We'll unload our John Doe at the morgue, Doc."

She closed her medical bag and stood. "My assistant will complete the necessary paperwork. I'm off duty until morning. Ella needs me."

Dad asked, "Sunny, can you pull fingerprints from an embalmed body?"

She removed her gloves and stuffed them inside a plastic bag. "Yes, unless the skin is completely macerated—soaked—or burnt to ash, or rotten to the point of liquification, fingerprints can still be obtained."

It wasn't my intention to rain on Dad and Dr. Sanders's parade when I said, "What if he wasn't killed in Enigma, and what if he wasn't embalmed by the Lewises?"

Dad and Dr. Sanders cast frowns toward me. He was unable to keep the annoyance out of his voice. "Leave it to my daughter to throw a wrench into what could have been an easy crime to solve."

"Sorry, Dad. I'll take that as my cue to go check the horse for clues."

Uncle Charlie stepped forward and linked his arm through mine. "Gittin' a little stuffy in here. I think I'll go with you."

Uncle Charlie isn't blood kin, but he and my dad have been blood brothers since they were children. They went to college together, served in the war together, and he would give his life for all those he loved. And years ago, he confessed that his father was Apache and his mother Inuit.

16

Charlie owns and operates the Whitehorse Saloon. He is an auxiliary deputy as well as chief of Enigma's volunteer fire department. As you can see, he wears many hats.

Once we were outside, I said, "Charlie, do you think there's something going on between my dad and Dr. Sanders?"

He answered with a grunt.

"You are an exasperating man, Charlie Whitehorse. Does that mean…yes, or no…or mind your own business, or all of the above?"

He chuckled. "It's not for me to say."

His laughter increased when I released an annoyed growl.

We let the moonlight guide us toward Barn B. Light flooded the barn's interior when he flipped the light switch. "What the hell…?"

"What is it, Uncle Charlie?"

"He's gone. I left the stallion right there in the first stall."

We trotted over to the empty pen. Uncle Charlie opened the gate. "There's no manure, either. It looks as if no animal has ever been in this stall."

I glanced around the enclosure. It was clean. I didn't want to say that maybe in all the excitement he'd put the horse in a different stall. Then again, I knew Charlie Whitehorse didn't make mistakes like that. "Approximately how long ago did you stable the horse?"

"About twenty-five, maybe thirty minutes."

"Hmm, that's enough time—"

He cut me off. "I know that look. What're you thinking, Little Sister?"

Uncle Charlie immediately brightened when I said,

17

"Thirty minutes is enough time for the killer to move the horse to another barn. Maybe our killer isn't as smart as he or she thinks."

"Yeah, a horse that size would leave hoofprints."

"Exactly! C'mon."

We carefully scanned both sides of the barn's wide aisle as well as the middle lane until we stopped at the rear doors. There was a pervasive quiet in the barn, and my voice sounded extra loud when I spoke. "Nothing!"

"Yeah, nothing, and the doors are shut, which means the killer didn't use the back entrance to escape."

"Let's check outside the front entrance. Maybe our killer *is* smarter than we think. Maybe he took advantage of the fact that we were all so distracted by the murder and the missing head that we didn't notice him when he led the horse out the front doors right under our noses."

Charlie removed a flashlight from his back pocket. He switched off the barn's interior lights and turned on the flashlight. "I've always heard that the insane are cunningly smart. Stay close, Little Sister."

"Don't worry, Uncle Charlie. I have no desire to become a victim."

Using a back-and-forth motion, he scanned the ground with the light's broad beam.

About the middle of the barn, Charlie swung around and faced the way we had come. He said, "What do you see, Tullah?"

"Nothing."

"Exactly. Nothing."

"It doesn't make sense, Uncle Charlie. There have to be prints! Horses don't sprout wings and fly away."

"Only in fairy tales, Little Sister. Only in fairy tales."

"Charlie? Tullah?" Dad's voice called out.

"Over here, Dad."

"Where's the horse?"

Charlie said, "Disappeared. We've been searching for hoofprints, and found nothing."

A cold wind kicked up, sending shivers through the thin material of my silk jockey costume. Dad said, "Tiny has cordoned off the area with yellow tape. Only the three of us remain. Let's call it a night."

"I'm for that. You and Tullah meet me at the saloon. I'll heat up some chili."

I glanced down at my costume. I had no desire to be seen in the saloon dressed as a jockey with a red winner's sash draped across my breasts. "You know how much I love your chili, Uncle Charlie, but if you and Dad don't mind, I think I'll pass. It's late, and I have animals that need tending. Besides, it will be morning before you know it, and I did promise Tiny I'd meet him at dawn with coffee."

"Punkin?" Dad wore a concerned frown. "Pacify your ol' man and spend the night with me or your grandmother."

I kissed his cheek. "Always the worry-wart. I'll be fine, Dad." I lifted my hand in a Girl Scout salute.

"Call me when you get home."

I heaved a sigh. Sometimes my dad forgets I'm a grown woman rapidly approaching thirty. "Yes, sir."

Chapter Three

River and Rascal greeted me as soon as I parked under the carport. Rascal is my impish teacup donkey. He certainly lives up to his name. River was the runt of a litter of black Labs and the owner didn't want him. It was the owner's loss and my gain, because River grew to a whopping seventy pounds of loyalty. I showered a little love on both animals before sprinting across the yard to my clinic. I'm ever so grateful that Dad talked me into having a security light installed. With the night's event of a headless body and a panicked black stallion scaring the wits out of everyone, I have to admit the long shadows cast over the yard left me a little skittish.

I did a quick walk-through and checked on my overnight patients—a pit bull recovering from a snake bite, and a Shetland pony suffering from laminitis. I scratched the little pinto's ears. "Well, Mr. Greedy-Guts, no more breaking into the grain bin for you. Next time you might not be so lucky."

The Shetland merely raised baleful eyes and sneezed his reply. I checked in with my answering service to let them know my schedule for tomorrow.

After I had showered and dressed for bed, I discovered that the events of the evening had left my brain churning with questions, which left me wide awake. My stomach also reminded me that a handful of candy ghosts and a couple of sugar cookies had left me wishing I'd taken Uncle Charlie up on his offer for a bowl of chili. After I'd indulged myself with a peanut butter-and-banana sandwich and a large mug of hot chocolate topped with a healthy dollop of whipped cream, I grabbed my laptop and climbed the stairs to my bedroom.

As follows my usual pattern when assisting my dad with a crime, I chose to create a murder board. For the title, I typed *Monster in the Dark*. After all, anyone ghoulish enough to hack off a person's head had to be pretty morbid, and the event had happened at night. I also uploaded the pictures I'd taken of the victim's body. It's too bad I wasn't able to get photos of the horse, which might have offered a clue to the owner's identity.

Victim: dressed like Brom Bones from "The Legend of Sleepy Hollow."

Age: undetermined at this time.

Gender: presumably male.

Cause of death: presumably decapitation.

Question 1) Was the victim killed before the head was removed?

Question 2) What is the significance of dressing the body as a fairytale character?

Question 3) Is there a specific reason the killer chose to flamboyantly flaunt the body on the eve of Halloween Eve?

Question 4) Why was the body embalmed?

Question 5) What motivated the killer to commit such a heinous crime?

Question 6) How did the killer get a fourteen-hundred-pound horse out of the barn without being seen or leaving any prints?

Question 7) Suspects?

Old Mr. Lewis, the undertaker, was in his early eighties and should have retired years ago. Arnie came to live with his grandfather after Arnie's parents divorced. When his father, Arnold Junior, died in a freak accident, it seemed Arnie's mother was content to have her son out of her life. Poor Arnie, a boy who was bullied because he was too shy and reticent to stand up for himself. He's a few years older than I am and still has trouble with looking people in the eye and communicating with them.

Maybe that was the reason Mr. Lewis hadn't yet retired. There was no one he felt he could trust to carry on the Lewis Funeral Home. It's not to say that Arnie wasn't business minded. He was smart and knew all the ins and outs of the funeral business, right down to preparing a cadaver for embalming. A groan escaped my lips. The local gossips would have a field day conjuring up nonsense that would point fingers at poor introverted Arnie.

I logged out, closed my laptop, and set it on the nightstand. River woofed and laid his paw on the edge of the bed. "No, you're not getting on the bed. You and your buddy lie down and go to sleep."

A little voice in my head suggested I lock the bedroom door. I leaned up on my elbow and scolded myself: *You're being paranoid. Stop it!*

I snapped off the light. The dark was velvety soft. With the window cracked, I listened to the soft chirr of the crickets and the night frogs' throbbing croaks, soothing sounds. For most of my life I had slept just down the hall, next to my grandmother's room, while this room had belonged to my mother and father. After her senseless murder, he couldn't abide living in the house and moved to town, where he'd renovated the upper floor over the sheriff's office into an apartment. When Grandmother ran the newspaper, she preferred being within walking distance of her office, saying it was more feasible than a daily drive from the country.

Except for the years away at college and medical school, I had lived my entire life in this house. Perhaps because I was approaching thirty, or perhaps due to the different attempts on my life, meshed with tonight's murder, I saw my life hanging on the cusp of the present. An overwhelming fog of loss embraced me. I tried to shake free of the bonds of anxiety that held me in wakefulness.

Perhaps the anxiety I felt had to do with my special gift. I'm not sure if I've possessed this ability my entire life and it lay dormant until after my mother's death, or if she had blessed me with it upon her death. Either way, I consider my empathic abilities, and being greeted at the most inopportune times by spirit animals, an annoyance and sometimes downright scary.

A dread filled me when at last I felt the pull of sleep. Eyes closed, I slipped into a dream. Alone in a darkened forest, I turned in a circle trying to get my bearings. A cloud wafted slightly to reveal the ghostly outline of a shanty. I ran toward it, but tripped and fell. A vine with gnarled fingers had wrapped around my ankle. I fought to break free and was relieved when I reached the shack and cautiously opened the door.

"Hello?" Silence greeted me. I was alone in an unlit room, or so I thought. When my eyes adjusted to the darkness, a rough-hewn table was set with three bowls. A beautiful little girl with long blonde hair sat at the table, eating from one of the bowls. She stared back at me and smiled. I knew her. She was—

I wasn't certain what startled me out of my dream, but I was fully awake, tensed, and listening. River emitted a low, throaty growl. He padded to the bedroom door. Rascal followed. A board on the front porch creaked, followed by a *tap...tap...tap*. Someone was knocking on the front door.

Easing out of bed, I opened the side table drawer and removed my revolver. I cracked the bedroom door and peered down the shadowy staircase. The tapping sounded again. Listening closely, I moved with great care. My dog and donkey nearly bowled me over trying to get around me. I followed, alert to the soft tapping. At the door, River whined and wagged his tail. Maybe it was my dad, but that didn't explain his furtiveness unless he didn't want me to know he'd come to check on my safety.

The revolver gripped in one hand, I drew a long, slow breath through my nose, and flipped on the outside light. I unlocked the door and cautiously cracked it open. I didn't know if I was relieved or angry. My voice rose when I said, "Dad!"

The porch was empty.

River woofed and pawed the screen door. A black object fluttered backward. Rascal released one of his little sneezing brays. With the shock of being abruptly awakened from a weird dream, and the expectation of seeing my dad, it took a few seconds for the cobwebs to clear from my brain. I pointed a finger at my animals and commanded, "Stay!"

I opened the screen door and was greeted with a series of high-pitched rasps from a large white-necked raven. I practically shouted, "Oh, no, not again." Ravens, especially those with white capes, are not native to Kentucky.

As if a bird would know I was threatening it, I waved the revolver at the raven. "Shoo! Go away. Whatever warning you have, I don't want to hear it."

The black passerine bird hopped backward, stopped, then cocked its head and looked at me with its beguiling ebony eyes. "Look, bird, you're too late with your warning. A crime has already happened." I fluttered my hands in a shooing motion. "So unless you can tell me the name of the murderer, go away, and don't come back another day."

From my studies, I know ravens can mimic the calls of other birds, as well as the speech of humans. The raven flapped its wings and rasped, "Nevermore!"

River lunged forward. Like an ethereal presence, the raven skittered backward, lifted its wings, and soared off into the night with one last throaty *kraa*, "Nevermore!"

I whistled River back inside the house and latched the screen door, and as an extra precaution, I slid the front door's slide-bolt lock into place after closing that door firmly too. I rubbed away the goosebumps rippling up and down my arms. Stopping at the bookshelf, I fingered through the titles until I found an old college literature book before sprinting upstairs to the warmth of my bed. I turned to Edgar Allen Poe's *The Raven*. It had been years since I'd read the poem which, even then, I found sad and dreary.

The rapid beating of my heart slowed, and I was able to draw in a deep relieving breath. I wasn't afraid for myself, but I was afraid of what was about to come. Before I opened that can of worms, I needed to know why the raven had visited me. Vaguely remembering the poem, I had no idea how to connect the poem's message to the current crime or any crime that might follow.

Opening the book, I smiled at the scribbled notes I'd made regarding the poem during one of Professor Hadley's lengthy, boring lectures. Overwhelming grief consumed me as I read each line. Maybe it was because of age, maturity, and life experiences that I now understood the meaning of Poe's words, even without my old lecture notes written in the page margins.

Like the poem's unnamed narrator, I had lost a loved one and was still struggling with overwhelming grief.

I closed the book, set it on the nightstand, and turned out the light. What did Poe's poem have to do with a dead person dressed like a headless horseman?

A vague sense of dread filled me.

Chapter Four

The two sounds that irritate me most, especially when I awake groggy and filled with dread, is the incessant cock-a-doodle-doo of a crowing rooster, and the racket of an alarm clock. I reached over and slapped the clock's buzzing sound of a herniated bee with laryngitis.

It was still dark outside. I chastised myself for volunteering to meet Tiny and Uncle Charlie at the crack of dawn when I'd rather stay snuggled between warm covers on a cold Saturday morning.

I rubbed the sleep from my eyes and propped myself against the pillows. Thinking to revisit Poe's poem, I reached for my college literature book. It wasn't on the nightstand, nor was it on my bed. I swung my legs over the side of the bed. River lifted his head and greeted me with sleepy eyes. Rascal roused and stretched his tiny gray body.

The animals were up and ready to go outside for their morning routine. That meant no lollygagging in bed. It dawned on me that the bedroom door was open. I could have sworn I'd closed and locked it after I returned from shooing the raven away.

After opening the doggie door and turning on the coffeemaker, I bumped up the thermostat to rid the chill that permeated the house, then hustled back upstairs for a quick shower.

A few minutes later, clad in jeans and a flannel shirt, I returned to the kitchen and filled a thermos with pumpkin spiced coffee. Before leaving to meet Tiny and Uncle Charlie at the fairgrounds, curiosity drew me to the living room. I was still troubled by the disappearance of my textbook.

Scanning titles of neatly aligned books, I spotted the textbook resting on the top shelf, collecting dust with the other books I hadn't read in years. Surely, I hadn't walked in my sleep and reshelved the book.

Mystified, I switched on the porch light and stepped outside. A blast of cold air greeted me. I don't know what I expected to find—a feather, perhaps, to prove the bird had been real and not a dream.

A dream?

Stranger things have happened to me. Once, an owl led me to a series of shallow graves, and a crow had helped get a confession from an aging actress who had committed murder. I had a strong feeling that fate was dealing harshly with me.

I rushed inside and locked the door.

****

Lights blazed at the main barn where last night's bizarre incident had taken place. I parked next to Tiny's patrol car and Uncle Charlie's truck. Frost-covered ground crunched as I tramped across the yard.

Except for the missing horse and the removal of the decapitated body, the barn's large interior remained much the way we'd left it last night. I grabbed three cups from the dessert table and filled each with steaming coffee from my thermos. Tiny pointed to the pink sack labeled Sweet's 'n' Eats. "Got 'em last night. I figured Patty might not be open this time of the morning."

Charlie helped himself to two chocolate eclairs. "By the way, Little Sister, Henry said after we finished up here to meet him at Patty's. He'll treat you to breakfast since you are giving up most of your Saturday to help with the investigation."

I looked forward to a stack of Patty's famous blueberry pancakes, laden with melted butter and maple syrup, with a side of crispy fried bacon. "Yum."

"Pumpkin spice." Tiny grinned as he sipped the steaming coffee. "A girl after my own heart."

"Yeah, and hopefully someday a special someone will rope and brand you."

We joshed around until we'd finished off the last of our early-morning treats. Uncle Charlie said, "With all this frost on the ground, there's little chance of finding prints—hooves or shoes."

"Tullah?" I looked up at the impeccably dressed deputy. He said, "With your special talent for finding the impossible, do you have any insights to what we should be looking for?"

I decided to keep quiet about the raven. I was still reeling from a dream that felt surrealistic. I shrugged. "Like any other crime scene, look for the unusual or what appears out of place."

Tiny said, "Yep, standard operating procedure. Let's split up. Charlie, you're a good tracker—you scout around the front entrance. I'll take both sides of the room."

Drawn irresistibly to the stage area, I recalled the girl dressed as Little Red Riding Hood. I tried to focus on what had specifically drawn me to her last night. The hood had hidden most of her face. Her fists were clenched, her body was tensed, and... I closed my eyes, trying to bring her into focus. A whole slew of questions flooded my brain. Who was she? Why was she angry? Why was she focused on the front entrance? Did she know the victim? Questions that added up to more questions.

I searched every nook and cranny. Nothing. No torn piece of fabric from her costume, no hand or foot prints left to disturb collections of dust. A slight noise drew my eyes upward toward the exposed rafters. Staring down at me was the white-caped raven. I remembered the dream I'd had. In spite of the cold, I'd awakened with my hand resting on my aching forehead, and the sheets tangled around my legs. I blinked to clear away the vision, only to find that in that brief second the bird had disappeared.

Charlie called out, "This is like looking for a needle in a haystack."

Tiny agreed. "I've got nothing. What about you, Tullah?"

Now still wasn't the time to mention the raven. On shaky legs, I joined him and Uncle Charlie. "Zilch. Let's check Barn B again. It's possible that whatever we overlooked last night might jump out at us today."

Tiny spoke into his lapel mic. "Nothing, Henry. Okay, right away."

From Tiny's answers, I knew he was speaking to my dad, who was inquiring if we'd found clues that might lead us to the killer. Tiny added, "Sure, I'll take care of it. Yep, she's here, and I told her you were treating her to breakfast."

A wide grin spread across the deputy's bulldog face—and I mean that in the kindest way. Tiny is as tough on crime as my dad, and like my dad, he has a tender heart when it comes to the people he respects and loves. "Hate to leave all the fun." He heaved a sigh. "Domestic violence calls are my least favorite. Henry said to enjoy breakfast and he'd catch you later. He also said to keep this area and Barn B off-limits to the public. If you don't find any clues, we'll do another sweep in a day or so."

Outside, Charlie helped the deputy slide the massive barn doors shut. Tiny gave a salute and sprinted toward his cruiser.

The sun had made its appearance. Treading on melting frost is like skating on ice. One minute I was up and the next minute Uncle Charlie's strong hands gripped my arms to keep me from falling. My only injury was a slightly bruised ego.

We stepped over the yellow crime tape. Instead of struggling with the huge doors, we entered the barn through the office entrance. My voice sounded extra loud in the empty enclosure. "Charlie, do you remember the old western movie where the outlaws covered their horse's hooves with burlap?"

He thought for a moment. "Sure, *Dark Sundown.* The posse couldn't pick up the gang's trail because there were no hoofprints to follow."

"Is it possible our killer put booties on the hooves and that's why we didn't find any prints?"

"Uh-huh, and there's the old trick of using sagebrush to sweep away hoofprints, and that's probably why we didn't find tire tracks last night."

"Is it also possible we're dealing with two people? I mean how feasible is it that one person, maybe a woman, would have time to put booties on four hooves, lead a horse out of the barn, load it in a trailer, get in a truck, and drive away without being seen?"

"A woman?"

I blinked. "Huh, what woman?"

"You said, 'maybe a woman.' Surely, you're not thinking a woman is our suspect?"

I heaved a sigh. "Anything's possible. At this point, Uncle Charlie, I don't know what to believe. Let's check to see if we can spot tire tracks."

There were no tread marks on the barn's wide aisle. We walked outside and around to the rear of the barn. While we didn't discover tread marks, there were slight pocks on the ground's surface. I squatted next to my godfather. He pointed to different-sized heel prints. Some overlapped, as if the wearers had stepped in one another's footprints. "What do you think, Little Sister?"

I hovered my hand over the prints, and then glanced over my shoulder. "I'm thinking that adults and children stood in line to use the port-a-potty." I pointed to where several footprints led toward and away from the temporary toilet stations.

He harrumphed. "Another dead end." He indicated toward the fenced area that separated the fairgrounds from a state-owned forested area.

Charlie glanced at his watch. "C'mon, I think we're spinning our wheels here. Besides, with it being Saturday and Halloween Eve, I've got to get back to the saloon. I'm expecting a large lunch crowd, and tonight it'll be hopping with a rowdy bunch."

"I wish you were going with us on the haunted graveyard tour. Dad and Tiny are both working, too."

"Are you expecting trouble?"

No sense stirring up trouble where there wasn't any. A sudden chill engulfed me. Deep inside, I sensed our killer wasn't finished yet. Maybe that's what the raven was trying to tell me. "I hope not."

Chapter Five

Every table in Sweet's 'n' Eats resembled an orange pumpkin. Patty Sweet, the owner, had decorated the café and pastry shop with cottony cobwebs, grinning pumpkins, and black cat cutouts. Rows of cupcakes swirled with orange or black icing and decorated with edible spiders and other creepy characters lined the pastry case.

"Tullah." My grandmother stood and waved me toward a booth. Her Cheshire-cat grin was a contrast to Ella's tired smile. I surmised that Ella had probably spent most of the night studying for an exam. Grandmother's wide beam, however, meant she was eager to share important information.

I spoke to several friends and clients as I threaded my way through the crowded café. Ed Shepard called out, "Hey, Doc, Henry got any leads on last night's murder?"

Harriet Henderson said, "I didn't sleep a wink last night." She tsked. "Horrible…just horrible."

Little Bobby Devers piped up, "I hope the sheriff didn't cancel the haunted graveyard tour. I like being scared." Bobby's mother immediately shushed her precocious nine-year-old son.

Kentucky may be known for its rolling green horse pastures, world-renowned bourbon, and awesome outdoor adventures, but those who know where to look may also find earthbound ghosts, paranormal activity, and real haunted houses in Kentucky. I can attest to the strange nightly sightings and sounds of Enigma's own Cedar Hill cemetery, where my mother rests.

A gruff voice spouted, "Yeah, what about that, Mayor? You gonna refund our money?"

In her youth, my grandmother was a tough crime reporter. Now that she's approaching eighty, she's mellowed a bit. As a Cherokee woman, she isn't easily intimidated by arrogant jerks. When she shoved back her chair and stood, I thought, Uh-oh.

"Is that you, Dennis Doolittle? Ah, yes, I see it is you." She pierced him with a dark look. "Let me assure everyone in this room that tonight's cemetery ghost tour has not been canceled." Her eyes were foxy and daring. "And you, Mr. Doolittle? I guarantee that it will scare the pants off you."

There are certain types of men that delight in frightening women. Dennis Doolittle suffered from an acute case of Napoleon Syndrome and was such a man. Anger swept across his acne-pocked face. His chair scraped against the floor as he shoved it back. As he attempted to rise, Patty came to the rescue. "Here, let me freshen—" She stumbled, and hot coffee sloshed from the brimming pot and onto his pants leg.

He yowled.

She snatched a rag from her apron and attempted to blot the spreading spot. "Oh, my, I'm so, so sorry. I'll get you a fresh cup."

In Doolittle's attempt to push her hand away, he knocked the pot out of her hand. I had to clap both hands over my mouth to hold back my laughter. The pot shattered when it hit the floor, and hot coffee splashed upward, further scalding the offending Mr. Doolittle. The expression on his face was priceless.

His voice roared with contempt. "You stupid twit! I'll sue you for scalding me!"

One of the men at Doolittle's table said, "Shut up, Dennis. You ain't suing nobody, 'cause if you'd kept your trap shut this wouldna happened. 'Sides, it was an accident. Now, c'mon, we got work to do."

The comment stopped Doolittle in his tracks. For a moment, I feared he would physically attack Patty, and I was prepared to come to her defense. Instead, he mumbled something I couldn't hear, then stomped toward the door.

The other tablemate stood. He doffed his cap and said, "Sorry 'bout that, Miz Patty. Dennis ain't got no manners."

Patty offered an innocent smile. "Thank you, Mr. Carruthers. If you'll step over to the pastry case, Myrtle will sack up a dozen cupcakes for you. On the house."

Dennis Doolittle stood poised as if he had something else to say. Instead, he stalked away muttering under his breath.

A waitress scrambled to sweep up the shards of glass and spilt coffee.

With a fresh pot of coffee in her hand, Patty sashayed to our table. She refilled our cups, including one for herself, and plopped down. She reminded me that my dad had already called in my order for blueberry pancakes with all the trimmings.

"That was no accident, was it, Patty?" My grandmother cocked an eyebrow.

Don't let Patty's last name fool you. She didn't get to be a successful business woman and vice mayor by being a shrinking violet. She cleared her throat. "Let's just say that it was a convenient…accident…and leave it at that."

I smiled. "Whatever it was, thank you for diffusing what could have become explosive."

A thought crossed my mind. Dennis Doolittle was small in stature. He had a volatile temper, and he had served time for nearly beating a man to death. Was it possible that he was our killer? "Do any of you recall seeing him at the dance last night?"

Grandmother pursed her lips in thought. "Why? Is he on your suspect list?"

Ella yawned. "With all the different costumes and masks, I could only recognize a few people, and he wasn't one of them." She shrugged. "Sorry."

"'Fraid I'm not much help, either," Patty lamented.

"Anyhow…" Grandmother beamed. "Patty and I have good news. With all the new industry in Enigma, and new tax revenue, we have enough money to hire another deputy."

"Does Dad know?"

"He does. I'm sure he'd want to tell you himself. Too bad he couldn't join us this morning."

Elation filled me. "What great news, Grandmother! Now maybe he and Tiny can slow down a bit."

Behind me, a man's timid voice said, "Tullah?"

Arnie Lewis was shy and reticent, a slim man whose hair was prematurely abandoning him. It was unusual for him to approach anyone. I swept my hand toward the empty chair. "Arnie, please, join us."

He hesitated. Wringing his hands, he continued to stand. "I'm sorry to intrude on you ladies. Tullah, the sheriff stopped by the office a while ago. Mr. Peebles said he wanted to speak to my grandfather and me. I-I was at the hospital."

In unison we all said, "Hospital?"

He nodded. "My grandfather had a heart attack. I spent the night in his room. I went by the sheriff's office a few minutes ago. Miss Joyce said he was on a call. D-do you know why he'd want to see us?"

Arnie and Mr. Lewis. Those were two names I could possibly strike from my list. When I touched his arm as a gesture of friendliness, Arnie jumped as if he'd been zapped with a cattle prod. Although I knew better, I assured him that my dad's contacting him was probably nothing serious.

He turned to leave, then turned back. "We've never been visited by the law. It makes me nervous. T-Tullah, it would set me at ease if you'd be there when I come speak to the sheriff."

Poor Arnie. "Sure. I'll make it a point to be there."

Patty spoke up. "Arnie, have you had breakfast?"

He said, quietly, "Oh, yes, ma'am, at the hospital."

He was visibly upset when he wished us a good morning and left the café.

I shook my head slowly. "Shame on me for speaking ill of Old Man Lewis. He's about as morbid as the funeral business. The way he's kept Arnie under his thumb is almost as bad as when the kids bullied him in school."

Grandmother offered a disgusted smile. "Arnold Lewis—shame on him for treating that poor boy more like a lowly employee than a grandson."

We all shook our heads in agreement. I had another thought: Keep the Lewises on my suspect list. Even the least expected commit crimes, and like Dennis Doolittle, Arnie Lewis was strong enough to lift a body onto a horse. And besides, Arnie knew how to embalm bodies. I made a mental note to add this fact to my murder file.

Chapter Six

After breakfast, I followed behind Ella's truck as we drove home. I pulled under the carport to my house, then met her half way in the yard between my house and the travel trailer she lives in. As my assistant, she finds it more convenient living next to the clinic than traveling from town, and she also wants independence. Not that she and her mother don't get along. They do.

"We both have time for a long nap before tonight's activities. How many more classes before you graduate?"

Without blinking she said, "Two, and then I'll take the state boards." She heaved a heavy sigh. "I'm not worried about passing my finals. It's the state boards. My advisor keeps telling us how difficult it is, and that most students don't pass it on the first try."

"Don't worry, Ella," I assured her. "You have an advantage over the majority of the students with your hands-on experience. You'll ace the boards and get your certification with flying colors. And then you'll officially be Dr. Ella Sanders."

She flashed me a weary smile. "I wish I was as confident as you."

I wished there was more I could say to reinforce Ella's belief in herself. "You need a break. Take a nap and then meet me around five. We'll grab a hamburger at the saloon before meeting Grandmother and Patty for the haunted cemetery tour.

"Sounds like a plan."

We waved and turned to our abodes.

I gave River and Rascal a little love while I strolled to the house. After checking in with my answering service, I resumed tasks I'd started a few days ago—paying bills, filtering through emails, and catching up on much-neglected correspondence. When that was caught up, I opened the murder file I'd begun last night and added Dennis Doolittle's name to the list of suspects. After closing my laptop, I tackled a few other chores I'd let slide. By noon, my sleepless night had caught up with me. Satisfied the house was in order, I climbed the stairs to my bedroom, where I sank down on my bed and drew up the covers. Enigma is a wonderful place to live, and I'm fortunate to be surrounded by loving family and dear friends. But my final thought was of Dennis Doolittle and his threatening demeaner this morning. My dreams reflected it—they were not pleasant dreams.

I woke to the alarm clock, groggy and out of sorts. I was determined to put the case aside and enjoy tonight's graveyard tour. Before leaving for town, I walked to the barn to feed the horses. For once, the post-surgery area was empty, leaving me with no patients to check on.

It was a typical fall day, the sky cobalt blue and without a cloud. In the waning sun, shafts of light flowed through the treetops. It was an evening to truly buoy my spirits, and they did need lifting.

I closed my eyes and allowed the sun to play over my face. When I opened them, I was no longer alone. Ella stood next to me. "You were right, Tullah, about the nap. I feel better already."

Ella is doll-like, extremely slender, and belies her

twenty-five years of age. She stands just a little taller than five feet, silky brown hair worn short, eyes to match the color of her hair. She's a bundle of energy and has a true compassion for animals of all temperaments. I felt fortunate to have her as a friend and future business partner. I only hoped that once she graduated and received her license to practice veterinary medicine that she wouldn't leave for a larger town and a more lucrative income, like my former protégée, Cindy Redfern, had done.

While we were feeding the horses, the weather shifted. Dark storm clouds moved swiftly along the horizon, blocking the sun every few minutes, then racing by and allowing it to shine through again. We completed our chores, and before leaving for town to dine at the Whitehorse Saloon, we freshened up and changed into suitable clothing for what promised to be a chilly night.

As I was backing the truck out of the carport, my phone chirped. Caller ID showed Grandmother's picture. "Hello, Grandmother. Want to meet us at the Whitehorse?"

"That's why I'm calling. I called Charlie to reserve a booth for us. He said the place was jam-packed and the noise level was rockin' the rafters. I've placed an order at the Crispy Chicken instead. You and Ella come to my place. Okay?"

"Thanks for letting me know. We'll see you in twenty."

I looked at Ella and said, "You heard?"

Ella nodded and smiled. "Food is food, and I'm starved."

We both laughed.

She said, "I missed last year's Halloween. Tell me

about the haunted graveyard tour. Should I be afraid?" Ella shivered and verbally expressed the cold she felt, with a "Brrr!"

I was matter of fact. "During the Civil War, Kentucky was a confederate state. There is a section of the cemetery where soldiers are buried. It's said that the cemetery is the site of one battle in which so many were killed their bodies were simply left to rot in the field. So now legend has it that these lost souls walk the graveyard at night trying to find their way home.

"Another legend, even more chilling, is about the Hillbilly Beast, which dates back to the days of Daniel Boone. The tales describe it as a hairy, smelly Bigfoot-like beast that howls. And then, there's the one about a child that was hanged as a witch. As the story goes, on Halloween night she reaches out through the iron bars that surround her grave and tries to pull visitors inside.

"People from Enigma have reported seeing flashing green orbs, shadowy figures, and hearing disembodied screams coming from the cemetery."

Ella hugged herself. "Even though I don't believe in ghosts, I understand why Enigma makes a big deal out of Halloween. It's certainly a moneymaking event."

I wheeled into an empty parking space in front of Grandmother's apartment. I cast an impish smile toward Ella. "After tonight, you might change your mind about believing in ghosts."

My vet tech opened the truck's door and slid out. "Oh, hush up. I smell fried chicken, and there's no such thing as a ghost." She playfully stuck out her tongue.

As guides and narrators of tonight's festive event, Patty, Dr. Ritter, and Grandmother were dressed in costume. Patty and Grandmother wore dresses and bonnets depicting the 1800s, and Dr. Ritter, dressed in black attire, a stovepipe hat, and shiny black boots, resembled an old-time funeral director.

Our dinner conversation centered around last night's victim. Patty wiped grease from her fingers. "Our volunteers have outdone themselves with the decorations. I sincerely hope nothing bizarre happens tonight."

Dr. Ritter helped himself to another crispy fried wing. He tsked as he lifted it to his mouth. "I don't think there's anything to worry about. Probably a sick-o wanting to flaunt his dastardly deed and used our event to fluff his macabre ego."

"What about tomorrow night when it's actually Halloween—won't it be dangerous for children to go trick-or-treating?" Ella wanted to know.

"We plan for that every year, Ella." Grandmother reached across and gave Ella's hand a reassuring pat. "We're hosting our annual trick-or-treat, all-you-can-eat BBQ, with plenty of free candy for the old and young kiddos. Besides, Monday is a school day, and the kids will be worn out from all this weekend's fun."

Dr. Ritter said, "Say, Tullah, do you mind if I hitch a ride? I don't see so well to drive at night. Getting old is hell."

I tweaked his wrinkled jowl. "Of course, especially for my favorite curmudgeon. There's plenty of room for all of us. And by the way, all of you look terrific."

Dr. Ritter wiped his nose. His eyes a little blurry, he said, "Before I retired, I had very little time for fun. If I did attend an event, like as not I'd be called away on an emergency." He took a sip of wine. "The old adage that time passes when you're having fun certainly holds true;

especially when you're with people who have become like family." He raised his glass. "Happy Halloween."

A quiet fell over Grandmother's tiny apartment. Nostalgia filled me as I was reminded of my mother's untimely, tragic death. We lingered for a moment. I cleared my throat. "I hate to be a party pooper, but we should probably get going."

Chapter Seven

The garden club and members of the volunteer fire department had once again outdone themselves with transforming the entrance to Cedar Hill cemetery to resemble the gates of Transylvania, complete with menacing gargoyles. They had spent a week decorating the grounds in a replica of faux stone walls with realistic cobwebs dangling from tree limbs. The sounds of eerie moans, howls, and rattling sabers were piped through a sound system, while grimacing jack-o-lanterns and flickering green orbs illuminated the shadowy expanse.

A bevy of volunteers from the community as well as the high school drama club were stationed in specific areas. I hadn't been privileged to see their costumes earlier, which added to the excitement.

Eager patrons waiting to be scared stiff had already formed a long line at the entrance booth. They would be escorted inside, in four groups of ten at a time, each group led by one of the narrators. Then fifteen minutes later, another four groups would be led inside. Grandmother and her team had organized each event down to a science. While patrons listened intently to the history of the cemetery and were regaled with various legends, costumed ghouls and headless soldiers and unearthly beasts appeared long enough to frighten the group and then quickly disappeared. This always elicited a series of screams from old and young alike.

At the end of each tour, guests gathered at one of the many food booths for hot chocolate and other delicious fare such as bloody fingers (hot dogs slathered with ketchup) or slimy intestines (spaghetti sautéed in olive oil). My personal favorite were the dragon eyes (large green olives stuffed with pimento).

Ella and I listened intently while Grandmother in her sing-song voice recounted a true historical legend. "In the 1900s, a woman and her six-year-old daughter were accused of witchcraft, but their trial was forgone. Instead, the townsfolk burned them both at the stake. The child, they said, had spewed vile threats and vowed to punish the accusers. Fearing the repercussions of their brash judgment, the townsfolk took precautions to prevent the child from returning."

Grandmother stopped and pointed toward a grave surrounded with sharp pointed metal stakes. "The child lies in a steel-lined grave, and the dirt was replaced with concrete and gravel. The gravediggers then put an interconnecting cross fence around it so her spirit would be trapped within the borders. Today, the fence is wrought iron and, if you look closely, has several spots that appear to be pushed out from the inside by a powerful force. Small footprints can often be seen in the gravel as well, according to those who have visited the site. The child-witch can supposedly pull people down into her grave."

Grandmother extended her hands as if she were reaching for the person closest to her, and said, "So watch out that she doesn't try to grab *you*."

Shrieks, nervous laughter, and compliments and thanks to Grandmother ended her portion of the tour.

I nearly wet my britches when a warm-breath-filled

voice whispered, "Great night for a graveyard outing, complete with a full moon and chilly weather."

"Dad, you scared the wits out of me!"

"Me, too!" Ella lamented. Her voice shook. "Tanti, are any of these stories true, or did someone make them up?"

Grandmother's tired voice said, "Legends are as true as the person who first told them."

We stood talking while Patty and Dr. Ritter finished leading their last tours. Several couples joined us. After all the compliments were handed out, the conversation turned to the headless horseman.

Budger Hilton, one of the wealthiest thoroughbred owners in the county said, "Mayor Crow, I'm surprised you didn't include Kentucky's own headless horseman legend in your repertoire of stories."

She offered a knowing smile. "Under the circumstances, Budger, my committee and I felt it was better to save that particular legend for next year. After all, we do recycle Kentucky's history and legends from year to year."

We moved away from the cemetery's entrance and toward the refreshment area.

Patty piped up, "Keeps it interesting. Folks don't like a rehash of the same-o-same-o year after year."

David Jensen, owner of Enigma's only radio station, stopped by with his wife. Brenda Jensen offered, "Wonderful as usual. I'm already looking forward to next year's event."

"Yeah. Just so you know, I never want to see another graveyard again. At least not until it's my time to go," Jason Baer, owner of the hardware store quipped.

Mists from earlier in the day had cooled the night. A

chill slithered through me. I grabbed my forehead and moaned. I felt like all the blood had drained from my body.

"What is it, Punkin? Are you ill?"

Punkin is the nickname Dad has called me since I was a child. "I suddenly have a splitting headache."

Grandmother fussed like an overly protective hen. "You're shaking like a leaf. Maybe it's the flu. It's going around." She commanded, "Paul, go get her a cup of hot chocolate."

"Stop!" I didn't mean to yell. "It's not the flu. It's…something…I don't know…" My thoughts were disjointed and I felt as if my legs wouldn't hold me up. "What time is it?"

Dad looked at his watch. "A few minutes before midnight."

An eerie howl rent the night. Hairs bristled on the back of my neck. "Dad, something evil is out there."

He smiled and put his hand out to touch my arm. "It's just a dog. Maybe you've had too much Halloween."

I backed away. "Don't patronize me." The howl came again. "I'm telling you something bad is about to happen."

Grandmother scolded, "Listen to her, Henry. She has the gift, and you know she's never wrong about these things."

A high-pitched wail, long and pitiful, erupted. We peered out over the dark property in the direction from which the eerie sounds had come.

All conversations stopped. A small child sobbed. And Dr. Ritter yelled, "Bubba, I thought I told you to turn off that dad-blasted sound system."

Bubba Graham growled, "I did."

We heard it again, louder this time, closer to a panicked scream. I pointed. "It's coming from the cemetery, or somewhere beyond."

"Merciful heaven." Patty hooked arms with Grandmother.

"I'd better see what's happening." Dad shifted instantly into law enforcement mode.

He took off at a lope, with the rest of us following. We raced to the cemetery, slipping on the damp grass, dodging tombstones and grave markers. As we ran, the clouds shifted and the moon briefly lit the area. I pointed toward a shadowy figure carrying a wicker basket and wearing a red cape with the hood covering the person's face. "There, it's Little Red Riding Hood!"

Dad shouted, "Halt or I'll use deadly force!"

Like a wisp of wind, the image disappeared into the woods. Clouds shifted, closing off the moon's glow, leaving the grounds pitch black. Grandmother yowled, then instantly cried out, "I'm okay. Just tripped over a grave marker."

I grabbed my cellphone and switched it to flashlight mode. I shined it around until I spotted Grandmother struggling to stand. "Dad, over here."

Dr. Ritter and Dad helped Grandmother, and, trembling, she assured us that only her pride was bruised. The screams had stopped by now.

"Sheriff Holliday, is that you?"

Dad swung around to peer into the darkness. "Who is it?"

A high-pitched voice answered, "Hailey Becker and Mark DeLong. Over here. It's terrible…really… really terrible."

We sprinted toward the sobbing girl. Dad said, "The tour is over. What are you two doing out here? It's after midnight."

The trembling girl lamented, "Please don't tell my dad. He thinks I'm spending the night with my girlfriend. We…that is…Mark and me…we wanted to be alone. You know how strict my father is. You won't tell, will you?"

"That depends. Did you see who was screaming?"

"We saw Little Red Riding Hood, and…" She leaned against the quaking boy. "It's over there."

Dad shined the beam of his tactical flashlight to where she pointed. She hid her face against the chest of her young boyfriend. We weren't so far away that we couldn't see what she was pointing at.

There in the pool of the flashlight's beam lay a motionless form dressed to resemble a wolf, and with an axe in the center of his forehead. But it was a man, not a wolf, and he was definitely dead, regardless of the fur pasted on his clothing. For a few seconds I was literally paralyzed with fear. "Dad, I believe it's supposed to be the wolf from the fairy tale 'Little Red Riding Hood.' "

Dr. Ritter slowly lowered to his arthritic knees and placed a finger against the victim's neck, which was covered with faux hair.

"Is he dead?" Dad asked.

Doc nodded his head. "Died instantly." He closed the eyes that stared at nothing. He glanced at his watch. "Tullah, mark the time of death at ten after midnight."

I simply nodded, with a small, "Um," as I opened the notes app on my phone. Had it not been so real and tragic, it could have been a scene out of a horror movie.

Dad and I joined Dr. Ritter next to the body. So as

not to contaminate the scene, Dad ordered the others to stand back. He pulled two pairs of latex gloves from his pocket along with an evidence bag. He handed me the second pair of gloves and put on the other, then leaned forward and removed a note pinned to the victim's chest. He shined his light on it and read, "Those you trust are often monsters in disguise."

Dad shook his head, wincing. "This is one of the worst crime scenes I've ever seen."

I agreed. This was getting grotesque. Well, more than grotesque.

"Bubba," Dad yelled.

"Right here, Sheriff, and I've already contacted Rita to bring the ambulance."

Dad checked the victim's clothing for pockets. His mouth a grim line, he gently rocked the body from side to side, searching for more evidence. There were no pockets on the furry costume, or inside the brown slouch hat that had fallen from the victim's head. Dad's meticulous search revealed nothing.

Bubba removed the cape from his Dracula costume and draped it over the bloody head. "What kind of fiend are we dealing with, Sheriff?"

Dad heaved a sigh. "Someone without a soul, Bubba."

Chapter Eight

Dad placed a call to his deputy, telling him, "We've got another one, Tiny."

I could only imagine Deputy Goodbody's answer. Dad ended the call. He said to the EMT, "Bubba, stay with the body until Rita gets here." He pointed to Hailey and Mark. "The two of you come with me."

A crowd of thrill-seekers marched toward us. In his authoritative voice, Dad commanded, "Listen up! To keep from contaminating the scene, I'm asking you to turn around and return to the parking area."

A snarky voice said, "Yeah, and what if we don't?"

Only a halfwit would challenge my dad's authority. Dad turned to face the direction of the voice. "Dennis Doolittle?

"Yeah, so what?"

"Unless you want to spend the night as my guest, you'll move along, peacefully."

Dennis Doolittle tried to stare my dad down and lost. He apparently decided that spending the night in jail wasn't worth the effort. Dad encouraged the two teens to walk ahead of him.

Mark DeLong lamented, "We didn't do nothing wrong, Sheriff. Honest."

Hailey followed up with, "What are you gonna do with us?"

"When Deputy Goodbody gets here, I'm taking the

two of you to my office. I'll need a statement. Then I'll call your parents."

Mark groaned. "We're so dead. I'll be grounded for a month."

I wanted to smack the acne-faced teen. "A person has just been murdered in the most horrific way, and all you're worried about is losing a few privileges."

"No, ma'am," Mark's voice quivered. "It's just...well...I wasn't thinking..."

"Hey, you there," Dad interrupted as he spotted a tall figure peering from behind a tree.

The tall figure hesitated, but with a crowd of people staring at him, he grudgingly obeyed.

Dad ordered, "Remove your hat and mask."

He reluctantly removed the broad-brimmed white Stetson and black mask, revealing George Hilton, Bart Hilton's twin brother. His face was pale, and his blond hair was plastered to his head. "I...I...I...didn't do nothing, honest," he stammered.

Bart huffed in a sprint to where we stood. His twin clutched his hands together in a tight knot and appealed, "I promise, I didn't hurt nobody. Tell 'em, Bart." He clasped both sides of his head and sobbed. "Hurt...head...hurt."

In a quiet voice, Dad said, "Just calm down, George."

Everyone in Enigma knew that sixty-year-old George Hilton once had a brilliant mind. That is, until he fell off a barn roof and cracked his head open when he'd landed head first on the edge of a cement watering trough. He'd lain in a coma for weeks. Unfortunately, when he awoke, the damage to his brain had left him with the intelligence of a mentally challenged child. Bart had taken care of his twin since the death of their aged parents.

"I'll need a statement from him, Bart."

The older twin by a few seconds simply shrugged his shoulders. "Good luck with that, Sheriff. There are days when he seems perfectly rational, and then there are other days when nothing he says makes any sense. Can we hold off a few days until he calms down?"

"Sure. In the meantime, if he remembers anything—anything at all relating to the crime—let me know."

Bart wrapped his arm around his sobbing brother. "Can I take him home now?"

"Of course."

George turned a tear-stained face toward my dad. "Are you mad at me, Sheriff Holliday?"

"No, George. You go home and get some rest."

A thought occurred to me as they turned and headed away. "What will happen to him if Bart dies first?"

Dad heaved a sigh. "I think you already know the answer to that, Punkin."

I did. The word *institution* stuck in my craw.

Rita had arrived. Dr. Sunny Sanders, as the local medical examiner, sat in the front seat. Rita flashed the ambulance's headlights several times, then rolled down the window and yelled at the crowd, "Coming through! Get out of the way!"

I wondered what was wrong with people that they stood blocking an emergency vehicle until Tiny arrived and whooped the patrol car's siren a few times. Dad approached the ambulance and spoke to Rita. I guessed he was telling her where to find Bubba and the body.

Meanwhile, little Amy Stoddard crawled on her knees in the grass and softly called, "Here kitty, kitty."

Amy's mother grabbed the four-year-old and scolded, "Leave that cat alone. It might scratch you."

"I want to play with the kitty, Mama."

A large black cat, back arched, hissed at the little girl. Large yellow eyes glared at the intruders in its domain.

A witch's familiar, I thought. The cat resided on the graveyard's grounds. I wondered if its appearance was an omen. Perhaps to another murder? The thought was unnerving.

A few minutes later, flashing lights appeared through the menacing Halloween-decorated gates and we were joined by the two EMTs, the medical examiner, and Deputy Goodbody.

A remaining few curious people inched toward the ambulance, trying to peer through the two end windows. Dad ordered them to get back. He waved Rita forward.

Deputy Goodbody stepped from the patrol car; a camera dangled around his neck. "Pretty gruesome, Henry. I've cordoned off the area with crime scene tape and spray-painted the area to mark the position of the victim, and I photographed several angles of the body. Do you want me to tent the area?"

Dad looked up at the dark sky. "Might be a good idea. Were you able to get suitable photos of the body?"

"Rita shone the headlights, and I was able to photo a good bit of the scene, even a couple of footprints. 'Course, there was a lot of trampling around the scene by folks on the tour. Not sure what the photos will show until I develop the film."

Dad huffed a frustrated sigh. "Can't be helped." He directed his attention toward Dr. Sanders. "Dr. Ritter noted the time of death, and the cause is obvious."

I spoke up. "Ten after midnight, Dr. Sanders."

She nodded and made a note on her pad.

Dad said, "Any information you can share about the first victim?"

Sunny Sanders offered a limp smile. "Only that whoever embalmed the body was a professional. We're doing a thorough inspection to include under the fingernails to see if we can collect evidence for DNA. We're working on it. Give me a few days."

"Dad, perhaps we should check the missing persons reports here in Enigma and surrounding counties."

"Good idea, Punkin. I'll get Joyce right on it."

When the ambulance drove off, one of the few remaining people asked, "Is there any reason for us to stay, Sheriff?"

Dad answered, "I know you're all tired. If you'll bear with us a few more minutes until we get your names, contact information, and where you were at the time of the alleged murder, then you can go home."

I drew Dad aside and spoke quietly in his ear. "What are you going to do about Hailey and Mark?"

Dad's cellphone buzzed. He held up a finger to motion for me to hold on to my question. "Go ahead, Joyce." He listened, then said, "Commissioner DeLong reported his car stolen? Did you get a description?"

He looked at me and said, "Tullah, write this down." He recited the description of a white newer model SUV. He spoke again into the phone. "Joyce, relate to Commissioner DeLong that his vehicle will be parked in front of my office within the half hour, and I have the perpetrator in custody. I'd also like you to contact Reverend Eban Becker. Tell him his daughter is at my office."

He disconnected. He quirked a smile toward me and then at the anxious teens. "Don't think I'd want to be in their shoes when their parents show up."

"Are you going to handcuff me, Sheriff?" Mark DeLong asked.

Dad cocked his eyebrow. "Why would I do that?"

The pimply-faced boy stubbed a booted toe against the ground. "I took the car without permission. That's stealing, isn't it?"

"How old are you, Mark?"

"Fifteen."

Dad scrubbed a hand across his cleanly shaven chin. "Do you have a driver's license?"

"My learners. Why, sir?"

"Technically, I could cite your father for allowing you to drive without the supervision of an adult. With him as one of the county commissioners…that doesn't look good come next election day."

I knew Dad was putting the boy on the hotseat. I also remembered the time he'd scared the beejeebers out of me for taking my grandmother's car without permission. It was all I could do to keep from laughing at the squirming boy's woeful expression.

"Oh, shi—I mean…oh, geez."

I could see Dad holding back the laughter. "No, son, I'm not cuffing you, although you and Hailey will ride with me to the office. My daughter will follow with your dad's car." He held out his hand. "Keys."

Taking that as a cue, I tossed the keys to my truck to Ella, and asked if she'd mind driving my grandmother, Patty, and Dr. Ritter home. She caught the keys in midair. "I'll meet you at the sheriff's office once I've delivered them safe and sound."

Chapter Nine

By the time we arrived at the newly constructed
sheriff's office, David Jensen stood waiting on the front
steps. I could almost hear Dad's groans. Mr. Jensen had
an overly inflated ego and fancied himself as a big-time
crime reporter in a county with a population of barely
seventeen thousand. He also had a penchant for
stretching the truth.

"We meet again, Sheriff. I've got pen and pad ready
to get the scoop."

Dad looked as weary as I felt. "Tullah, escort the
kids inside and get them settled." He directed a frown
toward the reporter. "Can't this wait 'til morning,
Jensen?"

I nodded. "C'mon, kiddos. Might as well get this
over with."

I could tell by the way Dad clenched his jaw that
Jensen was overstepping boundaries when he followed
us into the building. I spoke to the teens, saying, "Either
of you want a cup of coffee or a cola?"

"Look, you know me, Henry," Jensen told my dad.
"As owner of the radio station and a journalist, I know
people will start hearing rumors about this and that, and
then start making mountains out of molehills. It's always
been my philosophy to report a story as fast as possible
to let folks know the facts."

I prayed that the commissioner and the reverend

wouldn't show up until Dad had convinced Mr. Nosey-Body Jensen, who was always spouting off his first amendment rights, to leave. I could only imagine the scandalous, ambiguous truths he'd broadcast over the airways.

"Yes, Mr. Jensen, I'm well acquainted with your recounting of facts," Dad replied. "However, it seems to me getting *exact* details about the crime is more important. I'd appreciate it, Mr. Jensen, if you'd not make my job any tougher."

Jensen sighed. "As you wish, Sheriff." The radio station owner pointed his finger. "You'll keep me in the loop. Right?"

Dad merely nodded. I rushed to the glass door to politely hold it open for the bothersome Mr. Jensen. When we'd raced to the screams and found the body, the air had been charged with energy—the shock of the murder had adrenalin pouring through our veins. But now that the initial excitement had ebbed, a pervasive fatigue set in. I looked at the two teens slumped in their chairs, staring at one another with worried expressions while waiting for their parents. It had been a long night, and it wasn't over yet.

Dad unbuckled his holster and locked it inside a desk drawer, then directed his attention to the teens. "We're all tired, I know," he said, "but my daughter is going to take down some information from you. Try to remember what you saw, or heard. It doesn't matter how unimportant it may seem to you, just tell her all you can. You're free to go when your parents come get you. But just so you know, I'll probably need to interview you again in the next couple of days. So I'm asking, again, anything you remember even later is important. Jot it down, give me a call…don't wait. The sooner we catch this person, the safer our community can be."

It struck me, as I propped against the counter, making notes on what the two teenagers had to offer, that the people we interviewed at the cemetery were the most unlikely of suspects in a murder, but I also knew Dad had a job to do and would do it by the book.

When the glass door swung open, Commission DeLong and Reverend Becker entered together. By the scowls on their faces, I wouldn't want to be in Hailey's or Mark's shoes.

Commission DeLong growled, "What's this all about, Sheriff?"

I handed him the keys to his SUV and glanced toward his son. DeLong sputtered, "Mark? You?"

Dad tactfully said, "Tullah, escort everyone to separate interview rooms. Let the kids explain."

I directed the group toward a wide hall and down a corridor. The heels of our shoes on the wood-grained tile floors echoed off the vaulted ceiling. We stopped while I opened a door with frosted glass ingrained with what resembled chicken wire. "Commissioner DeLong, you and Mark can use this room." Two doors down, I invited Reverend Becker and his daughter into a similar room. Twenty minutes later, the two fathers, with kids in tow, returned to the front administrative area.

A small weary smile crossed Reverend Becker's face. "Thank you, Sheriff Holliday, for your discretion. Needless to say, I am embarrassed and ashamed of my daughter's behavior. I assure you her punishment will be appropriate, and she will be available to answer any further questions you may have."

Commission DeLong said, "At the moment, I'm

angry and disappointed. However, my son will be dealt with appropriately for taking my car without permission."

The Reverend agreed, too, that Hailey would suffer severe consequences for lying about spending the night with a girlfriend. "Are we free to take the children home, Sheriff?"

"Yes, they're free to go." He added, "I caution you not to let them leave town. We'll probably be interviewing all the prospective witnesses in the next couple of days."

Mark DeLong shot my dad a smug look. "Hey, Sheriff, my class is going on an overnight field trip to the caverns. My mom has already signed the permission slip and paid the fee. We're studying prehistoric culture."

Irritation laced my dad's voice. "Sorry, son, but I'm afraid this is one field trip you'll have to miss."

Mark grumbled, "You don't understand. It counts toward my history grade, and I need it to…" He lowered his voice and looked down at his shoes.

Commissioner DeLong's face turned scarlet. "You need it for what, Mark?"

The teen whined, "Pop, can't you use your influence?"

"Don't talk to me like that, boy! First you take the car without permission, and now I find out you're failing history?"

My dad interrupted smoothly, "We're all a little overwrought. Go home and get some rest. I'll be in touch."

Still fuming, both fathers marched their children out the door and into the cold night.

Joyce, Dad's office manager, saw to it that there was

always a fresh pot of coffee. I poured two cups. "I don't know about you, Dad, but I need caffeine."

Cups in hand, we trooped back to his office, with its new office furniture, where he removed his hat and bent to scribble on a notepad. "A reminder to myself to have Joyce check current missing persons here and in surrounding counties." He scrubbed both hands over his face. "I'm not aware of any new missing persons reports for Enigma. That means out of county, possibly."

I blew to cool the steaming liquid from my cup. "I'm glad Grandmother and her committee decided to cancel the haunted house."

"Yeah, two heinous murders in two days. Still, we'll need to keep a watchful eye on tomorrow's activities."

"Surely the killer wouldn't try anything in broad daylight."

Ella pushed through the entrance door. She looked as tired as I felt. "Everyone's delivered home safe and sound."

"I hope none of them have bad dreams tonight."

Ella laughed as she dangled the keys to my truck. "Not likely. Before I got to the main highway, Dr. Ritter was snoring, and not so quietly." She added, "Speaking of dreams, I'm exhausted."

"My thoughts exactly. 'Night, Dad." I kissed my father on the cheek.

Dad walked us outside to my truck. A worried frown crossed his forehead. "You girls make sure to lock your doors tonight."

Chapter Ten

The sun came up far too early on Halloween morning, even for this usually early-to-bed, early-to-rise animal doctor. I'd been early to bed all right, but it'd been early in the morning, not early in the evening. It was Sunday and my day off. My answering service would notify me of any emergencies. I was contemplating getting out of bed when the buzzing vibration of my cellphone jangled my nerves and forced me upright.

I yawned as I answered.

"Punkin?"

I put the phone on speaker. "'Good morning, Dad. At least, I hope it's a good morning."

"I take it you and Ella got home all right."

"Yes, we did, and our animals were happy to see us." I scooted against the headboard. "What's up?"

"Look out the window."

The sound of rain pelting against the window was both welcome and disappointing. "I can hear it. Does this mean the festival has been cancelled?"

"'Fraid so. The weather forecasts a front moving through with a hundred percent chance of showers all day and into tomorrow, followed with sleet and possible snow flurries throughout the week."

"I don't know whether to be relieved or disappointed. I'll give Grandmother a call later today."

"I'm sure she'll appreciate it. By the way, I have

Dennis Doolittle in jail."

"Really? What did he do?"

"Charlie said he was spouting off about knowing who the Halloween monster is. I'm holding him as a material witness."

I hmphed. "Maybe Doolittle is the monster."

"Not likely. He's not that smart. Just between you and me, his elevator doesn't always stop at every floor."

Dad's description of Dennis Doolittle was a slight exaggeration, but close enough. "Yes, but he's strong enough to throw an axe. Have you questioned him?"

"We had a few words after I brought him in. He was too drunk to make much sense. He's a smug son of a gun. Always wears a snarky smile."

"Yeah, he gives me the creeps. How long can you hold him?"

"I can hold him seventy-two hours unless I have reason to charge him."

"Do you—have a reason?"

I could envision Dad's smile when he said, "I do— disorderly conduct and destruction of private property. According to Charlie, Doolittle was hitting on some guy's wife, and the guy took offense, called Doolittle 'Shorty' among other unsavory names, and the rest is history."

"What about the Lewises—are they still on your radar?"

"Not entirely. The old man is still in the hospital. That rules him out for last night's murder. Still—" He paused.

"Dad, you might want to rethink about Arnie. I mean, we've known him his entire life. I don't think Arnie has the nerve to squash a roach, much less hack off a person's head and hide it, or sling an axe hard enough to split a human skull."

"I hear you, Punkin. For now, I'm keeping him on the list as a person of interest."

I heaved a heavy sigh. "When do you plan to start interviewing new deputy candidates?"

"Tanti spilled the beans, did she?"

"I guess she figured you'd take your time telling me. It's only because she wants the best for you."

He chuckled. "Yep, she's been more than a mother-in-law to me. Did she tell you there's enough funds to hire two deputies?"

"Two? Great news! You and Tiny have been overworked and underpaid long enough."

He snorted. "To answer your question, I'll be interviewing all week. In the meantime, hopefully, our monster won't claim another victim.".

"Enigma's off the beaten path. How many candidates so far?"

"Twelve. Mostly fresh out of the academy, but a couple of veterans from Paducah and Mayfield, one from Florida, and one from Illinois."

"Are you looking for experience or for people you can train your way?"

"Both. I'll use a veteran to relieve Tiny of the crime scene work, the rookie to man the office and handle minor offenses while I train him for the grittier stuff."

"Grittier as in victims with missing heads, and those stomach-roiling autopsies?"

Dad guffawed. "I should hire you to be my training officer. You're already tuned in."

This time, I laughed. "No, thanks. I'm happy doing what I do."

My phone chirped to signal another call coming in. "Grandmother's calling, Dad. I'll catch you later."

I disconnected and punched the answer button. "What's up, Grandmother?"

"It's storming outside, that's what's up." She huffed. "Patty, Paul, and other members of the garden club and I have spent the morning getting the news out that today's activities will be rescheduled—maybe in early November, depending on the weather. Do you know that some people had the audacity to suggest we apologize for cancelling, as if we have a special connection with Mother Nature?"

"Take a couple of deep breaths. Remember your blood pressure, Grandmother."

She was quiet for a moment. "The weather is supposed to get worse as the day goes on. I don't want you on the roads. Thank goodness Charlie has the good sense not to expect us today."

Since I was a child, Sundays had always been our family dinner day. None of us cooked, but rain or shine we usually met at Charlie's for barbeque or his special chili. "I understand your concern. Believe me, unless I get an emergency call, the only reason I'll go outdoors is to feed the horses and check on my post-surgery clients."

We chit-chatted for a few minutes, mostly discussing the recent murders and possible suspects. "Grandmother, I'm mighty sorry you and Patty had to see the victim last night."

"Me, too. It's weighed heavily on my mind. It just seems strange that something as gruesome as these two murders would happen in our quiet little county."

"Dad and Tiny are great detectives. They'll catch this psycho."

"Tullah, about your empathic gift, have you had any...you know...visits from the spirits?"

"Grandmother, I don't have a direct line to the spirit world." I hesitated over telling her about the raven. But why not? "I did have a visit from a raven."

"Really? *Corus corax* are not native to Kentucky. Do you think there's a connection between the bird and the killer?"

"Possibly. Something else, Grandmother. I think the killer's spirit visited me." I described the image that had appeared in my bathroom mirror.

"You should tell all of this to Charlie. He and I will make strong medicine to protect you."

A shutter banged against the house, reminding me to call a repairman to make a few necessary improvements before winter set in. "Don't worry, Grandmother. All will be well."

I dressed and padded downstairs to the kitchen. Something stopped me. What was it? I looked at my phone. In my mind, I replayed the conversations with my dad and my grandmother. I didn't recall anything out of the ordinary. Maybe after feeding my grumbling stomach my mind would be a little clearer.

After letting the dog and the teacup donkey out for their morning romps, I opened the refrigerator. Neither cereal nor grits and eggs suited my tastebuds this morning. Eyeing the box from Sweet's 'n' Eats, I grabbed it. Donuts are the one basic food group for law officers and veterinarians with a sweet tooth.

With a mug of steaming coffee, a plate laden with two glazed donuts and a chocolate éclair, I strolled to the living room, flicked on the remote to my new electric fireplace, and settled in my recliner. A jumble of thoughts about the Halloween monster raced through my mind. Wolfing down the two donuts first and following them with the éclair, I licked the chocolate from my fingers, grabbed my laptop, and opened the file I'd titled *Monster in the Dark*.

Chapter Eleven

After reading over my previously written details, I added the facts, as I knew them, from last night's homicide, and I mulled over Arnie Lewis and Dennis Doolittle as possible suspects.

Fact: Victim number two—hands, face, and chest covered with fake fur. Feet clad in fake wolf's paws complete with toenails. Slouch hat.

Name: unknown until identity is confirmed.

Method of murder: an axe embedded in victim's skull—close range.

Question: Did the victim know the killer?

Fact: Death—Instant

Motive: Unknown

Question: the note stated, "Don't trust strangers." Was the killer hurt by strangers?

My phone chirped, signaling a text. Ella wrote: *Univ. closed all week.* She added a smiley face emoji.

I answered: *Does this delay graduation?*

Ella: *No! Online classes. Woohoo! Text when U R feeding up.*

I answered with a thumbs up, and continued typing information into my murder file: Weather is an obstacle. Rain will wash away evidence.

Similarities: A) Both victims are obviously male. B) Both victims dressed as fairytale characters.

Two things happened simultaneously. First my

stomach rumbled loudly enough to wake the dead, and second, a lightbulb went off inside my brain. It occurred to me that *fairytale* was the obvious connection tying the two slayings together. Putting aside my hunger, I set my laptop on the end table, raced down to the basement, and switched on the light.

The dimly lit room was cold as a tomb. Chills invaded my body, and I had to force my teeth not to chatter as I rapidly searched bookshelves littered with old magazines and books of every topic.

"Aha!" I felt almost giddy when my hand reached to pull a dusty copy of Washington Irving's *The Legend of Sleepy Hollow* from the shelf. Next to it was the equally dust-ridden set of *Mother Goose Rhymes* and the *Brothers Grimm Fairy Tales*.

River joined me in the frigid room. He whined and bumped my hand as if telling me I had no business in this icebox. Snuffling brays drew my attention toward the cellar's open door. Rascal was obviously peeved that he was unable to join his buddy. I loaded my arms with the books and called for my black Lab to follow me. I also made a mental note to convert the basement into a livable room, complete with heat, another project to add to my handyman list.

Upstairs, I detoured by the bookshelf in the hallway and grabbed my old college literature book. I had a long day of reading ahead of me. Hopefully, I would discover a connection between the fairy tales and reality that eventually linked to the two murder victims.

After unloading my arms, I headed for the kitchen. It was definitely time for a grilled cheese sandwich, a bowl of tomato soup, and more coffee. My brain was a flurry of ideas to the point that I ate almost without tasting my food. Was the killer toying with us? If so, why?

After washing the dishes and setting them in the drainer, I returned to the living room and opened my literature book to Edgar Allen Poe's poem, *The Raven*. In one of the margins, I had scribbled a note, in red ink, saying "the poem symbolizes a mournful, never-ending remembrance."

I set the laptop aside and flipped open the modernized version of "The Legend of Sleepy Hollow." It'd been years since I'd read the story. I used a notepad to jot down page numbers and any thoughts that might lead me to a motive for dressing the victim like the headless horseman. Finishing the last page, I opened my laptop to create a new document, which I titled "Symbolisms of Fairy Tales and Other Information."

For several moments it was as if I were back in Professor Hadley's class answering exam questions. I organized my thoughts as I recalled the story, then typed:

"Traditional folklore holds that the Horseman was a Hessian trooper who was killed during the Battle of White Plains in 1776. He was decapitated by an American cannonball, and the shattered remains of his head were left on the battlefield while his comrades hastily carried his body away."

For emphasis, I underlined the part about the decapitated head and continued typing.

"Question: What does the Headless Horseman symbolize?

"Theory: The Headless Horseman is a major character in 'The Legend of Sleepy Hollow.' But the ghostly rider—and, especially, his head—may also symbolize the tension between reality and imagination, between the natural and the supernatural, held by many of the townspeople."

Again, I underlined the sentence about reality and imagination. In bold black letters, I added: "Insanity."

Engrossed in my theorizing, I nearly knocked the laptop out of my lap when a loud knock sounded at the kitchen door. River woofed. He and Rascal raced to the kitchen, and I followed to pull back the curtain that covered the door's window—Ella stood there, bundled up, her face barely visible under the sweater hat on her head, a scarf around her neck. I opened the door. "It's freezing. Did the heat in your trailer go out?"

She stepped inside. "It's past feeding time. I thought I'd better come drag you away from whatever you're involved in. Also, I've made goulash and jalapeño cornbread, if you're interested."

I glanced at the clock and then, grabbing my jacket, I apologized, "Sorry, Ella. I got lost in doing research and trying to come up with a motive for the murders. And, yep, goulash and cornbread slathered with butter sounds wonderful."

Our hands stuffed in jacket pockets, and heads down against the wind, we hustled across the yard to the clinic.

Ella's breath steamed when she spoke. "Sounds intriguing. Did you find anything interesting?"

"I'll tell you about it over supper."

In the barn, nickers greeted us as the horses stuck their heads over stall doors, eager for the feed they knew we would supply. I was glad I'd recently spent money to have the entire building renovated to include heat and air conditioning. Ella and I also blanketed the horses and let them out of their stalls and into the corral to run off a little pent-up energy before we settled them back in their stalls for the night.

Pogo and Ozzy, Ella's Chiweenies, were all wiggles and waggles when we stepped inside her trailer. We unwrapped ourselves, and while she poured two cups of hot chai tea, I explained my theory about the headless horseman and possibly how the symbolism of the story related to the first victim.

She handed me spoons and napkins. "It makes sense, Tullah. Are you thinking the murderer is insane?"

I mulled her question. "Possibly, either insane or a person who has lost touch with reality."

She set two steaming bowls of goulash on the fold-out table. My mind strayed a bit as I wondered how long Ella would want to continue living in these cramped but comfy quarters, or would she perhaps want to move to a larger city. "Ella, don't take offense." I hesitated.

She cast a curious glance in my direction. "Whatever it is, spit it out. I promise not to get angry."

"Okay, here goes," I huffed. "Once you are officially Dr. Ella Sanders, DVM, do you plan to stay here? In Enigma? Or...?"

She let the spoon settle in her bowl of soup and shot me a firm frown. "Tullah, I'm not going anywhere. Well, that is to say, I have been contemplating purchasing a piece of land, and building a house, but rest assured that I'm looking forward to a long partnership with you. Also, my mom and Uncle Tiny are here. Why would I want to leave?"

I shrugged my shoulders. "You could fall in love and marry."

Her hand acted as a stop signal. "Whoa. I'm not saying that I will never fall in love. I might if the right guy comes along. Trust me, he has to be *the* right guy. I might marry and have a half-dozen kids."

She lifted the spoon and savored a mouthful of deliciousness. Her tone grew serious. "I'm not Cindy Redfern, Tullah. I'd never use you the way she did. Your friendship means too much to me. I'm not sure I like how growth is changing our sweet little town, but warts and all, I love Enigma. I've planted my roots, and I'm here for the long haul."

I didn't know whether it was the hot soup that was causing my nose to drip, or the capsaicin in the jalapeños making my eyes tear up. Either way, I choked back my emotions. Ella was rapidly becoming the sister I never had.

I cleared the lump in my throat. "I have it on good authority that the five acres on the west side of me will be on the market soon. I was contemplating buying simply to keep from having some contractor possibly developing it."

Ella stood and gathered our dishes. She stacked them in the mini-dishwasher. "Really?" The excitement in her voice rose as she opened the refrigerator and lifted out Patty Sweet's signature pink box. "Which do you want—lemon curd or raspberry filled?"

I opted for the lemon-filled donut. She said, "I'm serious, Tullah. I'd be foolish to let this opportunity slip past. Right here, next to the clinic? Wow!"

I grinned as I stuffed my mouth with tart lemony sweetness. "Don't you want to know the price?"

Her shoulders slumped a little. "Drats, it'll be my luck the owner will want more than I can afford." She sat a little straighter. "Do you know the price?"

I grinned. "Believe me you can afford it." When I told her, she whooped and clapped her hands like an excited child. I continued, "I believe my grandmother can persuade Mr. Pickett to give you first and only dibs."

"Will you call her tonight?"

"Absolutely!"

Relief and elation filled me. Ella broke into my thoughts. "Tullah, my college adviser sent out emails advising all the graduating students that even though we'll participate in online classes until the university reopens, probably near the end of November, our last classes—at least everything in December—will be on campus." She sighed. "It's too far to drive every day."

"Where will you stay? Isn't it too late to get a dorm room?"

"Due to the circumstances, Dr. Campbell has arranged hotel rooms nearby. Four students to a room. We'll split expenses. Not the most ideal situation. Can't be helped, I suppose."

I tugged on my jacket and settled the sweater's toboggan neck over my ears. "That means you're still on track to graduate in December and then take your state boards in January."

A blast of cold air greeted us when she opened the trailer door. "Yes, I am. 'Night, Tullah. See you in the morning."

"As soon as Grandmother gets in touch with me about the property, I'll let you know."

I sprinted across the yard to the warmth of my house. As anxious as I was to return to my reading, I phoned Grandmother to relate the news about Ella's desire to purchase the property and my concern about a developer gobbling it up.

Grandmother said, "Don't you girls fret. Alvin Pickett plans to move to Louisville to live with his daughter. I'm sure he'll be thrilled to unload that large patch of weeds without having to go through a realtor."

With that settled, I returned to my recliner and opened the Brothers Grimm book to the story about Little Red Riding Hood and began to read.

"Once upon a time, there was a girl whose grandmother made her a red cloak, and thus she became known as Little Red Riding Hood. One day, when her grandmother was ill, Little Red took a basket of goodies and went to visit Grandmother. Her mother told her to stay on the path and not to speak to strangers. Upon meeting a sly old wolf in the woods, she ignored her mother's advice, and when he reared up on two legs and put his hands on her shoulders, she…"

Chapter Twelve

I leaned against the recliner and closed my eyes, allowing myself to drift into a netherworld. In my dream, Little Red Riding Hood was frightened of the wolf's leering grin and the way he smacked his salivating lips. She struggled to free herself from his strong grip.

An overwhelming sadness filled me. The wolf's bloodied face faded away, and in its place a raven sat on a porch railing. In many cultures, the raven, like the crow, is considered a symbol of evil and death. Somehow, I didn't feel frightened and didn't see the raven as a danger to me.

The bird blinked and squawked, "Nevermore!" before it fluttered away, and in its place was the face of the girl that had earlier stared at me from the other side of my bathroom mirror. Her liquid pale blue eyes filled with tears. Through her came the voice of my old college professor when he'd lectured about the symbolism of the raven representing Poe's own grief and his fears about his mortality. The girl's voice trembled when she spoke, "Nevermore!"

By the time I awoke, I wanted nothing more than to erase from my brain the girl's woeful expression and the images of a headless horseman and a bloodied man dressed as a wolf. The technicalities and hairpin curves of these murders were getting too much for me. I tapped the screen to awaken my laptop, and as if my fingers had taken a life of their own, I typed: There will be another murder.

Those words alarmed me, and I instantly hit the button on my cellphone that goes direct to my dad's private number. He answered immediately, "You and Ella okay, Punkin?"

Words gushed from my mouth. "Dad, I know who the killer is, and it isn't Arnie Lewis or Dennis Doolittle."

"Slow down, Tullah, you're talking too fast for me to understand what you're saying." He added, "Draw a breath. Did I hear you correctly about Arnie and Doolittle?"

I inhaled deeply, and blew out slowly. "The killer is a young woman."

"And you know this because…?"

My dad is a good man and stands up for his principles even though he despises my empathic abilities almost as much as I do. Nonetheless, these psychic abilities had helped him solve several seemingly unsolvable crimes. I briefly explained about the raven, and then said, "She came to me in a dream. I don't know her name, but she's for certain a sociopath with psychotic tendencies."

"In other words, she's cunning and dangerous."

"Yes, sir. And if she follows the modus operandi of serial killers, she will strike again."

"Does your special ability tell you that it'll be tonight, since it's Halloween?"

I wasn't exactly sure how to answer his question and hesitated while pondering my response.

"Tullah…?"

I knew when he used my given name that he was

serious. He said, "I'm not making light of this gift you have. If you know something, please tell me. I'm asking for your help."

"I don't think she will strike tonight, Dad."

"Serial killers usually don't deviate from their killing routines. Why do you think our suspect will skip tonight?"

I shifted in the recliner to relieve the pressure on my butt. "Even though we don't know the killer's identity, what I've surmised is that she thrives on the excitement of watching a crowd's reaction to the horror she's created. She enjoys showcasing her victims. That's why she chose the barn dance, and then the haunted cemetery tour."

I could almost see Dad pulling at his bottom lip, something he does when he's stewing over a difficult case. "That still doesn't explain why the suspect will skip tonight."

I sighed. Often when he asks this type of question, I doubt my innate ability. "The town is virtually shut down, and the Halloween fun day was cancelled due to inclement weather. There's no event, no crowd, no place for the killer to grandstand another victim dressed as a fairytale character."

Both Dad and I were silent for a moment, and I was the first to speak. "It's my opinion the killer is probably frustrated beyond measure. Serial killers usually get upset when their routines are interrupted. It's possible this break in routine will work to our advantage."

"Uh-huh, meaning the killer could get sloppy."

"Yes, sir."

"Any idea when the next kill will happen?"

I laughed. "Dad, just because I have empathic

abilities it doesn't mean I also have a crystal ball."

He joined in my laughter. "By the way, Punkin, we can rule out old man Lewis. Arnie called a half hour ago to let me know his grandfather didn't survive the heart attack."

I knew what it was like to lose someone you loved very much. My heart ached for Arnie. "I'm sorry for Arnie. What now, Dad?"

When my dad takes his time responding, I know he's searching for a suitable answer. He said, "I'll give Arnie a few days to grieve, and then I'll call him in for questioning. The fact that the first body was embalmed does keep him on my suspect list."

I was tired and having a problem focusing on my thoughts. I scrubbed a hand across my eyes. "Do you object to me sitting in on the interview?"

"Considering the boy's fragile mind, he might be more open with answers if you're there. I'll keep you posted."

I heard his phone ring, signaling another call coming in. "Hold on, Punkin, it's Dr. Sanders. She might have an update on the autopsies."

While I waited, I typed: Research symbolism: Headless Horseman and Red Riding Hood.

The phone clicked. "Are you still there?"

"Yes, sir."

"Sunny…that is, Dr. Sanders, had some interesting news." He paused.

"Do you plan to keep me in suspense?"

He cleared his throat. "Nope, just that what she revealed is a bit chilling, especially to my manhood."

His manhood? I wanted to laugh at the vision I'd conjured of him crossing his legs. "I'm listening."

"Both men had been castrated."

I sputtered out, "Castrated as in what I do to stallions and bulls?"

"Umm, no, as in completely whacking off their gonads. What do you make of that?"

Fully awake now, I sat in stunned silence. "That certainly puts a different spin on the case. In my opinion, it means our killer has a personal vendetta—a score to settle."

"I tell you, Punkin, I'm having trouble connecting the dots on this one." He continued, "What does your…ah…gift tell you about this?"

"*It* tells me that it doesn't take an empathic insight to suspect the killer is likely a woman. My best guess is a woman who has been severely abused by men, and her ultimate revenge is total removal of the genitals."

"A woman? Humph. On one level it makes sense. On a different level, I question a woman's ability to lift a cadaver on top of a horse or wield an axe with enough strength to split a guy's skull in two."

Dad had made a valid point. I sighed. "Maybe we're back to square one in our theories." We definitely had a mystery on our hands. I didn't know what else to say.

He sounded remorseful when he said, "I don't mean to make light of your ability, Punkin. I certainly respect and value this special gift of yours, and it's come in real handy several times. I hope you know I love and respect all of your talents, and I'm not doubting your theory that the killer is a woman. I just find it debatable."

"It's okay, Dad. There are times when I wouldn't wish whatever it is that I have on anyone, and then, other times, I'm grateful for my special ability, especially when it helps solve crimes."

"It's getting late, but one more question before I say goodnight."

"Okay, ask away."

"With that fertile mind of yours, why do you think the perpetrator, whether it's a man or a woman, dresses the victims in costume?"

This was a question I'd repeatedly mulled over, and I still hadn't come up with a viable answer. "I've asked myself that same question. I've been reading the fairy tales associated with the costumes. In my college literature class, we learned fairy tales and nursery rhymes have hidden messages or symbolisms."

"Interesting, but that's a little over my head, Punkin."

"It's easy, Dad. Here's a couple of examples—a white dove represents peace, and a red rose symbolizes love."

"So what you're saying is that once we figure out the symbolism of the stories, we'll possibly have a motive that can connect us with the killer?"

"You've got it, Dad. On a different topic—has Tiny had time to dust the saddle and blanket for prints?"

Dad made a sound of disgust. "Nothing. Our killer either has no fingerprints or wore gloves."

I tried to suppress a yawn. "I suppose the weather messed up last night's scene of the crime."

"Yeah, this weather front couldn't have come at a worse time. In fact, Tiny and I have already revisited the site looking for clues. The wind blew the tent over."

"And did you find anything?"

"Nada. Even the footprints from last night's crowd had turned to sludge. Good thing Dr. Sanders had already collected blood samples from the victim's clothing and entered those into the database. She's also checking dental records. She'll notify me when the results come in, and then we'll learn the deceased wolf man's identity. The headless horseman's ID may take a bit longer."

I felt his frustration. "On a different topic, how will this weather affect the deputy interviews?"

"It won't. I've set up interviews via Zoom, even though as you already know I have a love-hate relationship with all this new technology. I fully understand Joyce's frustration with trying to learn how to use her new computer and its updated program." He hmphed. "There's nothing like the good ol' days."

I laughed at the annoyance in his voice. "Zoom! Wow, Dad, I'm impressed."

He joined my laughter. "It's late. I'll catch you later."

"'Night, Dad. Let me know when you plan to question Arnie Lewis."

During our conversation a thought niggled my brain, a thought I decided to keep to myself until I was certain of my theory. The moment we disconnected, I reopened my laptop and clicked on the murder file. At the bottom of my list of suspects, I wrote: "Gay men? Who in Enigma fits this profile?"

I also typed: "Important note: I believe the murderer is possibly a young gay man; perhaps in his early twenties. He possibly wears a mask to hide his identity. His hair is the color of snow, eyes clear like blue liquid. He is afraid. Question: Why is he afraid, and who is he afraid of?"

I reread what I had typed. My mind went a little haywire. If the killer was really a man, then why was the image in the mirror a young woman? Was I wrong in my theory? Were my empathic powers out of kilter?

At 3 a.m. I awoke in a cold sweat. My dream had been one ginormous close-up of the headless horseman's head leering at me. It had beseeched, "Find me."

Functioning through a wooly brain fog as I climbed out of my recliner, I trudged upstairs and managed to shrug out of my clothes into flannel pajamas and crawl into bed before sleep hit me again. My last thought was, *Where is the head?*

Chapter Thirteen

Monday morning arrived gloomy, cold, and misty. It was six in the morning. After taking a hot shower and dressing in warm clothes, I padded downstairs to open the doggie door for River and Rascal. They were hesitant to leave the warm house, and I didn't blame them.

While the coffee brewed, I phoned Ella to invite her for French toast and scrambled eggs. She said, "How can I resist? I'll be over right away."

Speaking in an impish voice, I said, "It's a perfect day for mucking stalls, sterilizing the surgical area in the clinic, and taking inventory of medical supplies."

Ella snorted, then sighed. "Spoil sport." She added, "I take it we're not expecting much business today?"

"Hardly. Not in this weather. At least I hope there are no emergencies. Driving on slick roads isn't my idea of fun."

"Don't even think about it, Tullah. I'd rather stand knee-deep in manure than risk skidding into a ditch." She finished by saying, "Be there in a sec."

I opened the weather app on my cellphone. A chill raced through me when I read the expected temperature for the day.

My black Lab dashed through the doggie door, trotted to me, and dropped the newspaper at my feet. I patted him on the head and rewarded him with a treat. Not to be left out in the treat department, Rascal let loose a jealous bray. Actually, his brays sound more like suppressed sneezes. I scratched his long ears and gave him a veggie biscuit. I bake those especially for him.

While enjoying my coffee, I read the news on my phone. *Enigma's Halloween More Trick than Treat*, was the uninspired headline in the city and state section. A blurred picture of the headless horseman victim accompanied the article. Oddly, I didn't remember seeing anyone taking pictures, but then, in all of the commotion, I may not have noticed. The article was short and had little in it that I didn't already know. I was certain Dad was being guarded with any information he released.

The reporter stated that the two homicides were unlike any other murder. My name was included: "Dr. Tullah Holliday was able to subdue the panicked stallion. Will the killer strike again?" This simple question caused shivers to ripple through me. It all sounded so ominous in print. I didn't recognize the reporter's name.

A blast of frigid air filled the kitchen when Ella swooped inside. I pointed to the coffeepot as she shrugged out of her parka. "Help yourself."

"'Morning. Whatcha reading?"

I filled her in on the news article and on the late-night conversation with my father, plus the medical report from her mother.

Cradling the hot cup between her hands, she thanked me before saying, "Tullah, do you think whoever is doing the killing is local?" She hastened on, "Wouldn't it be awful if it's someone we know?"

While considering her questions, I walked to the counter and dipped slices of bread in the egg mixture and set them in the frying pan's sizzling butter. "Enigma has grown by leaps and bounds over the past couple of years."

I thought of the cliché about the good ol' days and regretted the way the town was changing. "Remember when we knew everyone who ate at Patty's café? I miss those days."

Ella slathered butter and poured a generous stream of maple syrup over the plate of French toast I'd set in front of her. Her brow furrowed as she loaded her fork with a drippy bite of syrupy bread. "So what you're saying, without saying it outright, is no, you think it's no one we'd know."

I didn't bother replying. Instead, I turned off the burner after loading my own plate. My mind was whirling when I sat down and automatically reached for the butter and syrup.

"Tullah, you didn't answer my question."

"Huh, oh, sorry." I filled my mouth and chewed. "I'm not sure. It could be a stranger, or it could be a local. We'll know when Dad and Tiny make an official arrest."

We bantered back and forth with the ease of friendship. I wasn't quite ready to share my suspicions about our killer's gender. We finished breakfast and loaded the dishwasher. Pulling on warm jackets and covering our heads, we sprinted across the yard to open the clinic. I was thankful again for the new HVAC system I'd had installed, with its automatic thermostat that kept the entire building warm in the winter and cool in the summer.

Our first course of action was to open the rear barn doors and then the stalls, to let the horses out. We laughed as they raced outside and frolicked like happy children. Ella went to the office to take care of long-overdue clerical work while I inventoried the pharmacy supplies and sterilized the surgical room from top to bottom. We left the most distasteful chore for last.

In between tasks, I assisted a variety of clients, over the phone, with solutions for the problems they presented, such as the feeding and general care of a new puppy, and how to calm a nervous dog so the owner could clip its toenails. When a sobbing client called about her sickly, aged cat, I thought it was time for Ella to become acquainted with counseling a client about euthanasia decisions and death of their pets. Euthanasia of a beloved pet is never easy, even for an old pro like myself. Most people think I get to play with kittens and puppies all day, but the patients I treat are generally somewhat on edge and not overly happy to see me.

Often, I'm called out in weather not fit for ducks, on my way to help a distressed mare with a difficult birth, or traveling to the middle of nowhere in the dark of night to set a dog's broken leg, or headed out to help pull a prized thoroughbred stallion out of a bog.

More of what I do is interacting with owners, developing diagnostic plans, interpreting findings, figuring out finances for what we need to do, talking on the phone, writing up records, mediating disputes with clients, helping with ordering hospital supplies, troubleshooting equipment, performing surgery and other procedures…and occasionally I get to take a break to eat or use the bathroom.

Ella blinked away tears as she grabbed a tissue and blew her nose. "This is the part of my job that I'm never going to enjoy. Mrs. Jenks is devastated about her cat. The poor old thing was nearly twenty years old. I tried to console her by telling her that Boo-Boo-Baby lived a long life and I was sorry for her loss." Ella sighed. "She wanted to know if I would come to her house and bury the cat. She didn't think she had the strength to do it herself."

This wasn't an unusual request, especially from elderly widows. "I hope you didn't agree, Ella. Look out the window. It's sleeting."

"You are an excellent teacher, Tullah. I remember last winter when Mr. Meier's dog died and the roads were closed due to flooding. Basically, I told Mrs. Jenks what you advised Mr. Meier—to wrap her cat in its favorite blanket, and if she has a shoe box, to place the body inside. Then take the box to the coldest area of her house to reduce the decomposition rate. I suggested this would give her time to plan for the necessary arrangements. I also told her that Boo-Boo-Baby was lucky to have had her as owner and best friend. My only doubtful part was whether or not I should tell her I'd call Uncle Tiny to take care of the burying."

"Did you tell her?"

Ella pulled a woeful smile. "Yes, because I knew he would. And he did agree when I asked him."

She was quiet for a moment. I waited, because death, animal or human, is never easy. She finally said, "In all my classes, I don't remember any of the professors addressing what to say to a grieving pet owner."

I glanced at the wall clock. It was well past five o'clock. The day had flown by. We'd tackled the entire clinic, leaving it spotless from top to bottom. "Book learning is wonderful, Ella, but you'll learn that compassion comes with years of experience."

I patted her on the back. She beamed when I added,

"You handled a delicate situation with grace and kindness. I'm proud of you, Ella."

We'd saved the yuckiest chore for last—mucking out the stalls, sanitizing the floors with bleach and water, then laying down fresh straw and filling the feed bins and water troughs. Once the horses had returned to their individual stalls, Ella and I removed the wet, dirty blankets. While currying my pinto gelding, I recalled the horrible leering image of the horseman's decapitated head. "Ella, if you were the killer, where would you hide a head?"

She peered over her horse's withers. "I'd dig a hole and bury it."

That wasn't exactly the answer I'd hoped for. "Think like the killer—wouldn't you keep it—like a prized trophy?"

She grimaced. "Tullah, that's just plain sick."

"You're absolutely correct. The person we're dealing with is severely mentally disturbed." I was curious to figure out what had happened to cause this extremism in the killer's life. Eager to get back to my psychology and literature books, I was impatient to close the clinic and return to the house.

Chapter Fourteen

After checking in with my answering service, Ella and I locked the clinic. Before returning to her trailer, she said, "I know it's only Monday, and too soon to hear from Tanti, but Tullah, as soon as she lets you know Mr. Pickett's decision about the land—"

"Don't worry, you'll be the first to know." I held up my hand. "Scout's honor."

She nodded and raced to open the travel trailer's door.

By seven, I'd made a good-sized dent in the mountain of paperwork I'd been avoiding for weeks. I decided another cup of cocoa would take the edge off my foggy brain. Before walking to the living room, I stopped at the bookshelf and retrieved my textbook of advanced psychology. Settling in my recliner, I flipped to the index and thumbed down to the psychopathy of a serial killer. Turning to the page, the multiple highlighted and underlined sentences brought back memories of intense lectures, and long nights of studying for a test.

After completing my internship as a medical doctor, I'd had an opportunity to treat a few criminally insane patients at a mental hospital in Florida. A couple of years into forensic medicine, I decided that animals were more my style and switched to animal science. I've never regretted my decision to become a veterinarian, but at no time in my career did I ever imagine I'd be referring to old textbooks to help my father solve a crime. A particular underlined paragraph seemed to beg for my attention. I read with interest: *A serial killer is typically a person who commits three or more murders, with the murders including a specific period of time. Psychological gratification is the usual motive for serial killing.*

The paragraph had answered the question of whether the killer would kill again. I skimmed down the page looking for the answer regarding what motivated someone to become a serial killer. I turned the page and found my answer in another underlined passage. In short, it specified that the FBI stated serial killers were motived by anger, thrill-seeking, and attention-getting, and the murders may be carried out in such a way as to make that motivation evident.

I stopped reading for a moment to let my brain absorb this information. My heart clutched when I read, *The victims may have something in common, such as gender, appearance, or race. Based on this pattern, the FBI focuses on a particular pattern serial killers follow that provides key clues in finding the killer and his or her motives.*

I asked myself a question—was our killer a sociopath? Once more, I searched the textbook's index until I found the page and turned to the chapter. Again, I was greeted with multiple underlined sentences in the section labeled Sociopathy vs. Psychopathy. The information disproved my theory by stating that a sociopath was generally disorganized when committing crimes. Enigma's Halloween monster was neither sloppy nor disorganized.

A folded piece of notebook paper lay nestled

between the pages. Curious, I opened it. No doubt these were additional notes I'd written, perhaps for test purposes. What I read was a treasure trove of information. I had labeled it *Four types of psychopaths*, and then written: *Clinical observations suggest narcissistic, borderline, sadistic, and antisocial.*

I set the textbook aside, opened my laptop to the murder file, and briefly scanned all previously written notes. Based on the latest information shared by my dad, I typed: "Do serial killers take trophies, and why?"

This question led me back to my textbook to read excerpts of case studies about such famous serial killers as Jack the Ripper, Jeffery Dahmer, and John Wayne Gacy. Each of these men had kept souvenirs.

Under the "why" question, I typed: "Trophies symbolize victory."

I added: "Halloween Monster Commonalities— both victims: male; complete removal of genitals."

After I'd closed the laptop, I opened my cellphone and scrolled through the picture file until I pulled up copies of the notes the killer had left on each victim, and printed them off. The first one read, "I am death, and I make all people equal." It was signed, "The Godfather of Death."

I made a notation in red ink: "This suggests the killer was made to feel inferior and needs to prove his superiority over the victims. 'Godfather' implies the killer is—male."

The second note read: "Friends are often monsters in disguise." Again, I made a notation in red: "The killer was obviously hurt by people he or she trusted."

River whimpered as he nudged my hand with his cold nose. I glanced at the clock on the fireplace mantel.

I'd been so involved in research and making notes that the time had gotten away from me. My eyes and body said it was way past bedtime. My brain, however, was wide awake.

"Another hour, River, and I promise we'll go to bed."

Rascal rose from his resting place and brayed. He bucked and farted as he scampered toward the kitchen. I heard the doggie door flap and knew he'd gone to relieve himself. River sat and stared at me with woeful brown eyes. I pointed my finger at him. "Go with your buddy. Go!"

There are times when my pets act like naughty children. When I stood, my body was stiff from the long period of sitting. I stretched to relieve the kinks in my back, then beckoned for the black Lab to follow. When I pointed to the doggie door, River reluctantly obeyed. I didn't blame him for not wanting to venture outside in the dark damp cold.

When my pets had returned, I shut down and locked the doggie door and returned to the living room to grab the textbooks and laptop. The animals followed me upstairs to the bedroom and settled in their beds. My brain was wired. I knew trying to force myself to sleep was fruitless and decided to do more research to answer the question of why the killer had dressed his victims as fairytale characters. The case—and I had begun to think of it as my case—had taken on a different twist.

Although lassitude tugged at me, I continued to read and make notes. There was evil happening in Enigma, and I intended to help my dad bring the monster to justice. Against my will, my eyelids took on a life of their own. I actually don't remember falling asleep.

Loretta C. Rogers

I watched myself enter a fog-shrouded wood. Silence surrounded me. I peered through the haze and saw nothing. I heard nothing. The effect of all the swirling mist was unnerving. It felt as if I'd entered a twilight zone. That's when I spied a red cape skipping through the woods. I raced to follow her, tripping over snarled roots. I called her name, "Little Red Riding Hood!"

She swung around and took two steps toward me, a basket hanging from her arm. She leered at me with a wolfish grin and licked her lips. A furry hand reached toward me, and I…

The cellphone rang.

My heart banged against my chest. The phone rang again. Reluctantly, I swiped the screen upward to answer.

"Hello?" I said softly, and then cleared the rasp out of my throat, and tried again. "Hello," I said firmly.

"Punkin, it's after seven. I thought you'd be up by now."

Surprised to find myself in my bedroom and holding the phone, I answered shakily, "What?"

"It's Dad. Are you ill? What's wrong?"

My arms had goosebumps, and I pulled the blanket tightly around me.

"Nothing's wrong, Dad. I was up late doing research, and I overslept." I laughed a little, still disconcerted over my dream. "In fact, I was in the throes of a nightmare when the phone rang."

"Wanna tell me about it?"

When I was a child, Dad would come to my bedroom to shoo away the monsters I believed were hiding under my bed. I felt myself relax. "About the

96

dream, it's not important, but about the research, I believe I've discovered quite a bit about our killer."

"Hm, sounds interesting."

"Dad, was there a special reason you called?"

"Yep, I plan to pay Arnie Lewis a visit this morning. You up to going with me?"

"You bet. What time?"

"Meet me at Sweet's 'n' Eats in about an hour. I'll treat you to breakfast while you tell me about your research."

"Does Arnie know you're coming today?"

"Nope. The element of surprise will keep him off balance, won't give him time to think about how he answers my questions."

"Sneaky, Dad. Without Dennis Doolittle, the suspect list is almost nonexistent. Did Dr. Sanders give you a timeline of when she'll get dental records on victim number two?"

"She didn't."

"Would it help if I contacted Vaneeta?" Dr. Vaneeta Sunreet is the chief of forensics at the University of Lexington and my former dorm mate when we were both students there.

"I'm not sure Dr. Sanders would appreciate your, ah, usurping her."

There was an undertone to his voice that I couldn't quite decipher. I wondered if Dad felt lassoed by Dr. Sunny Sanders' attraction. It'd been almost six years since my mother's tragic death. Six years was a long time for any man to remain true to a memory. Dad was a man who took deliberate, practical actions in his life. I liked Sunny, and Ella had become almost like a sister. It occurred to me that maybe I needed to give Dad a gentle nudge in the direction of courtship.

"Never mind, Dad. It's not my business to step in Dr. Sanders' business."

I envisioned him tugging at his bottom lip, that habit he has when contemplating an answer. Finally, he said, "Give it a couple more days, Punkin. She's working on overload as chief of staff, medical examiner, and handling autopsies, too. I'll ease it by her to see if she'll object to you contacting Vaneeta."

"Good idea." I paused. "I'll meet you in an hour. Are you treating me to breakfast?"

This time he laughed. "Don't I always?"

Chapter Fifteen

I parked in front of Sweet's 'n' Eats and walked inside. Several locals greeted me. I stopped to answer Mrs. Oldrich's concern regarding her little pug's asthma, and to hear Mr. Giolla's request to take a look at the new thoroughbred mare he'd purchased. "I'll be happy to, Mr. Giolla. Call my office. Ella will give you an appointment date and time."

I threaded through the crowded café to where Dad sat. He and a handsome blond-haired man wearing a crisp white shirt seemed engrossed in conversation. The man was on his feet the moment I said, "Good morning."

A wide smile heightened his freckled features. He gave me a long, appraising look. "You've changed a lot since high school, Tullah."

My mind was like a computer scanning through files of picture albums. He pulled a chair for me. His drawl was soft and easy. "Don't you recognize me?"

I looked at Dad, hoping for a clue. He offered a smug smile and a cocked eyebrow. A young waitress approached the table and filled my mug with coffee. She refilled Dad's cup and then said, "More for you, Mr. Kemble?"

He nodded his assent.

An idiot would have had to be blind to miss the invitation of her flirtatious smile and the extra sway to her hips when she left to serve another table.

In a tiny corner of my heart, I wanted to be a victim of love, slain by the power of romance and addicted to passion, and then his identity hit me. "Andy Kemble, eleventh grade rodeo team. You were first in— everything—" I neglected to include *even my heart*. "Your family moved before you finished out the year. Are you visiting Enigma?"

The same waitress arrived with a tray of food. She served Andy first—and made sure she rubbed up against him. I swear the freckles on his face lit up like red Christmas bulbs. It was a rarity for me to see a man blush. I swallowed back the laughter and concentrated on pouring syrup over the plate of pancakes she set in front of me.

Andrew waited until we were alone. "Actually, I'm here to make Enigma my home as Sheriff Holliday's new deputy." Andrew loaded his mouth with a healthy portion of grits and eggs.

"You drove through yesterday's weather for a personal interview? Brave."

"I arrived late Sunday night. I heard about the murder the next morning." He helped himself to another bite. "I phoned Sheriff Holliday—"

Dad held up his hand to interrupt. "Andy, when we're among friends, I'm more comfortable with you calling me Henry."

"Yes, sir. As I was saying, I wanted to be first in line for an interview. I called your dad, um, Henry, and here I am."

"Congratulations and welcome home. How long have you been in law enforcement?"

"As a master-at-arms in the Navy, six years. As a civilian, four years."

I suppose it's my inquisitive nature that caused me to ask, "I seem to remember that your father took a job in Bowling Green. Do you still live in Kentucky?"

"No, Texas. After my father died, Mom decided we should live on my grandpa's ranch, outside of Waco." A sadness filled his blue eyes. "And before you ask, my mother had to sell the ranch to pay for Grandpa's nursing home and medical expenses. He had Alzheimer's."

"I'm sorry about your grandfather. Will your mother move with you?"

"She remarried. Orville runs a feed-and-seed store. She's happy where she is. Besides, my sister and her husband are nearby, there. Mom has grandchildren to keep her from missing me."

A strained silence followed. I surmised that I might have wandered into a none-of-my-business area.

Dad cleared his throat. He said, "With Andy's credentials, I ruled out the other candidates. He will assist Tiny." Dad wiped his mouth and drew a long sip of coffee. "I still need one more deputy for the office." He sighed. "And, you might as well hear it from me…"

My heart thumped. I gave him a wary glance, praying the news wasn't awful. He said, "Joyce turned in her resignation this morning. She's officially retiring after Christmas."

Joyce had been around for as long as I could remember. In fact, she had practically trained my dad when he became sheriff. She was a fixture, and I couldn't imagine him running the office without her. I stammered, "She can't do that… I mean, of course, she can, but why?"

"I feel the same way, Punkin. She's been with the department for over forty years. Her seventy-fifth birthday is Christmas Day. In her words, it's time, plus she's tired of trying to keep up with all the new technology and computer programs."

I thought about my grandmother's and Patty Sweet's ages. Like Joyce, these wonderful women were valuable assets to the county. What would Enigma be without Mayor Crow and Vice Mayor Sweet's innovations, and how would my dad manage without Joyce's micro-management?

"Whoever you hire will have some big shoes to fill. Have you told Grandmother and Patty?"

"Didn't have to. Joyce told them before she told me."

A thought occurred to me. Maybe Dad wouldn't want me to accompany him to question Arnie Lewis, now that he'd hired Andy Kemble. "When do you officially start work, Andy?"

He dabbed his mouth with a napkin, folded it neatly, and laid it on top of his empty plate. "As soon as we're finished here, I'm driving back to Texas to load my gear. I'm on the job officially week after next."

Andy pushed from the table as if signaling the conversation was over. He reached out to shake my dad's hand. "I hate to rush off, but I'd like to get on the road before another front moves in."

He turned to me. "It was good seeing you again, Tullah. Once I get settled, maybe we can find time to go riding."

"Oh, you own a horse?"

"Nope, but I have it on good authority that you're an expert judge of horses. I hope it's okay to enlist you to help me find a good one."

I felt a ridiculous flood of warmth when he gave me

a brotherly hug. "Absolutely. Let me know when you're ready."

Andy picked up the ticket next to his plate. Dad said, "I've got it, Andy. Have a safe trip."

He waved and, with a purposeful stride, walked away.

Dad and I chatted for a moment about Andy and the hiring of another deputy and a new secretary. He pushed back his chair. "You ready?"

I nodded and followed him outside to his truck. The funeral home was a ten-minute drive from town.

****

The cloying fragrance of lilies permeated the Lewis Funeral Home, and the overwhelmingly sweet scent caused my head to ache. I don't know why I felt the need to whisper. It wasn't as if I was going to wake the dead. I had to suppress a giggle at the thought. "Do you suppose they're trying to mask the odor of embalming fluid?"

"Sure smells like it."

As if a ghost, he appeared from nowhere. "Ah, Sheriff Holliday—Tullah, I truly hope you're not here to make arrangements for a loved one. Not that we'd ever turn you away, of course." Bald, pot-bellied and bug-eyed, Mr. Peebles reminded me of an old-timey actor in creepy black-and-white horror movies.

Dad said, "Actually, we're here to see Arnie."

"Ah, yes, poor young Arnie. So sad about old Arnold. He and I were partners for more than sixty years. He left the business to me, you know."

"All of it?" I wondered if Arnie had been completely disinherited.

The way Mr. Peebles wrung his hands together,

along with his sinister smile, it didn't take empathic powers to know this man had a disturbing side to him. "Of course. Now if you'll excuse me, duty calls. I have last-minute details to attend to, before the next bereaved family arrives. You'll find Arnie's office down the hall. It overlooks the serenity garden."

Without another word, the mortician turned on his heel and disappeared behind a velvet maroon curtain trimmed with gold braid and tassels. Halfway down the hall we met a petite young woman. She appeared to be in her late teens or early twenties. There was a familiarity about her that I couldn't quite place.

"Good morning," I said.

Without looking at me, she merely nodded and disappeared behind a closed door. Although I could see only the curve of her cheek, I sensed she was deeply sad.

Dad interrupted my musing. "This is it."

He knocked, then opened the door. Arnie stood staring out a window, his hands clasped behind his back. He turned and simply said, "I've been expecting you."

Arnie pointed toward two dark brown leather chairs. Dad and I seated ourselves. I asked, "Who was the young woman we met in the hall?"

"I'm not sure. We get many visitors here."

His answer annoyed me. Arnie knew perfectly well I wasn't referring to a visitor. "To be more specific, she entered the prep room."

"Oh, that's Anne Brom, our cosmetologist. She's a miracle worker when it comes to performing magic on the dearly departed."

Dad said, "How long has she worked for you?"

"About six months." Arnie also volunteered that she worked as a stylist at the Beyond Beauty Salon, a newly opened beauty shop east of town. "She isn't in trouble, is she? I mean, we advertised. Not everyone wants to work on dead bodies. Anne didn't flinch when we introduced her to Enos Daoud. You remember how badly his face was burned when the gas tank on his tractor exploded? But you're not here to discuss Anne." He gave a heavy sigh. "You think I killed that man—the headless horseman."

Neither Dad nor I responded. There are times when it's best to let a suspect stew in their own juice for a few minutes.

Arnie stared as us in pure shock, his mouth open-gaped, at first, and then working. "Me?" the question was a squeak. "Oh, my God! Tullah, Sheriff, you can't *believe*... No! This is horrible. I'd never...never... Please tell me you don't think I'm the killer."

It wasn't a question but more like a statement of fact. Dad said, "At this point, we don't know what to believe. We're working every angle. The body was embalmed. Understand we're not accusing you, Arnie, but yours is the only funeral home in Enigma."

I'd known Arnie since grade school. He wasn't given to outbursts, but I suppose a person can be pushed only so far before they lose their cool. He stood abruptly and knocked over his chair. "What about Mr. Peebles, or even Granddad? I'm sorry, I don't mean to cast aspersions on the dead! Everyone thinks my grandfather was a kindly old man." Arnie's voice rose. "He wasn't kindly at all. He was a mean, tyrannical hypocrite, and I hated him. Do you hear me?" he yelled. "I h.a.t.e.d him! There I've said it. You can put the cuffs on me and haul me to jail, because anyplace is better than the prison I've lived in since my parents died and left me in his custody."

Beads of sweat lined his brow. Mild-tempered Arnie Lewis had morphed into a raging madman. And then, as if he'd run out of steam, he righted the chair off the floor, sat on it, and buried his face in his hands and sobbed. "I'm sorry. Forgive me. It's all been too much. Being accused of murder, along with Granddad's death, and...and..." He grabbed a handful of tissues and blew his nose.

I had to ask, "Did your grandfather cut you out of his will?"

When he answered, there was something new in his expression. "Whatever gave you that idea?" Before I could reply, he said, "Oh, Mr. Peebles must have told you that he inherited the business."

He grabbed a clean tissue and wiped his brow and face. "I am, in fact, a wealthy man. Granddad was a miserly geezer. He almost begrudged spending money on new equipment for the business. In fact, after he deducted room and board from my salary, I barely had enough money to buy new shoes or get a haircut." His laughter was deep and satisfied. "At least he was kinder in death than in life. I was the heir listed on his checking and savings account. Both of which bulged because of his stinginess; even with himself.

"Sheriff Holliday, I did not kill that man. When you're convinced that I'm innocent, I'm leaving Enigma and never looking back. In fact, I can't wait to get the stench of embalming fluids out of my nose, and I hope to never see or touch another dead body for as long as I live. I didn't choose this profession. It was foisted on me. I was expected to follow the generations of Lewis men who have been morticians."

The entire time Arnie rattled on, my mind was on Anne Brom. Dad's voice drew me out of my reverie. "Settle down, Arnie. I'm not arresting you. However, I'd appreciate your help with this case."

I caught the hint of a smile as Arnie released the tension in his shoulders. "Sure, I'll do whatever I can to assist you, Sheriff Holliday."

"Who besides yourself, your grandfather, and Mr. Peebles know the embalming process?"

Arnie looked skeptical, as if Dad was trying to trick him. I deliberately softened my voice. "It's not a trick question, Arnie."

He scratched the top of his balding head. "Sorry." He drew in a deep breath. "Sometimes we get students from the mortuary school who come to serve the necessary state-required apprenticeship." He tapped his chin. "It's been a couple of years since we've had one. I think his name was Davis Campbell."

Dad said, "Have you noticed any chemicals missing?"

"None that I can remember. But then, it's been a while since we've checked supplies."

Arnie's answer didn't satisfy me. I asked, "Is it possible for a person to sneak a cadaver into the building and embalm it without arousing suspicion?"

"I suppose. What I mean, Tullah, is it's not like we take inventory of bodies."

The nerve beneath my right eye began to twitch. I could feel it flutter at the way Arnie was looking at me. Not with boiling passion that ended up with two sweaty bodies tangled in sheets, but as a man desperately trying to control his emotions. "Tullah, we've known each other since we were kids. Remember you stepped in when those boys tried to bully me? Remember how I fainted when you bloodied Butch Tompkins' nose? Honestly, I can't tell you how many times I've vomited my socks off after working with the dead. Grandfather never missed the opportunity to give me the raunchiest cadavers to clean. He said I would get over it. He was wrong."

A soft rap at the door interrupted us. Arnie said, "I'm busy. Can it wait?"

The door cracked and a timid voice answered, "I'm sorry, Mr. Lewis. I wanted to let you know I've finished with Mrs. Hamilton and I'm leaving now."

Arnie went to the door. Through the opening, Anne stood in the shadow, barely visible. "I didn't mean to yell, Anne. We have two more coming in tomorrow. Are you available?"

Her reply was inaudible. Arnie shut the door. I said, "Arnie, would you mind giving us a tour of the prep room?"

Chapter Sixteen

Dad and I followed Arnie down the hall to the door labeled prep room. He opened it. "It's actually downstairs. We don't need as much air conditioning there to keep the cadavers fresh." He hmphed. "Another of Granddad's cost-cutting feats."

The farther down I descended the more my heart pounded, my throat felt constricted, and the hair follicles felt like needles piercing my skull. I wasn't squeamish at the sight of dead bodies. This weird sensation stymied me.

It was the loud tapping at the basement window that drew our attention. Arnie grumbled, "It's that blasted crow again. It's been tapping at that window for well over a week. I keep shooing it away, and even thought about shooting it. At this rate, the window will break."

My hands turned icy, and it felt as if I had tremors inside my head when I walked to the window. "It's not a crow."

Arnie called, "Whatever! Just don't open the window, for Pete's sake. The bird might have rabies or worse."

I knew different. This was no ordinary bird. This was the raven. I unlatched the window and eased it up, but not enough to allow the raven entrance. I spoke in the language of my mother's people. "Why are you here, friend raven?"

The bird with a white band behind its neck blinked. In a feminine voice, it said, "Nevermore…nevermore!"

"What does that mean, friend raven? Tell me."

The bird spread a wing. It looked as if it was pointing toward a tall black cabinet. The bird winked and, in a strangulated voice, squawked, "There."

In a blink, the raven disappeared. If Dad and Arnie hadn't also seen it, I would have sworn I was hallucinating. Maybe the chemical fumes in the basement were affecting my brain.

Arnie seemed shocked. "You were always a little strange, Tullah. I've heard about your ability to communicate with animals. I always thought it was a bunch of hooey, until now."

A chill overtook me. I had to grit my teeth to keep them from chattering. "Tullah, are you ill?" Concern filled my dad's voice. He removed his jacket and draped it over my shoulders.

I managed to say, "Dad, I know where the head is."

"The bird told you?"

The skepticism in his voice annoyed me. I pointed and said, "Trust me."

He walked to cabinet number ten. "What's in here, Arnie?"

I noted the worried scowl on Arnie's face. "Formaldehyde, methanol, ethanol—that's ethyl alcohol—and other solvents that we mix to create embalming fluid."

I looked at him standing there with his hands clutched against his chest. "Arnie, are the cabinets locked?"

"No, of course not, because the only people that ever come down here are myself, Mr. Peebles, and Granddad, when he was alive."

Dad pulled out his cellphone and switched it to record. He pointed it and said, "Arnie Lewis, do I have your permission to open cabinet number ten?"

Arnie glanced from Dad to me. Puzzlement and concern graced his face. He shrugged. "Sure, I've nothing to hide."

We walked around the embalming table to stand in front of the black cabinet. Part of me was curious to know for sure the head was inside. What if I was wrong? The other part dreaded it, because I knew exactly what sat on one of the shelves.

I almost cried out, "Stop!"

I kept quiet.

Dad reached out. It seemed like his hand moved in slow motion. He lifted the latch. The door squeaked as he opened it wide. A pair of eyes stared at me through hollow sockets. We had found the missing head. I heard screaming and wondered if it was my own, though not the words that followed.

Arnie shrieked, "Oh, my god! Is this some kind of sick joke?" He backed away from the cabinet and bumped against the embalming table. "Oh no…oh no, oh no, oh no," played on a continuous loop as he edged away from the head's gaping mouth.

He managed to reach the deep stainless-steel sink and grip the sides as he leaned over it. The odious smell from his puke caused my own stomach to violently roil.

I rushed over and grabbed a handful of paper towels. "Here, Arnie, wet these and wash your face."

He did more than splash his face—he stuck his head under the faucet and let cold water course through his hair and over his neck. I handed him a clean towel. He finally straightened and dried himself off. He stammered, "I'm sorry. It's so...I'm...oh, shit! I don't know how that got in there. It's him, isn't it?"

Dad was talking on his cellphone. "Yeah, Tiny. I'll need you to dust for prints. I don't think you'll find any, though. This place is squeaky clean." He turned his attention to Arnie. "I'll need a sterile plastic bag."

I pulled out my cellphone and snapped pictures at different angles. We'd found the headless horseman's head. Not a handsome face, but neither was it repulsive. Black hair, brown eyes. A nose that may have been broken, and lips parted wide enough to reveal a chipped front tooth.

Arnie sat on a straight chair. He twisted his hands together. "I swear, Tullah, Sheriff Holliday, I don't know how that got there. I can't bear to look at it." And then as an afterthought he stammered, "Somebody's trying to frame me."

I squatted next to the chair. To calm him, I touched his arm. The trembles in his body vibrated against my hand, and I knew he wasn't the killer. "I believe you, Arnie. Try to relax."

He sobbed a breath, and nodded. "I hate this place."

Dad and I covered our hands with evidence gloves. I used a pen to lift the flap of flesh around the head's neck. I said, "A surgeon couldn't have done better. An amateur would have mutilated the area around the neck. Look how precise the cut is all the way around."

"Uh-huh." He lowered his voice. "I'm not convinced that Arnie is as innocent as he claims."

I, too, whispered. "What about the grandfather? This isn't a recent surgery. The old man had the knowledge and the skill."

"That's a distinct possibility, Tullah."

I held the plastic bag open while Dad gingerly lifted the head and set it inside and knotted the ties to form a handle. "It's not anyone I recognize. What about you, Tullah? A client, maybe someone whose pet you might've treated?"

I shook my head. "No, sir. Doesn't look familiar at all. We're back to square one with suspects and identity aren't we, Dad?"

"Sure looks that way."

Dad set the sack on the table. He shook his head in a gesture of regret. "Arnie, could your grandfather have done this?"

Surprised shock and then revulsion covered Arnie's face. "Grandfather was a difficult man. He was capable of enormous verbal and emotional abuse. He was also an expert mortician."

Arnie looked down at his hands and seemed to concentrate on the lines in his palms before he turned his attention back to Dad and me. Weariness laced his voice. "I don't want to lay the blame on a man who can't defend himself, Sheriff, but it's possible."

A deep baritone voice called out, "Sheriff?"

"Down here, Tiny."

Dad's deputy eased down the steep steps to join us in the basement. "You found the head?"

Dad pointed to the white plastic bag sitting on the table. "Do you need help down here?"

"Nah, it's a small area. I'll dust every nook and corner. Maybe we'll get lucky."

Arnie spoke up. "Deputy Goodbody, even though we keep this area sanitized, you'll find fingerprints from me and from Mr. Peebles, and even my grandfather's."

"Thanks, Arnie. That's a big help."

Dad said, "I'll meet you back at the station, Tiny."

The deputy merely nodded and continued to set out the different colored powders used to dust for prints. I made my excuse to leave. "I need to get back to the clinic. Ella is handling things until I return. Otherwise, I'd offer to stay and help."

Tiny grinned with pride. "She's a fine girl. Smart, like me." He guffawed at his joke.

"Don't sell yourself short, Deputy Goodbody. Ella got her smart genes from both you and her mother."

"Say, a little birdie by the name of Tanti Crow said Ella's interested in purchasing the land next to yours."

"That's right."

The big deputy looked around as if keeping a secret. "If old man Pickett agrees to sell, Sunny and I plan to buy it." He placed a finger against his lips. "Shh, don't tell Ella. Let on that Mr. Pickett refuses to sell. We're gonna surprise her with it as a graduation gift."

I wanted to wrap my arms around this gentle giant of a man. "It's a bit of a cruel joke, but I'll play along." I made a tick-a-lock motion to indicate that my lips were sealed.

He rewarded me with a huge dimpled grin. "Henry, Charlie called and said to stop by the saloon. He's got lunch ready for you and Joyce." Then he said to me, "It's raining out, Tullah. Be careful on the drive home."

Arnie stammered, "Are you taking me to jail, Sheriff? Do I need a lawyer?"

Dad cast Arnie one of his *don't make me mistrust you* looks. "I'd advise you not to leave town for any reason. I'll let you know if you need a lawyer."

"Sure, okay, Sheriff. I'll stay right here. Um, I mean,

not here…in this room…"

"I know what you mean, Arnie." Dad worked hard to suppress a smile.

My cellphone vibrated. Ella's picture popped up on the screen. "Everything okay, Ella?"

"Everything except I'm starved, but I don't have much of anything left to eat at my place. There's nothing pressing here, if you don't mind doing a little grocery shopping for both of us."

Grocery shopping is on my "things I hate to do" list, but I assured her shopping wasn't a problem. "I have lots of news to tell you when I get home. Hold the fort down. I'll try to be there before dark."

I looked forward to telling her about Andrew Kemble, and about finding the head.

Chapter Seventeen

After completing grocery duty, I dashed into Sweet's 'n' Eat to load up on pastries. A young woman with hair the color of snow stood at the cash register. She was a pretty girl with a heart-shaped face. Her shoulders slumped a bit. I strolled to the pastry counter and pretended to peruse the vast array of goodies. Actually, I was covertly giving Anne Brom the onceover. I casually said, "Hello, again."

She stared as if seeing me for the first time. Her liquid blue eyes were empty of all emotion. They made my hide do a little goose step.

Her voice was throaty, almost masculine. "Have we met?"

"Not formally. My dad and I were looking for Arnie Lewis's office. You were in the hallway." I offered my hand. "I'm Dr. Tullah Holliday, local veterinarian."

She didn't return a courtesy handshake. "Of course."

"Arnie speaks highly of your work. You're new to Enigma. I hope you like our town." I was rambling to make conversation while racking my brain for clues to where we'd met before that hallway.

She paid for her purchase and turned. I stepped to partially block her from leaving. "You look familiar. Have we met?"

Her pale eyes flickered. She gave me a dark look. "Didn't you just say you'd seen me at the funeral home?"

She had me there. "I meant officially."

She reached out and flicked the braid of hair draped across my shoulder. Her skin was as pallid as her hair. "I don't know you. However, when I'm not at the funeral home, I work at Beauty Beyond. Your split ends need serious attention." She pushed past me and out the door.

Shazam! Not only had I been properly dismissed but insulted at the same time. It was all I could do to keep from kicking her in the butt as she walked away. I watched her open an umbrella and disappear into the foggy rain.

"Made up your mind, Tullah?" Patty's voice returned me to the present.

"Do you know her?"

"Anne? She's one of our recent transplants. Works at the new beauty shop." Patty Sweet shivered. "Gives me the creeps."

"How so?" I pointed at a tray of chocolate glazed donuts and held up six fingers.

"It's like she's a vampire scoping out the jugulars in my neck."

"You do have a way with words, Patty." I laughed and pointed at the tray of lemon-filled donuts. "Six." By the time Patty had bagged my order, raindrops were dancing up and down the sidewalk. While I waited for a break in the downpour, I said, "Patty, you know most everyone who comes into the café, so what do you know about Anne—where she's from, her age, parents, married or single…you know, the usual gossipy stuff?"

Patty filled a to-go cup with steaming coffee and handed it to me. She said, "Everything I know, I've already told you. Her name is Anne Brom, she's a cosmetologist, works parttime at the funeral home and at the beauty shop. She isn't particularly friendly." Patty added, "And she looks like death warmed over."

Dismissing Ms. Brom's facial features, I changed the subject. "I heard a rumor about a shopping center coming to Enigma. You're the vice mayor. Is the buzz true?"

Patty replenished her own mug. "Enigma has to grow or die, and as much as Tanti and I hate it, the trend is toward shopping centers. The bank is even contemplating adding a branch once the new plaza is built."

For a blazing second, I thought about the five acres that adjoined my property. I saw my home and clinic being razed and a shopping center with apartment houses erected on the spot. I thought the vision would leave me permanently blind; especially if Mr. Pickett refused to sell to Ella. Patty took my stunned silence for interest.

"You could parcel off your fifty acres, make a substantial profit, settle your debts, and have enough money to start over. It's no secret that Tanti and Henry would love to have you closer to town."

"Not gonna happen." I had lost my zeal for the containers of Uncle Charlie's prize-winning chili that sat cooling inside my truck, and for the taste of chocolate-covered donuts. "I have to go."

On my drive home, I envisioned my two-story house, the house my mother was born in, my clinic, crumbling under the blades of heavy equipment. I saw myself, my dogs and my horses, standing beneath the leafless branches of hundred-year-old oak trees as we watched our family home being ripped up by the roots.

I crossed the railroad tracks long abandoned by the train companies. Although modern times had caught up with Enigma, there was still a cultural distinctiveness to the county. Many of the shanties that had been built during my grandmother's youth had been torn down and replaced with brick homes. We had gained city plumbing, sidewalks, and streetlights. I drove down my long driveway, past the big oak tree that sheltered my front porch, and parked under the carport. I beeped the horn to let Ella know I was home. She opened the clinic's side door and waved.

I loaded my arms with grocery bags while River and Rascal waited patiently for me to walk up the steps and unlock the kitchen door. Setting my purchases on the counter, I glanced at the kitchen clock. It was time to close the clinic. Ready to shake off the cold and the gloom, I filled a kettle with water for hot tea.

Ozzy and Pogo dashed through the doggie door. My pets greeted them with woofs and brays. Ella opened the door. "I hope your day was more exciting than mine."

"Dull?"

She nodded. "Which bags are mine?"

I pointed to the table. "I've already set the cold items in the fridge. What was the most exciting thing about being on your own in the clinic?" I placed teabags inside each mug and filled them with boiling water, then emptied the container of chili into a pot to heat.

She laughed. "Shaving the hair off Dudley the great Dane's rump, to treat a hot spot. I can't wait to hear about yours." She looked over the brim of the cup and smiled at the pink box labeled Sweet's 'n' Eats. She opened it and removed a lemon-filled donut. "Dessert first."

I ladled chili into two bowls and topped each one with grated cheese. Uncle Charlie had also supplied us with a loaf of his special garlic bread. We sat in silence for a couple of minutes, enjoying our feast.

I brushed crumbs from my shirt. "Dad hired a new deputy."

"So soon? I thought he had a long list of potentials to interview."

I shoveled another spoonful of spicy goodness into my mouth and, between chews, said, "It turns out the guy he hired is from Enigma. He and I went to school together. His family moved away before graduation."

She waved her empty spoon in the air. "What's his name? Good-looking? Bachelor?"

"You're shameless, Ella. Bachelor— You asking for me or yourself?"

"Hah, you're the shameless one."

I gave her the shortened version of my friendship with Andrew "Andy" Kemble, then moved on to fill her in about finding the missing head. She rose to replenish our bowls. "I bet Arnie Lewis is close to a nervous breakdown. I've never met anyone before who has a permanent case of the tremors."

I plucked a glazed donut from the box and savored its chocolatey deliciousness. "You should have seen the expression on his face when Dad opened the cabinet." I related how Arnie had tossed his cookies.

"Did your dad arrest him?"

I licked chocolate off my fingers. "Not yet. Neither of us are completely convinced Arnie is the killer. Arnie claims he's being framed, and I believe him."

As we cleared the table, I related my encounter with Anne Brom.

Ella ran her fingers through her newly cropped hair. "She gives a great haircut, and that's all I can say. She will never win the Miss Congeniality award. There's something kinda odd about her."

I arched an eyebrow. "You and Patty seem to think alike. How so?"

Ella scrunched her face into a thoughtful frown. "I'm not exactly sure. It's like…" She paused. "It's like Anne is two different people, both feminine and masculine, at the same time." She flicked her hand in the air. "Crazy, huh?"

"Maybe she's really a man disguised as a woman."

Ella scoffed. "C'mon, Tullah. She's got breasts, and she doesn't walk like a man, or even have a five-o'clock shadow."

We both laughed. "I was joking, Ella. Seriously!"

"With you, one can never tell."

Ella rinsed the dishes while I loaded the dishwasher. She thanked me for grocery shopping as she gathered her bags. She hesitated at the door. "Tullah, have you heard from Tanti about the property?"

"Not yet." I truly wanted to break my promise to her uncle about the surprise he and Sunny had planned. "Don't worry. Old Man Pickett's probably mulling it over."

"I wish he'd mull a little faster. I'd like to know his answer before I leave on Monday." She shifted her load and reached for the doorknob. "Maybe I should give him a call."

I scrambled for an answer. "Give Grandmother a few more days. If Mr. Pickett thinks you're anxious, he might decide to jack up the price."

"Okay." And she hoofed it out the back door.

Chapter Eighteen

The moment the door closed, I rushed to settle in the recliner and open my laptop. I clicked on the murder file and typed a series of notes about finding the head and meeting Anne Brom.

On a whim, I decided to research the origin of Brom. The skin beneath my eye began to twitch when I read that in Gaelic "Brom" means "raven."

Was it realistic to think our serial killer would go so far as to disguise himself as a woman? I started to type "transvestite" but immediately deleted the word, disregarding the thought as ludicrous.

I was reaching for the phone when Dad's picture showed on the caller ID. He sounded worried. "You girls okay?"

"Sure. Why wouldn't we be?"

"We have a psychopath on the loose."

I bit back a snarky reply. "Yes, sir, I know."

"I'm not referring to the recent murders."

"I'm listening."

"Moments ago, I received a fax from Fayette County Sheriff's Office stating that a patient from Ohio State Hospital has walked away from the facility. The patient suffers from severe psychosis, is bipolar, and is considered dangerous."

"Dad, how does a patient with these traits simply walk away from a mental hospital for the criminally insane?"

"Apparently, he killed an orderly and stole the guy's clothes and ID badge and other credentials."

"Does this person have a name and a description, and do they say what method was used to off the orderly?"

"Yes and no. His last name is Comhghan. However, due to the difficult pronunciation the spelling was changed to Cowen." He emitted a sound of disgust. "That's all I have. Unfortunately, my new office didn't come with updated equipment. The antiquated fax decided to die before spitting out the most important information, and Joyce's computer is outdated to the point that it won't run the new programs."

I understood Dad's aggravation. He'd spent years working without an adequate budget, and I can't remember him ever taking a vacation. No wonder Joyce had decided to retire.

That didn't answer the question as to why Dad was concerned about safety for me and for Ella. Depending on the escapee's mode of travel, Ohio was almost five hours from Enigma. I reassured him not to worry. "We'll be okay, Dad."

After a few minutes of general father-daughter chitchat and feeling satisfied that I'd allayed his fatherly concerns, I said, "Dad, after researching fairytale symbolisms, I've come up with a theory that might explain why the killer dresses the characters the way he or she does."

"Great! I'm all ears."

"Not over the phone." I could almost see him rolling his eyes, and quickly added, "I promise it's not a wild goose chase, just a little complicated."

His voice softened. "You haven't been wrong yet."

Dad rarely paid compliments. This was blatant flattery, and I loved it. Suddenly, I felt very tired. There had been so little sleep recently. Added to that was the emotional trauma of being where someone had been brutally murdered, then finding the decapitated head and spending my every waking moment since then thinking about both murders and who might have committed them.

I needed a day off, but I knew that wasn't in the cards until I'd figured out more answers as to who these men were and why they had been murdered—and, more important, who'd done it. This wasn't the first time I'd been gripped by such a compulsion, and given my empathic abilities, it probably wouldn't be the last. I could have, and probably should have, put it out of my mind and been content with getting updates from Dad or his deputy.

I chuckled, because that wouldn't have been me, and if there's anything I've learned during my twenty-nine years, it's the need to go with who I am and not who I'd prefer to be.

"Dad, it's possible the killer is getting frustrated because the weather interfered with his ability to showcase another victim. Maybe whoever it is will mess up and leave clues that will lead to you nabbing him. I'm just thinking out loud, of course."

"It's a good thought, Punkin. It's also likely our person has already made his third kill and is biding his time for that right moment."

"This is why I'm a veterinarian and you're the sheriff. You're right. So when do you think this right moment might occur?"

"Halloween is over. November first and Dios Los Muertos (Day of the Dead) both passed without incident." He huffed a sigh. "That leaves the Veteran's Day parade, and Thanksgiving."

I wondered what secrets the raven held. It was a question the bird would never be able to answer. At our parting goodnight, Dad said, "Be careful, Punkin. Be wise with the people that need you to make barn visits, especially at night."

Before saying goodnight, I confirmed that unless an emergency called me away I would meet the family at the Whitehorse for our customary Sunday brunch. The family included Patty, Uncle Charlie, and now Ella.

My psychology classes from the University of Georgia had been a requirement even though I'd had no desire to spend my time listening to the sordid problems of people who'd screwed up their lives and wanted an audience to whine to. I had studied psychology because it was easy, interesting. Like many other students, I'd also hoped to find answers to a few of my own problems without having to spill my particular soul-searching to anyone else.

Being fortunate enough to have two wonderful and loving parents didn't shield me from being called derogatory names and receiving hate notes because of my Native American heritage. I had found no answers, but I had learned many fascinating things about the human animal. One of the questions I'd pondered in class was the ability of a human to commit an act considered a horror.

The underlying thesis of the class had been that each and every person is capable of anything, given the right circumstances. I knew this to be true. My mother's beautiful face loomed before me. Her brutal murder had been senseless, and in essence had been swept under the rug to the point that it was now a cold case. Apparently, the New York police department had its own discriminations.

Put in the right situation, I could probably kill, too.

It had been a long day. An eventful day. I closed my laptop and unlocked the front door to stand outside looking up at the pristine wintery sky, then peered down the long driveway that led to the main road.

In my profession it always grieves me when I have to euthanize an animal. I was overcome with the reality that a person in Enigma had committed two brutal murders.

Neighbor or stranger? Someone was crazy…or unbelievably vicious. Whoever did it was still at large.

I'm not a fearful person by nature. With my dad being the sheriff, I was probably the safest person in the county. I willed my senses into alert status and, as soon as I stepped inside, I locked the door, then hurried to the kitchen to secure the locks there.

I saw by the kitchen clock that it was nine-thirty. It felt like midnight. I trudged upstairs, pulling off my flannel shirt as I went. I managed to shuck off the rest of my clothes, climb into my pajamas, and crawl into bed. Yet as much as I willed sleep to come, it eluded me. My mind drifted to the suspects. Old Mr. Lewis was dead. Dennis Doolittle was sitting in jail awaiting trial. That left Arnie Lewis. When he was in high school with me, he and I had shared several classes together. But he would have mood swings. He'd be hyper excited and follow me around jabbering, and then he'd get all quiet and sullen and just stare at me, until finally I had confided about his behavior to my dad, who then paid a visit to the principal. Mr. Lewis came and got Arnie and, I think, had him committed for a while, not just because of me but because he'd already been in trouble for touching boys and girls in the wrong places, plus he had developed some strange habits that creeped me out. He'd never hurt anyone, that I knew of, though he made a bunch of students nervous.

I was concerned that Arnie was beginning to repeat that pattern, and if he was involved in these murders, I needed to heed Dad's warning to watch out.

Chapter Nineteen

Wednesday morning swooped in clear and cold. I stood at the stove frying bacon and listening to the news. The November election was right around the corner. Candidates for the Senate were answering questions on this morning's talk show. To me, both men sounded like salesmen trying to convince the viewers to buy their product. I watched while I ate breakfast, but then switched over to the weather channel while I loaded the dishwasher. The weatherman announced the temperature and said to expect more rain over the weekend.

I looked out the window. The clouds had lightened a little. With the clearing weather, I expected an overload of appointments. I grabbed my jacket and left the house to walk across the yard to the clinic. Ella sat at the desk with the phone to her ear. She glanced up and waved. The coffeemaker was on and the pot was full. I poured two cups, reached into the small refrigerator to grab a carton of creamer and laced Ella's with a generous dollop, and set a cup in front of her.

We had a steady stream of walk-in clients with an array of suffering pets, from a bee sting on a severely swollen nose to a case of roundworms. The phone rang constantly for booking appointments. In fact, Ella and I worked through lunch, and my stomach was making squeezy noises, reminding me I was hungry. I visualized a plate of chicken-fried steak slathered in gravy, with a heaping side of garlicky mashed potatoes. Unfortunately, all I had to choose from was an assortment of frozen dinners. I had never mastered the art of whipping up fine cuisine. My specialty was in heating leftovers from Sunday family dinners or nuking microwaveable meals.

I stretched the kinks out of my back. It was good to leave the surgical room and the scent of anesthesia behind after I'd cleaned up from docking the tails of eight registered Doberman puppies. I filled my lungs with fresh air.

We were soon busy again. Dark-thirty finally arrived. Ella and I had worked two hours past our normal closing time. We were getting ready to walk out the door when the phone rang. Ella said, "Let the service pick it up, Tullah. It's been a long day and we're both exhausted." She added, "And hungry."

I agreed. "Let's go to the Whitehorse Saloon and indulge in one of Uncle Charlie's hamburgers with a side of onion rings. My treat."

She grinned. "You don't hear me arguing, do you?"

It had been a long and eventful day. I hadn't forgotten that my friend and assistant was about to leave. "Ella, how am I going to handle the office and the patients when you leave next week?"

I pulled onto the highway and turned in the direction of the Whitehorse Saloon. Ella said, "I've given it lots of thought, and the only idea I've come up with is perhaps the high school has students in the DCT program who'd love to get out of class and gain a little hands-on experience in a veterinarian's office."

It wasn't a bad suggestion. "Diversified Career Track, of course. Ella Sanders, you are a genius."

Her mouth turned downward to form a glum smile. "Save the flattery until after I graduate and take the state licensing exam."

I was about a mile from the Whitehorse when my phone rang. Dad was calling. I put the phone on speaker. "What's up, Dad?"

"Have you had supper yet?"

I looked at Ella and smiled. "No, sir. In fact, Ella and I are minutes away from the Whitehorse."

The seriousness in his voice piqued my interest. He said, "Come to the office. I've ordered from the Crispy Chicken."

"Has there been another murder?"

"None that I'm aware of."

"Then why are we meeting at your office?"

"Privacy. Too loud and too many listening ears at the Whitehorse."

I remember when the busiest nights at the saloon were Friday and Saturday. To keep the business alive, Uncle Charlie had begun serving his award-winning chili, BBQ sandwiches, and hamburgers during the week. These days, and with the town's growth, finding a parking space was difficult every day. I was happy for my godfather. Goodness knows, he deserved the financial benefits from the increase in business. Yet I was enveloped by a sense of loss for "the good old days" when we didn't need to elbow our way to a booth or wear earplugs.

I hesitated to ask if this was a private meeting. I glanced at Ella. She nodded her understanding. "Dad, you did hear me say that Ella's with me?"

"Yep. I'll call and order another plate. She knows the drill—just like any doctor that takes an oath of confidentiality, whatever she hears or partakes in doesn't leave my office."

Ella leaned toward the phone. "I understand, Sheriff Holliday. You don't need to worry about me."

I drove past the saloon's crowded parking lot and merely shook my head. Wednesday night and folks were parking on the side of the road. Ella turned to look over her shoulder. She said, "It's only a matter of time before a chain restaurant comes to town and gives Mr. Whitehorse some competition."

The sight of a vacant lot that had been clear cut of massive oak trees disgusted me. A sign displayed the promise of one business lacking in Enigma, a hotel. I made a mental note to meet with the town council about writing an ordinance that forbade businesses to strip the land of trees. "More people—more crime. Maybe, by then, Uncle Charlie will be ready to sell out and retire."

I drove under the "Welcome to Enigma" sign and down main street. Businesses had American flags displayed, and traffic cones were stacked on sidewalks waiting for workers to set them out to mark next week's Veteran's Day parade route. I parked, and we hurried through the chilly air and up the steps to the new government building that housed the sheriff's office, interrogation rooms, and holding cells. Across the street, the old sheriff's office, with its second story that was my dad's apartment, looked sad and dilapidated.

A high schooler from the Crispy Chicken met us at the door, his hands filled with two large sacks. I dug in my jacket pocket for a bill to tip him while I relieved him of his burden. He thanked us. "Hey, Doc Holliday, you nab that killer yet?"

I resisted rolling my eyes. "Sheriff Holliday and

Deputy Goodbody are following leads."

"Some of the kids at school said we should form a posse like in the olden days and go after the guy."

I wanted to laugh at the sixteen-year-old whose face had glowed with embarrassment when his baritone voice unexpectedly shifted to a high squeak. I displayed a serious frown. "This isn't the Wild West, Bert. Going off half-cocked is dangerous, and someone could get hurt." I also warned, "It won't go well if Sheriff Holliday gets wind that you kids are forming a vigilante committee."

The boy's face deepened to a darker shade of scarlet. "Oh, no, Doc, we're just talking. You know, kid stuff. We ain't really serious." He stammered, "I-I gotta get back to work." He turned on his heel and sprinted away down the sidewalk.

"You going to tell your dad, Tullah?"

"Yes."

Deputy Goodbody sat at the reception desk. I handed him the bag with his name on it. He pointed. "Henry's waiting for you."

"Is he in a mood?"

Tiny Goodbody rewarded us with a belly-deep chuckle. "No more than usual. I think this case is getting to him."

Ella said, "Tullah, I'll sit with Uncle Tiny. The less I know about this case, the less likely I am to have nightmares."

I handed her a sack. "Totally understood."

I regretted not having my laptop. Having the murder file at my fingertips would have been helpful. Thoughts invaded my mind as I turned the knob to Dad's office. He greeted me with his usual fatherly smile and waved me to a chair. "Wanna eat first, then talk? Or eat and talk?"

I pulled a chair closer to his desk. "Talk and eat." I removed the chicken baskets and drinks from the sacks and set them on the desk. "Dad, Bert Howard, the kid that works for the Crispy Chicken, implied that some of the boys at the high school have hinted at forming a posse. Those are his words, not mine. I thought you should know."

"Kids and their crazy ideas. 'Preciate the heads up. I'll contact Principal Garrett and Coach Devane, as well as Sergeant Walker, the ROTC instructor. The last thing we need is a bunch of half-cocked kids running around the county with loaded guns."

Dad scarfed down most of the french fries before saying, "About this symbolism theory of yours, what have you surmised?"

Hot, greasy chicken had never tasted so good. "The Headless Horseman, of course, is a major character in "The Legend of Sleepy Hollow." But the ghostly rider— and especially his head—also symbolize the tension between reality and imagination, between the natural and the supernatural, the belief in legend and myth held by many of the townspeople in the story." I paused to wash down my bite of food with a gulp of cola.

Dad listened with interest. "Okay, what does the big bad wolf in Little Red Riding Hood's story symbolize?"

"The wolf is the symbol of pride, vengeance, secrets, and self-denial. He hides, waiting to take his revenge when opportunity comes. Nothing stands in his way when you anger him.

"It just so happened that the wolf was ready to eat Little Red Riding Hood when the woodsman came by. He heard Little Red Riding Hood scream, grabbed his axe, and killed the wolf."

Dad removed a wet-wipe packet from the sack and cleansed grease from his hands. I gathered our trash and excused myself to the ladies' room. Upon my return to his office, we continued our discussion.

"You know, Punkin, I'm just a small-town sheriff who majored in football when I was in college." For a moment, he seemed lost in thought. "If I'm re-elected this term, it might be wise for me to enroll in some online criminal psychology courses. Growth brings more than additional tax revenue—it brings crime and sophisticated criminals, too."

It worries me when Dad is silent. I watched him thump a pencil against the desk, and waited. He leaned back in his chair and folded his hands against his chest. I feared he was thinking about retiring, but I swallowed back the words.

He finally said, "What else?"

I blinked and recovered from my thought. "The central theme of Little Red Riding Hood is to be careful of those who are predators and who want to take the most valuable things in life away from others for the purpose of feeding their own selfish needs. In other words, don't trust strangers, or even people you have come to trust.

"Dad, the fact that both victims were male and their genitals were completely removed… It's my opinion that our killer was brutally mistreated, possibly as a child. This is definitely an act of revenge."

"That's damn sound reasoning, Punkin. Any man that'd steal a child's innocence needs to be castrated."

The long day was catching up with me, and I was almost too tired to appreciate Dad's emotion. "What's really disturbing is that whoever our killer is, he probably had no one to protect him from these fiends."

"Yeah, that happens more than we know." Dad massaged his temples. "You have an opinion as to why the victims were dressed in costume?"

I pulled my thoughts together. "At this point, only the killer can answer that question. My thoughts are that somewhere in his childhood, he lost touch with reality and sought refuge in fairy tales.

"There's something else, Dad. It's about the raven. I believe this particular bird is connected to the murders. I'm not sure how, just that it appeared before the first and second murders, and then, you were there when it tapped on the basement window—"

"Yeah, and that was when we found the missing head. Why does it say, 'Nevermore'?"

I stood and wandered around the office before sitting again. "In Poe's poem 'The Raven' the main message is that grief can overcome a person's ability to live in the present and engage with society. He or she is probably a loner, and this is why I'm certain we're dealing with a psychotic."

Tiny's voice came through the intercom. "Henry, Sunny's on line one. She has the information we've been waiting on."

I pushed the reply button. "Ella, you okay?"

"Sure. Take your time. I'm listening to a podcast on my cellphone."

Dad put the phone on speaker. "Evening, Sunny. Tullah has been enlightening me about the psychology of symbolisms."

Dr. Sanders and I exchanged greetings, and then she said, "Finally, I have the identities of both victims. Forensics apologized for the delay. With the approaching holidays and budget cuts, the process is moving slower than usual."

Dad said, "Understandable."

She heaved a sigh. "Here's what I have. The headless guy is Nathaniel Pilcher, and the wolfman is Larry Parrish." She continued, "Parrish was easy, due to his dental work. Pilcher, on the other hand, was healthy as a horse, no pun intended, Tullah."

"Love your humor, Dr. Sanders."

"Tullah, I wish you'd call me Sunny."

"Yes, ma'am."

Dad interjected, "How did you identify Pilcher?"

"Even though he'd been embalmed we were able to extract a small amount of DNA from his organs. It took a while to get a match."

When she hung up, Dad said, "I'll run the names through the Kentucky Bureau of Investigations to see if Pilcher and Parrish are in the system."

Chapter Twenty

We had already said our goodnights. Dad followed me to the reception area, and Ella and I were about to leave when the phone rang. Call it empathic instinct or being nosy, I delayed my exit through the door. Tiny looked up and said, "Henry, it's Malachi Dotson."

Dad said, "Stay on the line, Tiny. I'll take this in my office."

I waved my final goodbye, and was ready to follow Ella outside when Tiny's voice drew me back. "Tullah, Henry thinks you need to hear this."

Ella yawned. "I'll wait for you in the truck, Tullah."

Dad came out of his office, and joined Tiny, who was propped against Joyce's desk. When she's off duty, the deputies pull double duty at answering the telephones or walk-in traffic.

"Anything wrong in Dixie County, Dad?"

"You know the headless horseman's horse, the one that mysteriously disappeared?"

"What about it?"

"Malachi said the owner had reported the stallion stolen. Get this—it's worth over a million dollars."

Tiny and I both released amazed whistles. I crinkled my face and turned in Dad's direction. "I'm surprised the owner didn't have an all-points bulletin out on the horse. Why is Sheriff Dotson just now getting around to notifying you?"

"Because the owner lives in Dixie County, Malachi naturally figured someone from the area stole the horse. When his investigation didn't turn up anything, he decided to widen his search. Get this—the thoroughbred has DNA ties to Man O' War."

This information elicited another whistle. "Shazam, Dad. It's been over a week." Then I backtracked. "Of course, if the horse is insured, the owner isn't out anything if Sheriff Dotson doesn't find it. Maybe the owner is guilty." I shrugged. "Just saying."

It's rare, but there are times when, if a thoroughbred stallion isn't earning its keep by winning races or producing winning foals, the owner will find a way to dispose of the animal in order to collect the insurance money.

"I mentioned that to Malachi. However, he said the owner stated she was at a sale in Louisville and didn't know the horse was missing until she got home a few days after Halloween. Even then, she didn't visit the barn until a couple of days later."

"And the barn manager didn't notice the stallion was missing?" I didn't bother keeping the sarcasm from my voice. "Yeah, right."

Tiny spoke up. "Henry, I'll check our list of known horse thieves in the county. It's altogether possible the animal has already been sold and shipped out of the state. For all we know, it might be on its way to the Middle East or Europe, especially France."

Or the glue factory. I didn't say it out loud, and the thought caused me to shudder. "Did Sheriff Dotson say where the horse was when it was stolen?"

Dad nodded. "Yep, I specifically asked. According to the owner, it was in the stallion barn. Malachi said he went out to the farm to investigate, and the stall was the last one at the rear of the barn."

"We all know that stallions are fairly fractious, especially during breeding season. Not just anyone could walk in, snap on a lead strap, and walk the stallion outside. And, obviously, it had to be either loaded in a trailer or saddled and ridden off the property." I thought for a second, then asked, "Did Malachi happen to say the horse was gray?"

"Yep, here's the description—gray, seventeen hands, stallion, five years old. Four black stockings. Serial number tattooed under top lip—B19047."

I mused for a moment. "I wonder where the killer got enough boot black to cover a horse that large?" I added, "I've treated a number of gray stallions but none from Dixie County. I also keep a log of all the serial numbers of pure breeds I've treated. I'll check and let you know in the morning if this particular tattoo number is in my file."

****

Anne Brom was on my mind as I drove home. During our conversation about symbolism, I'd forgotten to mention that in the Gaelic "Brom" meant "raven." I shook it off because Anne Brom didn't fit the profile of a psychotic. Although she wasn't particularly friendly toward me, she did have a job that required a modicum of social skills. I mentally crossed her off my list of suspects, which left me with Arnie Lewis as the one and only person of interest.

While keeping my eyes on the road, I said, "Ella, do the names Nathaniel Pilcher and Larry Parrish ring a bell?"

"Not unless they've brought animals to the clinic for

treatment. I can check the files. Why?"

I related the information her mother had shared with us about the murder victims. "Dad's running their names through the KBI database. If either of them has committed a crime, it'll show up, which will hopefully give us a motive for the killings and lead us to the killer."

"What if they don't? Have a record, either one of them, I mean?"

I glanced at her. "Then we're back to square one."

The extra-long day had caught up with us. It was as if we were both too tired to talk, and we rode the rest of the way in silence. I turned down the driveway and pulled in front of the trailer so Ella would have enough light to get inside. She opened the truck door and slid to the ground. "First thing in the morning, I'll contact the guidance department at the high school to see if we can recruit a student to help until I graduate. Do you have a preference—male or female?"

Gender hadn't crossed my mind. "Honestly, it doesn't matter, as long as they can follow directions, answer the phone, and show up on time."

Chapter Twenty-One

I wasn't particularly looking forward to this day. It meant that tomorrow was Ella's last day for the next four weeks. The cold November wind bit at my face as I hustled to the clinic. River and Rascal raced ahead of me. Gandalf, my black-and-white pinto, stood at the fence and whinnied. I spoke to him. "It's too cold to go for a ride. Wait until it warms up."

As if not to be left out of the conversation, the other three horses raced up to the fence and stretched their long necks. I walked over, reached into my coat pocket, and drew out carrot chunks for each of them.

Ella greeted me the moment I entered the office. "Good news, the school counselor said she had the perfect student for us. She said he's smart, reliable, and that he jumped at the opportunity to spend the next four weeks working with you."

"Interesting. I kind of thought a girl would be more interested in office work." I shucked out of my jacket and put on a lab coat. "Doesn't matter. When will he start?"

She glanced at the wall clock. "This morning. I told her nine o'clock. He'll work four hours, three days a week."

I helped myself to the coffee and wrapped my hands around the warm mug. "Why don't you take tomorrow off? I imagine you still have packing to do."

Ella quirked her lips to one side. "I'm all packed,

and my truck is loaded. Besides, I'm not leaving until Saturday. It won't take long for me to settle in, once I get to the hotel where the university is setting up the December graduates."

"I've been thinking. Maybe we should change the name of the clinic, especially since you're becoming a partner."

"No way, Tullah. I appreciate the thought. People know and trust Holliday Animal Clinic. Let's not monkey around with changing the name."

"You'll at least need your own office, and we should think about hiring an administrative assistant. With you handling the small animal end of the business and me taking care of the large animals, neither of us will have time for office duties."

Ella agreed.

A timid knock at the entry door interrupted our conversation. We glanced at each other and shrugged. Usually, people didn't bother knocking, opting to walk right on in. I went to the door and opened it.

One of the delivery boys from the Crispy Chicken stood outside. "Jeff?"

"Yes, ma'am. Mrs. Fauntroy said you needed a student assistant."

I invited him in. "Do you drink coffee?"

"No, ma'am. Hot tea or ice tea. And I really love colas." He pointed to his pimpled face and shrugged to indicate the reason for the acne.

"Ms. Sanders and I drink copious amounts of coffee. One of your duties is to keep the coffeepot full. We need the caffeine to keep us going, especially on super-busy days."

I motioned for the gangly lad to take a seat, hoping

to ease his obvious nervousness. "Jeff, Mrs. Fauntroy implied that you really wanted this position. Care to tell us why?"

"Well, ma'am, it's no big secret. 'Bout everyone in Enigma knows my family is poorer than dirt. I'm the first one to graduate. Heck, my daddy and mama can hardly read and write. I've also been saving the money I make at the Crispy Chicken 'cause I want to go to college. I'll be the first in the family to do that, too." He shifted as if uncomfortable to reveal his family history. "Anyhow, my granny said she had a little money tucked away, and she'd help with my tuition. Honestly, Dr. Holliday, working with you will look good on my college résumé. I'll do a real good job." His face turned beet red as he looked down and tried to tuck his feet under the chair.

My eyes followed to a pair of tattered tennis shoes. I both admired and felt sorry for the teen.

Ella asked, "Do you aspire to become a veterinarian, Jeff?"

Concern shadowed his fair features. "No offense, ma'am, but I've had my fill of horse sweat and horse manure, and travelin' around the race track circuit. Groomin' is 'bout all my daddy and uncles know. I'm staying with my granny so's I can finish school."

He squirmed a bit, waiting for a comment. "Does this mean you don't want me to work here?"

Ella and I exchanged smiles. I said, "Whatever your career goals are is none of our concern, Jeff. As long as you show up on time, keep the files organized, and the appointments up to date, we're satisfied." I thought for a moment. "If you don't mind telling us, what *are* your career goals?"

He offered a glimmer of a smile. "I want to become

a teacher, ma'am. There's a great need for education in the Appalachians. Illiterate folks get taken advantage of more often than not. I know firsthand."

"Teaching is an admirable career, Jeff. One thing, though—I'd prefer you call me Dr. Holliday."

"Yes, ma'am." He chuckled and blushed. "Uhm, Dr. Holliday."

"Dr. Sanders will show you how the office works." As far as I was concerned, Ella's new title was Dr. Sanders. I had no doubt she would ace the state boards, which would officially give her the title.

At noon time, our new office assistant had caught up with the pile of neglected filing and had gone through the long list of lip and ear tattoos. Jeff had found none that matched the number on the missing horse. When it was time for him to leave, he said, "Thank you for this opportunity, Dr. Holliday. I'm looking forward to Monday."

He grinned. "Dr. Sanders, I sure wish you luck with your final exams, and thank you for being patient with me today. This is a new experience, and I really liked it."

Once he was out the door, I said, "My heart goes out to that boy. He's to be admired for working to break the mold of his family history."

"College tuition is expensive. Lots of students don't finish because working and studying is tough. They burn out."

A thought occurred to me. "I'll make certain that Mrs. Fauntroy helps Jeff with grants and possible scholarships."

I picked up the phone and dialed my dad's office. Joyce answered, "Sheriff's Office, how may I direct your call?"

"Hey, Joyce, it's Tullah. What is Dad going to do when you retire?"

She tsked. "He'll manage. And to make sure he doesn't call me, I've booked a month-long cruise." She added that she had already interviewed several candidates and had narrowed the field down to two. "Henry and I'll make a decision soon. I want plenty of time to train the person before my last day."

We both laughed. "Is Dad in?"

"Sure, hang on." In her usual manner, she refused to use the intercom and yelled, "Henry, Tullah, line one."

When he answered, I filled him in about my student helper, then said, "About the tattoo number, I've never treated that particular horse. Did Malachi say if he'd checked with Cindy Redfern?"

"Yep, Dr. Redfern has no records of treating the animal. Another dead end."

"We're striking out on this one, Dad. My guess is we'll never find the horse."

He agreed. "Finding the stallion is merely a blip. It doesn't help with our case."

"I suppose it's too early to hear from the KBI?"

"Might take as much as twenty-four hours. Hopefully, tomorrow."

Ella answered her cellphone. Her loud groan and the tears welling her eyes caused me to say, "I'll catch you later, Dad."

Before disconnecting, Ella said, "Thank you for letting me know, Mayor Crow."

"What did my grandmother say that's got you so upset, Ella?"

She huffed a sigh. Her shoulders drooped. "Mr. Pickett sold the property. The sale is final." She sniffed.

"I had my heart set on buying it."

The look of disappointment on her face pierced my heart. I nearly broke my oath of silence to tell her that she'd been punked by her mother and uncle. I patted her on the shoulder. "Don't worry. There'll be other properties that you might like better than the one next door."

"Sure. Let's go eat lunch. I need to drown my sorrow in a bowl of chili."

Just as we were about to call the answering service to let them know we were going to lunch, the phone rang. Ella answered, and she jotted a name, address, and animal on a slip of paper. She said, "Dr. Holliday will get there as soon as possible."

Although the information was on the paper, she read it off. "Mare has been in labor for over twenty hours. The owner says he's certain the foal is breech." She handed me the slip.

I read the owner's name. "Cadillac Farms. I hope the mare isn't Jessabelle. I've warned Bob Cadillac that she's too old."

I grabbed my coat. "This may take a while. I'll see you in the morning."

My hospital truck is fully equipped and is, in essence, a traveling pharmacy or even a hospital. Except for an operating room, most everything I need is inside the truck. I peeled out of the driveway. As I drove, my mind wasn't on the mare, but I would do all I could to save her and the foal.

I mentally counted the days from the last murder. A new weather front was moving in. Local forecasters were predicting up to four inches of rain, with flooding in lower-lying areas of the county. I suspected the killer was growing frustrated at a missed opportunity to flamboyantly showcase another victim. The empathic voice inside my head warned that the killer was tired of waiting.

Halloween was over, so would the victim be dressed in a costume? Would the raven contact me? In such deep thought, I almost missed the road that led to the Cadillac farm.

Chapter Twenty-Two

Feeling satisfied with what I'd achieved, I cleared Enigma's town limits and decided on the spur of the moment to stop at the Whitehorse's drive-through window for a large black coffee and whatever food Uncle Charlie could whip up fast. I was wired from saving the aged mare's life and delivering twin foals. A slow drizzle coated the windshield, and the weather had turned colder.

"Out kind of late, aren't you, Doc?" Vera Jones asked as she opened the drive-thru window. Even as a teenager I'd loved the thick white coffee cups and the hamburgers Uncle Charlie made.

"Goes with the job, Vera."

"It's after ten. You look beat. The crowd has thinned out. Why don't you come in and sit a spell?"

"I'm too tired, Vera. What's in the kitchen that you can throw together without much fuss?"

"It's Thursday. We've got BBQ leftover. How 'bout a big ol' sandwich?"

"Sounds good to me." While she called in the order, I said, "Vera, do you know Nat Pilcher or Larry Parrish?"

Vera loaded a sack with napkins and extra sauce. "Lots of men come and go in the saloon. If they were rowdy, I'd remember them." She handed me the to-go cup. Her voice had taken on a bit of an edge. "Are they connected with the murders? Should I keep an eye out for them?"

Vera had worked for Uncle Charlie less than a year. I'd come to know that she enjoyed creating fantasies. "Nothing to fret yourself over, Vera."

She looked at me as if she could discern the truth behind my curiosity. She gave a short little snort of agitation. "I know. It's all hush-hush, and I'll read about it in the paper." She left to fill my order.

My cellphone chirped, signaling that I'd received an email. Hoping it was from Dad with information about the dead guys, I resisted the urge to open the app. Maybe it was the late hour, or maybe that I was exhausted. Whichever, Vera's voice startled me. She scoffed, "Caught you napping with your eyes open, didn't I? Drive safe, Doc. Even ducks don't like this kind of weather."

I handed her the money and told her to keep the change. As I drove away, I couldn't resist the aroma of onion rings and reached inside the sack to grab a few.

Rain pelted the windshield. I concentrated on the road as I drove through the night. When I pulled up to the house, I regretted that I hadn't left the kitchen light on. It occurred to me that even with my dog and donkey waiting on the steps, it was almost more than I could abide, to be walking into a dark house alone.

Once inside, I shut down the doggie door and locked the kitchen door. Too tired to sit at the table, I ambled upstairs. It wasn't customary for me to eat in bed. Tonight, I'd make the exception. Shucking out of my clothes and boots, I donned a pair of flannel pjs. I plumped up both pillows and leaned against the bed's headboard.

After a generous gulp of coffee, and several

satisfying bites of sandwich, I opened the email on my phone. Dad had written: *KBI report—Pilcher and Parrish were disqualified as foster parents, their licenses revoked by the state of Ohio for habitual child neglect. There are other charges non-related to the abuse offenses. Your 'revenge' theory is right on target.*

I responded: *I wonder if Arnie Lewis has a connection to them? Remember when his grandfather sent him away? Can you check to see if either of the deceased worked at a sanitarium or private school?*

It was almost as if Dad was waiting for my reply. He answered immediately: *Will do!*

I remembered that Dad had received a fax from the Fayetteville Sheriff's Office, and immediately sent another email: *Dad, any more information from Fayetteville Sheriff's Office about escaped patient?*

Just because I felt the need, I filled him in about enlisting a student aide to help in the office while Ella was away, and about delivering the twin foals. I signed off with a smiley-face emoji. He answered with a thumbs up.

I scarfed down the rest of my sandwich and finished off the last drop of coffee. I'm not one of those people bothered by caffeine keeping them awake. Suppressing a yawn, I decided to research Anne Brom. I had looked deep into her eyes, and what I saw startled me. It was like looking into a cavern of evil. I googled her name and came up with nothing. I checked in the white pages for name and address. It was as if Anne Brom didn't exist.

Dad responded to my email: *Waiting for return call.*

Before completely crashing, I walked downstairs to the kitchen to dispose of my dinner trash, then to the bathroom. I returned to bed and switched off the lamp.

I lay in the dark with the quilt pulled over my ears and thought about the case. The case—and like all the others, I had begun to think of it as *my* case—had taken a different twist. We now had a solid motive with one viable suspect. Like a complicated puzzle, I needed to find the missing pieces to solve the crime.

Chapter Twenty-Three

Masks distorted their faces, making them appear like half-formed creatures. More terrifying than the grotesque smoothness of their features was the absence of any emotions. The eyes were dulled behind the masks, and all semblance that mark humankind were blunted, metamorphosing them into nightmarish monsters.

The violent thrums of a raven's black wings beat around my head as the bird squawked, "Nevermore... Nevermore...Nevermore!" I could not seem to move from the doorway. Helplessly, I watched, a thin soundless screaming rising in my throat.

I came out of the nightmare suddenly, as I always do, with a wrenching motion that brought me up, gasping frantically for air.

With desperate urgency I flung myself to the bathroom. I slipped out of my sweaty pjs and stepped into the shower. The blast of cold water took my breath, and I stood under it until my body trembled from the cold and the water had lost its shock.

Finally, I turned the water off, stepped out, and wrapped myself in a thick blue towel. I moved carefully, keeping my mind off the details of the dream, as one would walk warily through burning embers with bare feet.

As I moisturized my skin with cream, *It's happening soon* popped into my head. Driving that thought from my mind, I focused on getting dressed. With the time change, it was still dark outside—too early to open the clinic and too late to crawl back into bed, even if I dared do so.

I opened my cell phone, allowing my finger to hover over the call button. Doubt stopped me. What if my dream was simply a nightmare and not an omen? I closed the phone and set it on the night table next to my bed. There was no need to bother my dad at this hour of the morning.

By the time I'd finished the routine of putting on makeup and braiding my hair and was ready to get dressed, the shock of the terrible dream no longer seemed unbearable. It was not gone. No, it lurked somewhere in the dark corridors of my memory, waiting until I was relaxed before another memory of it would come again. I had learned to occupy my mind quickly with something—anything—else when those empathic flickers flared inside my brain.

Dressed and ready to greet the day, I retrieved my phone and tucked it into the back pocket of my jeans.

While I waited for two waffles to toast and the coffee to perk, I decided to check my email, hoping for more information from the Fayetteville Sheriff. Nothing!

Soon I was enjoying the golden-brown waffles, and when finished, I indulged in another cup of coffee.

Dawn was breaking and the air was filled with moisture when I left to open the clinic. I thought about the case as I unlocked the door. Flipping on the light, I paused at Ella's desk and perused the appointment book. Almost every time slot was filled. Unless an abundance of cancellations occurred, today promised to be extra busy. I pressed the button to turn on the coffeemaker. A rich aroma filled the office.

I filled my cup and walked to my office to sit in the leather chair. I looked at the photograph of my mother, Josie Crow Holliday. I stared at the picture, thinking how my father had often told me that I got my streak of stubbornness from the Scots-Irish side of the family.

I lifted the picture and sat quietly, thinking of my Native American heritage. My grandmother and mother were full Cherokee. My mother was beautiful and artistically gifted. Her kindness knew no limits. My grandmother, Tanti Crow, proudly proclaims that I inherited my gift of inner sight from *Koga*, the great spirit.

I looked into Mother's gentle eyes. Her death was an ache in my bones. My spirit wept for her. I murmured softly, "I promise to find your murderer." As I spoke, I heard the outer door of the office open and then close. Getting to my feet, I walked quickly out of my office to find Jeff settling down at Ella's desk.

"Oh, morning, Dr. Holliday," he greeted me with a slightly startled look. "I didn't know you were in your office." The carrot-haired high school senior with the soft brown eyes said, "Anything you need right now?"

I gave him a quick look. "I didn't expect you until Monday."

He shrugged, and his freckled cheeks pinked. "Today is Dr. Sanders' last day. I've got a lot to learn about the office before I go back to class this afternoon. It's okay—that I'm here—isn't it?"

Before I could answer, Ella breezed in. "'Morning, Tullah. Jeff, I've typed a list of instructions for you." She pointed to a desk drawer. "Actually, it's more like a book." She smiled wanly.

He opened the drawer and lifted out a notebook filled with different colored tabs. He shook his head as he opened it and rifled through the pages. "Wow!"

I was quick to reassure him. "Mrs. Fauntroy says you're a fast learner. It's not as complicated as it looks."

Ella nodded toward the ringing phone. "Go ahead, answer it."

Jeff answered in a clear voice, "Good morning, Holliday Animal Clinic, how may I help you?"

Ella and I each gave him a thumb's up. We watched him scan the appointment book as he said, "Rabies shot. We have an opening today at eleven o'clock. Thank you, Mrs. Drummond. Oh, and what's your dog's name?"

We watched him log the information on the appointment page. Before Ella or I could comment, the phone rang again. It definitely promised to be a busy day.

****

Before turning out the lights, I phoned my answering service to advise Julie that unless it was a matter of life or death to forward all emergency calls to Dr. Redfern in Dixie County. Wild horses couldn't drag me away from Ella's sendoff dinner.

Friday night and the Whitehorse Saloon was jam-packed as Ella and I threaded our way through the mob of people to a door labeled Private Room. Uncle Charlie—I'm sure with Vera's help—had decorated the room with bright red streamers.

The moment we walked in, revelers sang "For She's a Jolly Good Fellow." Uncle Charlie led Ella to the head of a large table and seated her. On either side of her sat her mother and her uncle. Platters of BBQ ribs, bowls of potato salad, and pitchers of beer, wine, and colas lined the table.

As usual, Ella and I had missed lunch. The sensation of my stomach digesting my backbone drove me to take a seat. My stomach's long deep growl seemed to signal it was time to eat. Rib platters were passed around and plates loaded.

Dad filled my glass with cola. I gave him an appreciative look. "I'm glad you could make it. With you and Tiny here, who's minding the office?"

"Andy. It's sure nice having an extra deputy."

"Have you hired the second deputy, and what about Joyce's replacement?" I filled my mouth with a generous bite of potato salad.

"Hired the new secretary this morning. Janice McElroy. I'm still interviewing for a second deputy. Most of the fresh-faced guys are looking for glory, not small-town dullness, and most of the experienced cops are too close to retirement."

My eyebrows shot up. Before I could sputter out my comment about the new secretary, he answered, "I know. Old Sheriff Henderson's daughter. She moved back to Enigma after her husband was killed. She has no encumbrances, and she understands how the law works, plus she's computer literate."

"I hadn't heard that she was back."

Dad laid a bare rib bone on his plate and grabbed a fresh meaty one. "With the hours you keep, you have no social life."

Not wanting to hear another lecture, I redirected the conversation. "Any word from the Fayetteville sheriff?"

Dad dabbed his mouth with a napkin. "I finally reached him this morning. The patient who walked away from the state hospital is considered dangerous. Male, approximately five foot six, slight build, fair complexion, dark blonde hair, blue eyes. Most significant feature is a large fibrous burn scar on his left cheek. His name is Bonny Cowen, age twenty-four, could easily pass for sixteen."

I rolled my eyes. "What parent in their right mind would give a boy a feminine name?"

"Beats me. What's more interesting is his backstory."

"I'm listening."

"Cowen is a twin. Apparently, accidently or purposely—the information wasn't clear—the kid set the house on fire. Both parents and the twin sister were killed in the fire."

This information stunned me. "Let me guess—he spent years being shuffled from one foster home to another."

"Yep, and I see the cogs churning inside your brain."

"You know me too well, Dad. The Cowen kid killed Pilcher and Parrish, and I think we both know why those two monsters were divested of their genitals."

The cellphone in my back pocket buzzed, vibrating against my hip. I chose to ignore it. Dad shifted in his chair. "The sheriff faxed Cowen's picture." Dad removed his work phone from his shirt pocket and opened it. He scrolled through the pictures and turned the phone toward me. "Recognize him?"

"No, sir, but I don't get into town that often. What about Patty or Grandmother?"

He shook his head and returned the phone to his pocket. "Tiny and I have shown the picture around to most of the local business owners. Based on the fact that the first victim was embalmed, I showed it to Arnie."

"And?"

"Nothing."

"Several questions come to mind. What drew Pilcher and Parrish to Enigma, and did they have jobs? If so, where? Also, if the Cowen kid murdered them, how did he know they were in Enigma?"

Dad and I both knew the answers to these questions were a vital part of the puzzle. We ate in silence, until I leaned close and whispered, "I dreamed about the raven last night." I didn't bother to elaborate about the nightmare.

Dad was tense and serious. "You think our killer is ready to strike again?"

"No, sir. I think he already has."

Chapter Twenty-Four

The party had wound down. Dad and Tiny had returned to work. Ella and I said our goodbyes. She had decided to spend the night in town with her mother before getting an early start on Saturday.

I was about to leave when a feathery ghost touch on my arm stopped me. "Tullah, is my old bedroom available?"

I cast a curious look at my grandmother. "Are you planning to trade your apartment and move back to the country?"

"Smarty pants. No, it happens that tomorrow my apartment is being fumigated and I need a place to stay for a few days."

"You never have to ask, Grandmother."

On the drive to pick up her suitcase, I commented about how upset Ella was over the news that Mr. Pickett had sold the property to someone else. "Please tell me you were pranking her."

I parked in front of the apartment door. Grandmother handed me the key and said, "I'm sure Sunny and Tiny would feel awful knowing how badly the news upset Ella. It's true, old man Pickett sold the property, but to Sunny and Tiny. I was only playing along with their request to keep quiet."

I slid out of the truck.

Grandmother said, "The overnight case is next to the

door."

On the drive home, we discussed everything from Dad's new deputy to Joyce's retirement and the hiring of a new secretary. I resisted thinking about all the wonderful things I could imagine happening with Andy.

The house was cold as a tomb when we finally arrived home. I helped Grandmother inside, jacked up the thermostat, and carried her suitcase to the bedroom. I returned to the kitchen. "I need to do a last-minute check on the animals. I'll put fresh sheets on the bed when I return."

"What about a cup of hot chocolate and a blueberry scone?"

"Sorry, Grandmother, my cupboards are bare." I have no idea why I compared my shelves to those in a nursery rhyme.

She merely gave me an indulgent smile and reached inside a large tote bag she'd set on the dining table. "Never fear. I'm always prepared." She lifted out one of Patty Sweet's signature pink boxes.

When I returned from the clinic, Grandmother had already placed fresh sheets on the bed. She and I retired to the living room with our treats. "Grandmother," I asked, "why don't you have inner sight?"

The question didn't seem to surprise her. "It was not written in the stars."

"I don't remember having this ability when I was a child. It seemed to appear after Mother's death."

Her voice was soft. "Tullah, you were who you were before my Josie put the stamp on you. You came out of the womb with the gift. No help for it, not in the past, and not in the future. As a child, you were not ready for the heavy responsibility and were shielded from it by a protective bubble. Your mother's death, pardon the cliché, burst the bubble."

"But, Grandmother, I don't want this gift. It's a heavy burden."

She drained the last of her chocolate. Her voice grew serious as she laid her hands against my cheeks, almost touching her nose to mine. "My Josie was the world to Henry, to you, and to me. She was pure goodness and did not deserve to have her life stolen from her. This gift that you so despise has aided your father in solving many crimes. I believe the Great Spirit Father is preparing you for a long and heartbreaking journey—yes, even a dangerous journey." Her voice trailed off.

Her words frightened me. "If you mean to comfort me, you're doing a terrible job."

"Go upstairs and soak in a hot tub, Granddaughter." She gathered our cups and saucers. Before walking to the kitchen, she said, "Put some salts in the water. Aromatherapy. Your great-great-grandmother, Chenoa, knew about all that back before the Trail of Tears. Nothing is new; it all recycles." She lifted her eyebrows and smiled.

"Chenoa is a beautiful name. What does it mean, Grandmother?"

"It means "White Dove," which symbolizes peace, prosperity, and new beginnings."

I headed upstairs to the big old bathtub that I intended to fill with enough hot water to swim in. I wished I had known my great-grandmother.

****

I woke from a troubled sleep to find a shy sun peeking through my bedroom curtains. It was Saturday. I wanted to burrow back under the pillows, but the fragments of my dreams were like pinpricks. I didn't have a full recollection, but the overall atmosphere of the dreams had been darker than a raven's wings. I had traveled down a muddy road to a big old creepy house. In the dream a silhouette of a girl shrouded in black stood on the porch, holding a head in one hand and a bloody axe in the other. Her eyes were blue and blazed with fury in a mostly monochromatic dreamscape.

Out in the night sky, the fiery tip of a stick wrote the name *Mother*. I stood in a bevy of ravens, their necks ringed with white. The terrible whir of their wings sounded like a whispered plea of mercy. And I was suddenly one of them. One of us would die. We knew it and hung low to the ground.

I awoke with Grandmother shaking me and calling my name. "Tullah…Tullah…wake up."

I was sweaty, and my legs were tangled in the sheets. It took a few minutes for me to realize I was in my home, in my bed, and safe. Grandmother wrapped her arms around me. In Cherokee, she crooned softly as she rocked me the way she had done so many times when I was a little girl frightened by a nightmare I did not understand. Her dark eyes gazed into mine. "Tell me about the dream, Tullah."

I shook off the last of the tremors, and related what I remembered of the nightmare.

In response, she told me, "Long years ago, even before I was born, our people considered ravens as carriers of evil because they consorted with witches. Raven are sneaky, unkind, and evil creatures. I believe your dream is an omen."

"Grandmother, the name 'Brom' in Celtic means 'raven.' "

"You are speaking about Anne Brom, and you think she is connected to the murders?"

"I don't know what to think, Grandmother. Dad believes the killer is a man." I grabbed my heavy chenille housecoat and pulled it on, tightening the belt around my waist. "In every dream I see a young woman, which leads me to believe the person we're looking for is young and female." I shook my head. "I don't know, Grandmother. It's confusing."

"Come downstairs. The coffee is ready. What would you like for breakfast?"

That was an easy question. "Biscuits with sausage gravy, and eggs over light."

I showered and dressed. When I entered the kitchen, Grandmother stood looking out the window. When she turned to look at me, her eyes darted away. For a split second, fear seemed to spark in her eyes.

"What is it, Grandmother—what has frightened you?"

"You spoke of the raven in your dream. Just now, there was a raven at the window. I'm afraid for you, Tullah."

I tried to speak, but it seemed my throat was frozen, the words blocked. The cup she was holding fell from her hands and shattered. The black liquid spread across the yellow linoleum in the shape of a raven, and for a moment I could only stare at it.

Grandmother made no effort to move. She looked at me, waiting. "What does it mean?"

I bent down and picked up the broken fragments. "I don't know," I said, although in my subconscious I knew it was another warning.

She clutched at my arm. "Leave this alone, Tullah.

Call Henry. He's paid to take risk." She faced me, and for the first time she looked old, her voice tired. "Keep this up and you'll end up either in the emergency room or the morgue. I can't lose you, too, Granddaughter."

There was no point in denying that I shared her fears. "Grandmother, you told me this was my destiny. I have to believe that if the Great Spirit Father gifted me with this curse that he'll also protect me."

"Yes, of course." She forced a smile as she placed hot biscuits on the table. "Just promise me one thing."

Oh, no, here it comes, I thought. "I need to hear your request before I can commit to such a promise."

"You are my only grandchild. Before you get too old to bear children, I'd like a great-grandchild to spoil before I die."

Her request was not what I'd expected. I scoffed and grabbed two hot biscuits from the pan. "I need a husband first."

She scooped a generous ladle of gravy over the steaming bread. Mischief lit her eyes. "What about Andy Kemble? I seem to recall the two of you were an item in high school."

I spooned generous dollops of strawberry jam on top of the gravy. "You are totally outrageous, but I love you just the same."

The dream tucked away, we enjoyed our breakfast. "Grandmother, it's been a while since you were out to visit Banjo. Care to join me at the clinic?"

I filled a sack with baby carrots. We each grabbed an umbrella to shield us from the misting rain as we maneuvered around mud puddles on our way to the side door that led to the stable's interior. Banjo, Moon, Jupiter, and Gandalf stuck their heads over the stall doors to greet us, and we rewarded each horse with carrot sticks.

Moon is Grandmother's brown-and-white pinto gelding, a good-natured horse. Nothing rattles him. Grandmother opened his stall and removed the cold-weather blanket. She crooned as she curried him. She said, "When I retire, I plan to spend more time riding Banjo."

It had been a while since I had ridden. "I wish the weather wasn't miserable. A good gallop might help clear my head."

Grandmother's cellphone rang. She looked at the ID and said, "It's Patty. I hope it's not some foolishness with the city council."

She left the stall and shut the gate. I finished grooming Banjo, my father's appaloosa, and covered him with a fresh warming blanket. Then I moved on to Gandalf. Gandalf had belonged to my mother. He and I are a good match. We're both a little high-strung and stubborn.

I heard Grandmother say, "That's very interesting, Patty. Thanks for the info." She added, "Yes...yes, by all means call Henry, and I'll fill Tullah in."

After she disconnected, Grandmother helped me finish currying my horse.

"What do you need to fill me in on?" I tossed a warming blanket over the black-and-white gelding's sleek back.

"Let's finish up. Patty's bringing lunch. Maybe she should be the one to tell you."

I wanted to grit my teeth and growl. Like my horse, I didn't like surprises. I grabbed a pitchfork and filled each stall with fresh hay while Grandmother moved about, filling each horse's feed bin with sweet oats.

The rain had stopped by the time we'd finished our chores. My biscuits and gravy had worn off. I looked forward to whatever food and news Patty was about to deliver.

Chapter Twenty-Five

As we crossed the muddy yard that separated the clinic and barn from the house, River and Rascal joined us. River carried a stick in his mouth. I accepted the stick and gave it a good toss. With Rascal close on his playmate's heels, they raced to retrieve their prize.

Grandmother's laughter filled the yard. "I swear that little donkey thinks he's a dog. So cute."

Her laughter faded at the sound of a car coming down the drive. "That must be Patty."

Patty parked her silver sedan next to the front porch and stepped out. She opened the trunk and retrieved a large picnic basket. I rushed to relieve her of the load. She shivered and verbally expressed the chill she suddenly felt.

"It's nippy," I said. "Let's get inside."

Grandmother held the door wide for us to enter, and that included the dog and the donkey. We walked to the kitchen, where I set the basket on the table. While Patty busied herself lifting out paper plates, napkins, a box of chicken salad croissants, and a container of potato salad, Grandmother set a fresh pot of coffee to brewing.

I loaded my plate with two croissants and potato salad. Patty removed another box. She smiled as she lifted the lid. "Boston cream donuts."

As soon as the coffee perked and our cups were filled, I said, "Patty what was so important that you

167

couldn't tell us over the phone?"

She bit into her sandwich and chewed thoughtfully. I knew she was toying with me and refused to allow myself to get frustrated. Finally, in a conspiratorial voice, she said, "You know Rita Ainsworth that owns Ainsworth Realty? Well, to make polite conversation while she took her sweet time selecting the donuts she wanted, I happened to ask if she'd sold any property lately."

Patty took a moment to consume another bite of croissant. I thought to myself that I wished she had a fast-forward button. Impatience knotted in my stomach. "And what did Mrs. Ainsworth say?"

Patty heaved a dramatic sigh. "You know the two dead guys?"

"Pilcher and Parrish?"

"Yes, them. Rita said they had approached her about leasing a house, at least five bedrooms with two or three baths, and something close to town but not in town."

I made a hurry-up motion with my hand. "Did you ask her why they wanted a house that large?"

Patty quirked a smirk. "I sure did. That's when Rita said the guy named Pilcher stated that he and his new partner wanted to convert the house into a private school with specialized tutoring services."

She wiped her mouth with a napkin and grabbed a donut. "Henry had already showed me the *real* pictures of those men, you know, without the costumes—that's how I knew who Rita was talking about. She absolutely gob-smacked when I told her the men were the ones that had been murdered."

After a deep breath to digest what I'd just heard, I said, "That answers the question as to why Pilcher and

Parrish came to Enigma."

Patty bemoaned, "Those poor men. Only a monster could kill in such a horrific way."

"Horrific my ass!"

Grandmother and her best friend exchanged curious looks, then looked back at me. Grandmother gave me her tell-the-truth glance and said, "What are you not telling us, Tullah?"

"Those men were creeps in the worst way!"

The word "creeps" caused both women to shudder. Patty squished her Boston cream donut hard enough to squirt yellow cream over the front of her blue shirt. I rushed to the sink to wet a handful of paper towels to blot the spot. I also refilled her cup with coffee.

Grandmother offered a mild chastisement. "It isn't nice to speak ill of the dead, Granddaughter."

I refilled her cup and replenished mine as I related what Dad had learned about Pilcher and Parrish from the KBI files.

Grandmother nearly spewed coffee across the table. Her eyes narrowed to angry slits. "Forget what I said earlier. I take it all back. Merciful heavens! Somebody should've whacked their gonads off a long time ago."

My effort to laugh and swallow at the same time ended in a coughing jag when the coffee went down the wrong way. "Somebody did, finally, Grandmother."

At the women's confused expressions, I explained that when Dr. Sanders had removed the costumes from the bodies to prepare them for autopsy, she had discovered that both men had been completely divested of their genitals.

After a moment of silence, Grandmother put her hand on Patty's arm. She spoke in a low calm voice.

"What did Henry say when you told him?"

"Not much. He thanked me and said I'd given him a helpful bit of information."

"Cherchez la femme."

"I'm assuming you're speaking French. What does it mean, Tanti?" Patty asked.

"It means that Tullah thinks a woman committed the murders."

"Why is that, Tullah?" Patty wanted to know.

"In my psychology classes, we learned that most murders are crimes of passion. I believe it was Alexander Dumas who said to look for the woman in the case."

Patty stood to gather the paper plates and wadded napkins. "I suppose whacking off men's wing-wangers is certainly a crime of passion."

I didn't try to contain my laughter as I hugged her. "Patty, you do have a way with words."

As the day slipped past us and the sky began to darken, I was concerned about Patty's poor eyesight. "Patty, would you like to spend the night? There's a twin bed in Grandmother's room."

She insisted she could see well enough to make the twenty-minute drive to town and her apartment. She also promised to let us know that she had arrived home safely.

After I'd toted the picnic basket to her car, Grandmother and I stood on the porch and watched until the silver sedan's red lights disappeared down my long driveway.

My cellphone rang, and I groaned when I glanced at the caller ID. "My answering service."

Grandmother held the door while I walked inside with the phone to my ear. "What's the emergency, Julie?"

"Sorry, Tullah, I know it's Saturday and technically your day off, but a Mrs. Estelle Gardner phoned. She has an old horse that's laying down. Mrs. Gardner said that she's in her eighties and disabled. She has no way of getting the horse on its feet or to the clinic and asked that you come to her place. I told her there was an extra charge for after hours and weekend barn visits. She said the horse had belonged to her son, who died last year, and it was her only connection to him. She also said she'd pay double if you could come tonight. I have her on hold. What should I tell her?"

I pointed to a slip of paper and a pen lying on the table next to my recliner and motioned for Grandmother to write as I repeated the address and telephone number. "I'm not familiar with that road, Julie. However, tell Mrs. Gardner I'll try to be there within the hour."

"Will do, and again, I'm sorry to bother you, especially since it's beginning to rain again."

I assured her it wasn't a problem. When I disconnected, I said, "I'm not familiar with Frogmore Road. Are you, Grandmother?"

She thought for a moment then shook her head. "It doesn't sound familiar."

I opened my phone and said, "Hey, Google," and spoke the road name and number. I laughed when several addresses for Sussex, in England, popped up. "Maybe I'll have better luck with the GPS in my truck."

"Tullah, I'm going with you."

"Grandmother, it's raining and cold out there, and you'd get bored sitting in the truck waiting until I'm finished. Depending on the condition of the horse, this may take several hours."

"I'll take a blanket, a pillow, and one of your

mystery novels." Anxiety filled her eyes. "Don't argue."

In truth, a knot had developed in the pit of my stomach, and it wasn't from the three donuts I'd consumed earlier. Although I had no connection to the two murdered men, past experience with killers told me I had to be cautious.

While I waited for Grandmother to gather her coat, blanket, and pillow, River emitted a low growl. The hackles on the back of his neck rose. And then...a *tap...tap.*

Absurd, but the sound sent alarms racing through my bloodstream. "What is it, River?"

The black Lab reared with his front paws against the kitchen sink. His body tensed, his growl low and throaty. I immediately switched off the kitchen light so the perpetrator couldn't see inside the house, and to also give me better vision. I leaned closer to the window to peer outside. I saw no one—nothing. The tapping sounded again.

I grabbed the baseball bat next to the door.

Grandmother whispered, "What is it, Tullah?"

"Until I find out, go in the bedroom and lock the door."

"Should I call Henry?"

"Not unless you hear me scream."

I held the bat ready and eased the back door open. River and Rascal nearly knocked me down as they burst past me. River's frenzied barks escalated.

My breath nearly left me when I spotted the raven. It had fluttered away and was sitting on the roof of my truck. For a moment, I felt paranoid and vulnerable.

"What do you want, Raven? And don't say, 'Nevermore.' "

The bird cocked its head as if understanding my words. River made a giant lunge and landed on top of the truck's hood. The bird flapped its black wings and flew away.

"Tullah?"

I turned to see Grandmother's darkened outline standing in the doorway. "I'm okay, Grandmother."

I had to admit I was a bit shaken. "It was the raven, Grandmother. Are you ready to go?"

She flipped on the light. "Give me a minute to gather my things."

Chapter Twenty-Six

While I waited for the engine and the interior of the truck to warm, I programed the address into my GPS. A map appeared on the screen with dotted lines. I scrolled to enlarge the image. In small italic letters was the word *vacated.*

"Vacated…what does that mean, Grandmother?"

Her explanation left me stymied and suspicious. I mused aloud, "Why would Mrs. Gardner live on a road that the county no longer maintains, that's considered inaccessible?"

I didn't wait for Grandmother's response because I knew the answer. I immediately dialed my dad's direct number and placed the phone on speaker. He answered, "Everything okay, Punkin?"

"Dad, there's been another murder."

"And you know this how?"

I quickly related the incident with the raven at my kitchen window. "And when I programmed in the address for Frogmore Road, it came up as vacated." I'd nearly run out of breath and had to do a deep inhale.

Dad said, "Come to think of it, I do remember Frogmore Road. It's been abandoned for years."

Grandmother leaned toward the phone. "It's been such a long time that I'd forgotten. About fifty years ago, a man from England bought the property. He aspired to build an upscale subdivision, and he did construct a few two-story houses, but he never permitted the road. Due to constant flooding, and lack of assistance from the contractor and the county to build retention ponds, and due to insurance problems, the owners eventually abandoned the houses." She hesitated, then spoke slowly as if choosing her words carefully. "Henry, I'm not sure, but isn't a portion of Frogmore Road in Dixie County?"

"Come to think of it, I believe you're right, Tanti."

I breathed deeply and controlled the dread that crept inside of me. "This is crazy…plain crazy. Something is out of kilter here. If no one lives on the road, then why would the caller give me that particular address?"

Grandmother was quiet in an instant. She didn't have to answer. I knew without evidence that we'd find Estelle Gardner—if that was her real name—dead.

"Maybe you should stay here, Grandmother. I can't guarantee what we'll find."

"I know you're not a cop, Tullah, but you've grown up with law enforcement, and have had very bad things happen to you. Don't forget that as a retired crime reporter, I've seen my share of dead bodies." She reached for the seatbelt and snapped it in place. "Your instincts have always panned out. I'm going."

Dad's voice came through. "We won't find out if another crime has been committed if we sit here jawing about it. Tullah, meet me at the end of your driveway. I'll flash my lights when I get there. You can follow."

"Roger that, Dad."

"Wiseass."

When I parked at the end of my driveway, it dawned on me to make sure I had my pistol. I leaned over and opened the glove compartment. The light showed it was securely in place. In ten minutes, a set of headlights flashed. Dad slowed his old four-wheel-drive 4Runner. I answered by flashing my own lights before pulling in behind him.

"Grandmother, does Estelle Gardner's name ring any bells?"

In the dim light, I watched her shoulders shrug the answer. "Sorry, my memory isn't as good as it used to be."

I followed Dad when he turned off the main highway onto a narrow county road. In the distance sat a lonely convenience store with two gas pumps and an awning that looked like a tornado had had its way with it. It wasn't a place that inspired a desire to stop. We passed Gross Knob Hill. What connection did Estelle Gardner have with Pilcher and Parrish?

Grandmother interrupted my thoughts. "We're headed toward Dixie County."

"I wonder if we should contact Sheriff Dotson? This is his district."

As if reading my mind, the phone chirped. Grandmother leaned forward and hit the speaker button. "Go ahead, Henry."

"Do you have any clients out this way, Tullah?"

"No, sir. I don't get out this way very often, and when I do, I've never noticed a sign for Frogmore Road."

I heard him say, "Tiny, turn on the spotlight so we don't miss it." Then he said, "Tullah, depending on the condition of the road, we may need to park and walk in."

There was no evidence of houses, no lights, or at least none that could be seen from the highway. The idea of traipsing down a dirt road in the dark was not appealing. Visions of stumbling into a nest of moccasins or a pack of wild dogs filled my head.

"Dad, what'll I do if this turns out to be a legitimate call—will my four-wheel-drive make it down the road? I'll need my equipment."

Dad slowed his vehicle and turned in the direction of the spotlight's wide beam. He said, "We'll worry about that after we assess the situation."

I followed his 4Runner as he turned off the main highway. We drove as far as we could down a narrow lane. Overgrown brush scrubbed the sides of our vehicles, and low tree limbs scraped across the windshields. My anxiety increased.

Dad's truck taillights flashed, then went out. "This is as far as we can go, Punkin." His voice came through the phone. I shut off the engine and opened the door of my truck. The night had grown colder, and there was barely a glimmer of moonlight. It was a night for hot chocolate next to a cozy fire, curled up with a mystery novel.

I grabbed my flashlight, opened the door, and stepped down to the ground. "Stay here and lock the doors, Grandmother."

"Listen." Grandmother held up her hand. "Did you hear that?"

The idea of a killer shuffling in the underbrush made my body prickle with fear. I once again issued the command. "Stay in the truck."

She slid to the ground and moved a little closer to my side. "No way. I'll feel safer with all of you. Henry and Tiny are expert shots."

Something moved in the underbrush—the crackle of a stick, the shush of leaves being moved or crunched, and what sounded like a soft grunt. I whispered, "Wild hog."

We joined Dad and Tiny. Dad said, "Stay close."

He needn't worry about us straying away. Briars snagged our legs as we bravely ventured farther into the woods. I was thankful for my leather boots. Grandmother tripped and almost went down. I caught her by the elbow in time.

The noises had stopped. I sidled next to my dad. Grandmother lamented, "We're sitting ducks if the killer has a nightscope or other tactile equipment, and malice in their heart."

Her anxiety increased my own jumpiness. If there was a horse that needed treating, I didn't relish the idea of tramping back to the truck to get my medical kit.

Dad held up his hand and signaled for us to stop. I flashed my light in his direction as he pressed the earbud closer to his ear. He answered in a whisper. When he disconnected, he said, "I had Deputy Kemble run Estelle Gardner's name through the system."

All attention was on him. In my heart, I already knew the answer. When he said that she'd once been a foster parent and had served time for misuse of funds allocated for the children in her care, my brain was going a thousand miles a minute as I shifted pieces of the puzzle into a solution. All I knew for certain was that we'd find Estelle Gardner's body when we got to wherever we were going.

Movement to our right made us all freeze. Dad flashed the beam of his light in that direction. A dark ripple of energy flashed through the trees. Grandmother reached out to grip my hand. She said, "I've never been afraid of the woods, but my heart is racing with fear."

"There's no such thing as the bogeyman," I said, though I hadn't meant to say it aloud.

Dad said, "C'mon, let's get this finished."

Whatever creature was out there beat its wings about my face. I shrieked and didn't care how ridiculous I sounded. Dad shined the light in my direction.

The raven squawked, "*Nevermore!*"

Dad removed his cowboy hat and batted at the bird. Once again, the raven squawked before fluttering away.

The timbre of Tiny's baritone voice deepened when he said, "There's the old house."

Dad's flashlight beam followed Tiny's. In the distance I spotted the old antebellum-style building. Once a beauty, she had lost her glory. The white paint was cracked and peeling, and long shutters with missing slats sagged from the front windows. An overgrown thorny hedge blocked our way to the house.

Dad and Tiny shined their lights, looking for a path. I pointed. "There."

We found a narrow trail through the worst briars. I instructed Grandmother to tuck her hands inside her pants pockets to keep the thorns from pricking her flesh. I did the same. As we approached the house, the distant sound of cows lowing drew my attention. I wasn't familiar with any cattle ranches in this particular area.

We all stopped and listened. I said, "It's coming from the back of the house. Let's check it out before we go inside. If there's a barn, maybe we'll find the missing horse."

We left the briars behind and set out toward the rear of the abandoned dwelling. Dad and Tiny's beams danced up and down in the night. In the distance, across a raggedy yard, sat a barn with a partially collapsed roof. A large door hung askew on its hinges. Rank and file, we followed Dad to the dilapidated building. He and Tiny unholstered their weapons, with Dad instructing

Grandmother and me to stand back.

Tiny stood to one side of the door with his weapon ready. Dad called, "Sheriff Holliday. Anyone in there?"

Nothing. Not even a nicker. Dad had to crouch and enter the opening sideways.

Tiny motioned me forward. He shined his light while I squeezed through the narrow entry. Grandmother opted to stand next to the big deputy. Dad flashed the broad beam of his light around. Massive cobwebs hung from the rafters. Once a nice barn, it was now a home to wild critters. A rat scurrying across my boot elicited a startled shriek.

"You okay?" Dad shined his light about.

I shuddered. "Rats. Nasty creatures." I pointed to the bales of moldy hay. "Home to snakes."

We hit gold—or I should say manure—when we looked inside a middle stall.

I scouted the darkened interior until I was satisfied it was safe to enter, and used the toe of my boot to check the dung's freshness. "With the number of clods littering the area, I'd say the horse was a stallion."

"Why's that, Punkin?"

"Stallions often 'scent mark' their territory, which means they poop more than mares and geldings."

"I can tell by your expression that something's churning inside your brain."

I walked back to the aisle. "I'll tell you in a minute. Shine your light to see if there's a rear door."

In my experience, most enclosed barns had double rear doors that generally opened into a large corral or into a pasture. There was, and it stood wide open.

"Sheriff, you and Tullah okay in there?"

"Yeah, Tiny. Meet us around the back of the barn."

It didn't take long for Dad's deputy and Grandmother to meet us. Tiny said, "You didn't find a horse?"

I grinned inwardly. "No, something better." I pointed. In the distance ghostly lights illuminated the horizon. "Do you think those are coming from Enigma's fairgrounds?"

Dad and Tiny switched off the beams. The shadowy glimmer of lights grew a tad brighter. In the stillness of the night, the mooing we'd heard earlier drifted to our ears. We moved across the raggedy expanse of lawn covered by dead limbs and a blanket of leaves. About a hundred yards on, we found what was left of a narrow dirt road.

"Damn straight, Punkin. That's Enigma's 4-H fairgrounds."

"Dad, I'll bet my life savings this is how the killer got the headless horseman to the Halloween party and the wolf to the graveyard without being seen."

"Yep, the woods line the rear of the fairgrounds. If it were daylight, I believe we'd find evidence that would prove the killer used this old road. We're dealing with a cunning individual. Someone familiar with the area."

I agreed. "Do we know if Pilcher, Parrish, or Mrs. Gardner ever lived in Enigma?"

"If they did, they were clean. No arrest records, not even a speeding ticket showed up for Enigma or Dixie County."

"Then how did the killer know about this place?

"That's the million-dollar question, and we may never know the answer."

Grandmother spoke up. "When we get back to the truck, I'll give Patty a call and have her check voter registration records. If they ever registered to vote, it'll show addresses."

We retraced our steps across a once lovely yard that had boasted of hydrangeas and azaleas. The porch creaked with age as we stepped on the boards.

Dad reached for a rusted doorknob. The door squeaked when he shoved against it. Tiny stood to one side with his revolver ready. Dad called out, "Sheriff Holliday from Enigma. Mrs. Gardner?"

Chapter Twenty-Seven

At first, I thought it was a mannequin. You know, like the ones used in store windows. There was no blood. She was sitting in a chair with her back toward us. The room reminded me of a scene from a horror movie.

Dad said, "Mrs. Gardner?"

I thought about the time I'd been on the movie set of *Lights...Camera...Murder* where the stunt man was killed, but in this act, there were no supporting actors. In the distance, a dog barked, and there was no movie director to call, "Cut!"

I swallowed the bile rising in my throat. The beats of my heart echoed inside my ears. I eased around the table. Oh, God! She was real. She was once...like flesh and blood and bone...just...oh, God! The woman I had thought was a mannequin was a corpse.

It was only the extreme brutality of her death that made her appear as if she were not, as if she was some creation of the most brilliant and lurid mind working in a Hollywood special effects studio.

A heavyset woman, clad in an old-fashioned granny dress, her wrists and ankles wrapped with silver duct tape, securely bound to the chair's arms and legs, and with a double strip of tape that sealed her mouth shut, stared vacant-eyed at an empty soup bowl.

She appeared to be in her early sixties. Fleshy jowls, perfectly manicured fingernails painted ruby red, and a faint floral scent of perfume mingled with the putrid odor of rotting flesh.

Dad gasped against the offensive smell. "How long do you thinks she's been dead?"

Like my dad, I placed a hand over my nose. As much as I dreaded looking at her, I studied her bloated face. "She appears to be in stage three of rigor."

Grandmother asked me to explain what that meant.

Behind my hand, I drew in a deep breath to clear my nostrils of the foul stink. I spoke between parted fingers. "Twenty-four to seventy-two hours after death the internal organs decompose, and then three to five days later the body starts to bloat and blood-containing foam leaks from the mouth and nose. Eight to ten days after death, the body turns from green to red as the blood decomposes and the organs in the abdomen accumulate gas."

Dad mimicked the way I'd covered my nose and spoke through his parted fingers. "At least a week?"

"Yes, sir, and this amount of deterioration is what attracted the rats."

Our presence had disturbed an apparent feeding frenzy. A hoard of rats scurried across the table, from out of the woman's mass of gray hair that had once been fashioned into a bun, and from the cleavage of her ample breasts. It seemed that hundreds of the filthy vermin scampered about the room seeking safety from the beams of light.

Before I could hold her back, Grandmother stood next to me. She began to keel over. I quickly caught her—bracing myself—and steadied her.

"I'm s-sorry," she immediately apologized.

"It's all right, Grandmother. I completely

understand," I assured her.

A rat the size of a chihuahua dog leapt from the table. I used the palm of my hand to bat it across the room before it landed on my grandmother.

At first, I thought there had been no blood. Now there was red around the...around the places where the rats had feasted on the corpse's face, neck, arms, and hands.

Dad folded Grandmother against his chest. She moaned. "This is truly horrible and cruel and tragic."

Naturally the way we'd found the body was gruesome, to say the least. Dad rasped, "Tullah, who is she supposed to be?"

In the aftermath of shock, I misunderstood his question, and said, "Estelle Gardner, I suppose."

Even lawmen are not immune to such abject cruelty. Quiet emotion filled his voice. "No, Punkin, I meant what storybook character."

When I didn't answer, he said, "Are you all right?"

My stomach roiled. I didn't want to look at the woman. The rats had feasted on her eyeballs and nose, and other parts of her face.

Tiny excused himself. We heard his retching before he reached the back door. It was one of the worst crime scenes we'd ever seen, and we all knew it.

I racked my brain searching for a nursery rhyme to fit the murdered victim. "Sorry," Tiny apologized when he reentered the room. Dad brushed it off because he, too, had been a little green around the gills.

"Tiny, if you can get a signal, put in a call to Deputy Kemble, and Dr. Sanders, and we'll need the ambulance, too. If you can't make contact, go back to the truck and use the radio."

"Dad, how will they ever find this road, especially in the dark?"

For a moment, he was pensive. "Yep, you're right." He looked at his deputy. "Tiny, use your best judgment with making sure the crew doesn't get lost, then lead them back here."

The big deputy scrubbed a hand across his face. "Sure thing, Henry."

I sensed he was grateful for the short reprieve from the crime scene.

"Dad, the killer left notes on the horseman and the wolfman. Serial killers don't usually deviate from their pattern."

I steeled myself and stepped closer to shine my light across the table. One last brave rodent sat in the middle of the soup bowl, apparently searching for a morsel of whatever had filled it. In its effort to avoid being harmed, the creature knocked the bowl over while making its escape. Too bad the rat didn't know it had inadvertently exposed a vital clue—the killer's note.

I gingerly lifted the slip of paper and held it between the nails of my forefinger and thumb. Before I deposited it into the plastic evidence bag, I said, "Dad it's the Mother Goose rhyme about the old woman that lived in a shoe."

Dad zipped the bag shut. "Read it."

I cleared my voice as I smoothed the plastic across the paper with its typed words. "There was an old woman who lived in a shoe. She had so many children, she didn't know what to do. She gave them some broth without any bread, and whipped them all soundly and put them to bed."

I hated the thought that popped into my mind. "Dad,

look at the distance from the chair to the table, and the way the body leaned toward the table as if the victim was trying to reach the bowl." I grimaced. "Based on the poem, it's possible that as a child the killer and perhaps other children were starved, and this is his revenge."

Grandmother said, "When I was a crime reporter, I worked a few foster parent cases that involved child neglect and worse. It's not a comforting thought."

Right then, I'd rather have been tending a sick animal than looking at the corpse. I had no desire to continue looking at the woman's face, at the mutilation left by the rats. Not so long ago, she had enjoyed a manicure at a beauty salon, and had probably laughed, and her eyes had sparkled. But now she sat like a broken doll discarded by a disgruntled, sadistic child.

Thinking about the other two victims, did this accurately describe the killer? I opened the note section of my phone and wrote: *a) are there more victims; b) are the victims and the killer from Enigma; c) if not, how did the killer know the victims were in Enigma;* and my last notation: *clues other than nursery rhyme symbolism.*

Later, I would transfer these notes to the murder file I had created on my laptop.

Dad looked at me as if he were worried about me. I answered with a weak smile, "A little rocky, but okay."

It seemed hours had passed. I had escorted Grandmother to the front porch with instructions to signal when she either heard or spotted the forensics team. It's unusual for my stubborn grandmother to easily acquiesce, but I believe she had decided she'd rather take her chances in the dark than remain in the same room with a corpse.

I followed Dad up a set of stairs to the second floor.

187

We searched the three bedrooms and a bathroom. Nothing. Dad shrugged as if to say such things happen.

"We'll come back tomorrow when there's enough light and continue our search."

"Sorry, Dad, much as I'd like to help, I have a full schedule, and with Ella away, I—"

"It's okay, Punkin. You've helped more than you know." He emitted a low chuckle. "Besides, it's time to see if Andy is tough or fluff."

Grandmother shouted, "Henry...Tullah...they're coming."

I walked to a bedroom window and through a broken pane watched orbs of lights bobbing up and down like giant fireflies approaching the house.

Chapter Twenty-Eight

Grandmother opted to return to her own apartment and rode back to town with Dad and Tiny. A sense of relief washed over me when I drove under the carport and was met by River and Rascal. I unlocked the kitchen door and, after greeting my pets, rushed upstairs to the bedroom.

I needed a shower—big time.

But coffee...first. I turned on the electric brewer.

I headed to the bathroom and stripped down, turned on a spray of wonderful hot water, and was ready to step into the shower when I heard a sound.

I froze. It sounded like a tap, difficult to hear over the running water, but there had definitely been a sound. Otherwise, River wouldn't have growled.

I was careful. Being the daughter of a sheriff had taught me to be observant. Over the years since my mother's death, with my increased empathic abilities, I had become more cautious.

I knew I had locked the kitchen door. I had even double-checked before coming upstairs.

But that sound...

I listened again. It was almost as if someone had entered the bedroom.

I remained still and listened. Grabbing a towel and wrapping it around me, I eased to the bedroom, trying harder to listen, to hear.

River let out a loud woof, then charged out of the bedroom and down the stairs, with Rascal hot on his tail.

I searched for a weapon and settled on a spray bottle of toilet bowl cleanser. I wasn't going down without a fight. In the kitchen, River stood at the sink, bouncing up and down on his hind legs, barking frantically. However, his tail was also wagging. Whatever was out there apparently didn't pose a danger.

I grabbed his collar and commanded him to hush his racket. In the silence came the familiar *tap…tap…tap*.

I immediately switched off the kitchen light. As soon as my eyes adjusted to the dark, I peered closely out the window. Staring back at me was—you guessed it—the raven. For a moment, I felt paranoid and vulnerable. Did I have enough emotional fortitude to see another maimed body?

I rapped at the window. "Go away…shoo!"

I poured myself a mug of coffee. I was still wearing the towel, and the water was still crashing down in the bathroom. I headed upstairs, careful not to spill my coffee. The dog and the donkey followed, and once they were in the room with me, I slammed the door and locked it before sinking onto the bed. I wanted to forget about the headless horseman, the wolfman with his head split in two, and the vacant eyes of an old woman's lacerated face.

I breathed deeply, scooted against the headboard, and sipped my coffee. It seemed my empathic communication with certain animals was increasing. Whether it was real or a product of my imagination, I gave myself a shake, finished my coffee, and went into the bathroom to indulge in my hot shower.

I allowed the water to bead over my head, down my

face, and over my body. I wanted to stop seeing the bodies of dead humans.

****

My alarm rang; it seemed to be coming from far, far away. I awoke with a start and slid off the bed, landing hard on my butt. I had no idea where I was or why I was on the floor. River whined as he licked my face, and Rascal tried to get into my lap.

This was too humiliating. Sane veterinarians didn't fall out of bed. Yes, I was an animal doctor, not a psychic, not a cop. I pushed off the floor, and gave myself a good mental shake. It was time to dress, fortify myself with coffee, and open the clinic. I had a full day of appointments.

Real or a product of my imagination, the vision of the corpse dressed as the old woman in the shoe filled my head. I forced myself to erase the ugliness from my mind. With a shudder, I readied for the day and headed to the kitchen, wondering why the damn bird had paid me another visit. If there had been another murder, surely I would have felt it.

I opened my cellphone and dialed. When he answered, I blurted, "Dad, the raven visited me again last night. Has another murder been reported?"

"Punkin…Tullah, slow down. You're not making sense. What's this about another murder?"

I sucked in a deep breath, and holding the phone to my ear, I poured a cup of coffee. I forced myself to speak slowly, and again, related about my late-night visitor. Dad responded that so far, no new murders had been reported.

"Andy and I are on the way to the hospital. Dr. Sanders is performing the autopsy this morning.

Afterward, we're heading back to the house to dust for prints and search for clues. You want to join us?"

"Wish I could, Dad. Full day scheduled. In fact, it looks like I'll be working long after dark-thirty." Way too busy for this small county. I glanced at the wall clock. Almost time for the first patient to arrive—a dalmatian puppy with what sounded like iris sphincter dysplasia. Which, if that was the case, surgery was warranted.

"Catch you later, Dad. Let me know the autopsy results."

I'd been raised by a great father who had always reassured me that a girl or a woman could do anything she chose. As such, I'd met whatever challenges came my way, with the humility to accept help when necessary.

Today was Monday, and Jeff, the student aide, would arrive for his first official day of work.

I beckoned River and Rascal to follow me outside. I scanned the window ledge and the fence line, and even the barren tree limbs. No raven.

I didn't like the feeling of being so…

Haunted.

My lungs hurt from sucking in the frigid air. "C'mon, River…Rascal. We have work to do." Hunched against the cold, my hands tucked inside my jacket pockets, I jogged to the clinic, the dog and the donkey jogging after me. The autopsy was on my mind. It was hard to accept that the body jostled on a gurney and down a dark, wooded lane had ever been a real woman, with no chunks of flesh gone and no horde of rodents feeding on her.

Once inside the office, I strolled to the surgery to

prepare for a possible operation on the Dalmatian. While I waited for the rush of patients, I opened my phone and scrolled to the pictures I'd taken of Mrs. Gardner's body. I'd seen brutal things before, but the torturous cruelties in these three murders seemed above all else. I attached the latest photos to an email to Dad and hit Send.

Part of me wanted to attend the autopsy. The other part of me was obligated to the profession I cherished and the clients that kept me in business.

****

I was thankful for Jeff. Having him man the office took an enormous load off me while Ella was away. In fact, if he agreed to attend Enigma's community college, I'd happily offer him parttime employment.

At the end of the busy day, I settled in my recliner with a cup of hot cocoa, opened my laptop to the murder file, and was copying and pasting the notes from my phone into the file when my cellphone chirped. A quick glance at the caller ID prompted me to immediately answer; otherwise, I would have let my answering service screen the call.

"Hey, Dad, did Andy survive the autopsy?"

Henry chuckled. "Like an old pro. That boy's a keeper."

I hastened on because I didn't want to hear what a great catch Andy Kemble would be, or how my social life was like a barren desert. "Great. Did Dr. Sanders give you immediate results?"

"Frankly, I wished you were there. She used a lot of medical terms." We fell silent for a moment. Then Dad was speaking again. "She didn't give us much more than what we already know. The victim had been held for several days. Evidence from the raw edges of flesh confirmed she had been fed on by rodents.

"Also, from the trace amounts of material in what pieces of the digestive tract could be found, she hadn't eaten for several days before her demise."

I listened to Dad repeat a litany of horrid and grisly details of Dr. Sanders' clinical dissertation. When he had finished, I said, "So, basically, she was starved to death."

"That's about the size of it. The deep gouge wounds on her wrist indicated that she had tried to free her hands from the arms of the chair."

I envisioned the rat that sat inside the bowl that appeared to have been set strategically in front of the corpse. "And with the chair legs screwed into the floor, she wasn't able to scoot forward to get to the food. What a terrible way to torture someone."

I could almost visualize Dad giving himself a mental shake. "There's more. Dr. Sanders pulled a set of prints. Andy ran them through KBI and came up with a match. The victim is definitely Estelle Gardner."

"What about family? Any next of kin?"

"We have a list. Tiny is working to decide just who that might be—especially with her being a foster parent. You have any feelings on this, Punkin?"

"Only that it's strange no one has filed a missing persons report for any of the victims."

"I know. Three damned corpses in the matter of days apart. What the hell is happening in my town?"

It wasn't a question that required an answer. I knew exactly how he felt. As a mayor trying to breathe life into a dying town, my grandmother along with the town council and the county commissioners had inadvertently opened Pandora's box.

I knew that, in criminal cases, bodies could stay in

the morgue up to thirty days, or longer. "Ask Dr. Sanders if anyone has claimed the bodies of Pilcher and Parrish. Knowing who would do that might lead us to possible suspects. And you might want to ask Arnie Lewis if anyone has contacted him about funeral arrangements for any of the three victims."

A thought came to me. Except for Arnie Lewis, we had no persons of interest. "Dad, have you run Anne Brom's name through KBI?"

"The strange girl we bumped into at the funeral home? No. Have I missed something?"

"You haven't missed anything, and I don't have a reason for suspecting her—just call it a—feeling."

"I trust your instincts. Of course, anything is possible."

My day had been full and exhausting, yet it had been normal. And like my day, the conversation had come to an end. The yawn slipped out before I could call it back. "Sorry, Dad."

"Busy schedule tomorrow again?"

"You know it. Before I hang up… With murder number three, it's bound to have made the news. Are you prepared to meet a barrage of reporters?"

He growled. "Reporters, the bane of my existence? Thankfully, Joyce still has a few days left before she retires. Hopefully, she'll teach Janice how to field annoying questions without giving away confidential information."

"Good night, Dad, and let me know what comes up about Anne Brom."

I trudged upstairs, taking my laptop with me. I knew I needed to rest. The problem was that my mind and body were at war with each other. My body demanded sleep, but my mind refused to turn off. Three victims—two men and a woman; all connected to social services, all former foster parents with less than stellar reputations. This killer must be stopped, and we hadn't begun to scratch the surface.

After dressing for bed, I snuggled against the headboard and opened my computer to the murder file. I wasn't sure why I felt irritated. I'm a veterinarian, not a cop. I don't have an egotistical need to be the one to solve the case. But I knew Dad wanted this murderer taken down, and fast.

I typed: *a) Need a list of all children in the care of Pilcher, Parrish, and Gardner; ages, dates in care and with whom. b) Reports of child abuse…names of child or children. c) who filed the complaints.*

I closed my laptop, turned out the light, and drew the heavy quilt up to my chin. I'd cleared my mind of nagging questions and was drifting off to neverland.

Neverland!

Much to my chagrin, my eyes widened. I groaned. River roused from his bed. I assured him I was okay. It occurred to me that when the raven had tapped on my window, it had not squawked the word, "Nevermore."

I grabbed my laptop and typed: *Neverland is an imaginary place; a fantasy like the characters in the Brothers Grimm and Mother Goose. The raven last night merely tapped on my kitchen window without speaking its favorite word—Nevermore. Does that mean the killer is finished with his revenge? Will there be no more murders?*

I was bleary-eyed with exhaustion. We were definitely dealing with a brilliant mind. In most murder cases, law enforcement generally looked close to home for suspects during their investigation. Husbands, boyfriends, lovers. By the very nature of it, this case was different. Pilcher, Parrish, and Gardner didn't fit the usual profile.

River bumped my elbow and whined. Animals have a way of communicating, and he was telling me to turn out the light. I sighed deeply, reached over and patted his head, then closed down my laptop.

Chapter Twenty-Nine

Tuesday morning arrived with a vengeance. It was still dark outside when River barked and Rascal brayed. I rolled over and pulled the quilt over my head to shut out the noise. When I didn't respond, River jumped on the bed and tried to tug the blanket from my head.

"Go away, River. It's not time to get up."

He raced out of the bedroom. His barking grew frantic. I forced myself out of bed and grabbed my bathrobe. A glance at the clock told me I still had two hours of sleep left. I also knew that my dog wasn't a frivolous yapper. Without turning the light on and before I opened the doggie door to let him and Rascal outside, I leaned against the kitchen sink to peer into the darkness.

Parked under the security light sat a large white paneled van with satellite dishes on the top. The WKYB logo indicated the truck belonged to a news station from Lexington. I gritted my teeth. Bruce Webber was a bane to lawmen, and more than a reporter—he was a sensationalist who capitalized on embellishing the stories he wrote. He didn't care who got hurt in the aftermath of his reports as long as it raked in the dollars.

I disliked disturbing my dad at this hour of the morning, but it couldn't be helped. His voice was groggy with sleep when he answered the phone. "What's the emergency, Tullah?"

I apologized for waking him at five in the morning.

"Our old buddy Bruce Webber and his crew are parked under the security light in my yard."

Reporters, journalists, and the morbid curious always pressed the limits of privacy and confidentiality. Bruce Webber and the rag media he worked for were the worst. "I'm surprised he hasn't camped out on our doorsteps before this. What do you want them to know, Dad?"

He cleared the rasp from his voice. From the tone, his aggravation was clear. "Doesn't matter what you tell Webber, he'll only blow it out of proportion. Tell him that we're using all available resources to find the perpetrator of these crimes. It won't do any good, but impress upon him that it's important he doesn't whip people into a frenzy of panic." Then as if his head had cleared from a sleep-dazed fog, he added, "Stay inside. Don't turn on any lights. I'll send Andy out asap. It's best to have a deputy with you. Maybe that asshole will think twice about misquoting you. And, Punkin—keep your cool."

My previous run-in with Webber had resulted in a lawsuit for assault and battery. However, the judge said Webber couldn't hold me responsible for my little donkey kicking him in the shins, or my horse stomping Webber's drone to pieces.

While I dressed, I kept the animals in the house. There was no need to alert Webber and his crew that I was awake and stirring around. I made my way to the living room and found a vantage point at a window to watch for Deputy Andy Kemble.

The usual drive time from town is twenty minutes. It seemed forever before I spotted the red light on top of Andy's car. He was approaching without a siren. Smart,

I thought.

I rushed to the kitchen window. Once he'd parked alongside the news van, I grabbed the double leashes and snapped them in place on the dog and donkey harnesses. I had no doubt my pets would remember Webber, especially since he'd kicked Rascal. There was no need to invite trouble.

My animals lunged against their tethers and nearly dragged me across the yard. I greeted Andy. "Thank you for coming."

Webber and his cameraman exited the van. I made the introductions, "Mr. Webber...Deputy Andrew Kemble with the Enigma Sheriff's Department." I didn't bother to hide the sarcasm in my voice. "Deputy Kemble, this is Bruce Webber, famous for overly embellishing the news, creating unnecessary alarm, and abusing animals."

River snarled and sprang forward. I had to brace myself to keep from being yanked off my feet. Webber backed against the van. He yelled, "Get that beast away from me, or I'll..."

"Or you'll what, Mr. Webber?" Andy spoke with soft authority.

Webber didn't answer. Instead, he motioned for the cameraman to hand him the microphone. He cut a cautious sideways glance toward the deputy.

Andy asked, "Why are you here, Mr. Webber?"

Webber whipped out a handkerchief and wiped his nose. "Why, to obtain information about the serial killer, of course."

Not to be deterred, Andy said, "I would advise you to direct all questions concerning police matters to Sheriff Henry Holliday. Doctor Holliday is a private citizen and as such has no authority to release information concerning active or ongoing cases."

Webber sneered, "Yeah, but—"

"No '*but*,' Mr. Webber. If you persist, I can haul you in for harassment. However, because Doctor Holliday is a consultant on the case, Sheriff Holliday has given his go-ahead for her to cooperate…within reason."

This was the same Andrew Kemble I knew in high school. Direct. No nonsense. Except the years and life experiences had matured him. I was glad he had returned to Enigma as Dad's new deputy. He looked at me and nodded.

Andy removed a small recorder from his coat pocket. He held it forward. "This, gentlemen, is a tape recorder. Like you, I will record your questions and Doctor Holliday's answers. Understand, this is merely a precaution to ensure that Doctor Holliday's statements have not been altered or modified. Any questions?"

The incredulous expression on Webber's face was priceless. I had to restrain myself to keep from hugging Andy. He quirked a smile and nodded.

We stood in the dark and the freezing cold. I suppose I should have invited them inside the house, or at least the office, for coffee and warmth. However, give Webber an inch, and he'd milk it to his advantage.

I was serious and fluid when I spoke. Yes, we were sorry to report that a third victim, probably attacked by the same perpetrator, had been discovered. We understood the public's and the media's concern and implored them to understand that, in an active investigation, only so much information could be given out. I suggested the public should take extreme care under the circumstances, and if needed they should also fully cooperate with law enforcement during the investigation.

Webber said, "Doc Holliday, rumor has it that the victims have been butchered. That the murders are connected to nursery rhymes and fairy tales, and possibly similar to the unsolved Jack the Ripper cases that occurred decades ago. Do you agree?"

He shoved the microphone forward, practically under my nose. I disliked the slang use of my title, but I refused to be baited. "Mr. Webber, we're not making comparisons right now to any serial killers or their modus operandi."

There was derision in his tone. "Yeah, it's like the law to withhold information. We know about the whacked-off head, and the other vic's head split in two by an axe."

I refused to be angered or swayed to any emotion by his smirking. "As you've gleaned, Mr. Webber, there is nothing normal about these murders. The savagery and brutality, and the display, is to incite the public and to taunt law officers."

Webber said, "Would you describe them as heinous?"

I thought to myself that I had never seen such barbaric horror of the victims and the way they had been displayed. My head hurt, and I wanted to reach out and slap the sneer from the reporter's face. I forced an expression of calm. "The very act of taking a human life is always horrible."

Andy came to my aid. "Sir, our units have scoured the county for hours. We will keep news coming to you with all possible speed, just as we will catch this killer with all possible speed." He placed a hand at my elbow. "Now, if you will excuse us, we—"

Webber had no intention of excusing us. A barrage of questions followed a I turned toward the house.

Andy stepped forward. "You've had your time, Mr. Webber. I suggest you pack your gear and leave the premises. Sheriff Holliday is available to answer more questions."

"It is my constitutional right to inform the public of—"

Andy's expression was intense. "No, sir, it is not your constitutional right to harass a private citizen who has been more than forthcoming with her cooperation. If you refuse to vacate the site, then I will read you your rights, place you under arrest, and impound your van and equipment. Do I make myself clear?"

Again, he held the tape recorder forward.

Webber said grimly, "Yeah, abundantly."

We stood in the yard and watched until the news van's taillights disappeared. The cold had seeped through my jacket. "Andy, would you like a cup of coffee?"

He smiled. "You don't need to ask twice."

I released River and Rascal from their leashes. Andy said, "Your pets seem to have a distinct dislike for Webber."

While we walked toward the house, I regaled him with my first encounter with the reporter. I said, "Webber doesn't like animals. Heck, I'm not even sure he likes himself."

"I've met a few like him. You handled yourself like a pro."

We removed our jackets and settled at the dining table. I filled the mugs. "Cream and sugar?"

Andy answered with a wave. "Black."

We were quiet for a moment. I joined him at the table. "What's your take on the murders?"

He spoke over the rim of his cup. "You're sure a straight shooter, Tullah. You haven't changed a bit in all these years." After another gulp of coffee, he went on. "Back to your question—although these are crimes of passion, we can rule out romance or sex."

Thoughtful and tired, I sipped my coffee. "Dad and I are at loggerheads. He thinks the murderer is a man, and I'm almost certain it's a woman."

Andy nodded. "Henry told me about your symbolism theories, and that the murders are acts of revenge, which supports the passion idea."

I agreed. "Even when the killer is captured, I don't think we'll ever know all the facts."

He rolled the cup between his hands. I sensed there was a question he was hesitant to ask.

I waited.

"Tullah, Henry told me about your, ahm, your—"

"My weird connection with animals and how I know when murder has happened?"

Andy looked uncomfortable. "Did you have this when we were kids?"

I gave him the abbreviated version of my mother's untimely death. It was a subject I'd rather avoid. "Anyhow, Grandmother says I was born with this gift— or curse—and that I will likely die with it. Just understand that I am not a psychic." I offered to refresh his coffee. He held the cup forward. I said, "Does knowing this make you uncomfortable?"

He looked at me curiously. "Your gift is a rarity, Tullah. Embrace it."

"You didn't answer my question."

He lifted the cup to his lips. "A little taken aback, but uncomfortable? Not in the least."

Andy leaned forward to prop on his elbows. "Here's a question for you, Tullah. Do you think the killer will strike again?"

"If I said yes, it would be pure speculation." There was no need for me to add, "Unless the raven shows up and says, '*Nevermore.*' "

Chapter Thirty

Jeff arrived a few minutes before nine. I was stymied, because it was Tuesday and his schedule was every other day. I sensed he was nervous and attributed it to his first official day as a student office aide.

"Good morning, Jeff. It's Tuesday. Does your counselor know you're here?" I handed him a blue folder filled with office procedural instructions. "There's coffee and soda. Feel free to help yourself, and don't be afraid to ask questions."

He twisted his hands together in a nervous gesture. "Yes, ma'am. She knows, and I've checked in with my homeroom teacher." He shifted from one foot to the other, his discomfort obvious. "Ah, Doctor Holliday, I do have a question."

"Ask away."

"Well, ma'am, uhm, Doctor Holliday, my grades are good enough that I can take an early graduation. I hadn't planned to, but I'm, ah, wondering if, you know, with Miss Ella—"

"Jeff, just spit it out."

He heaved a deep sigh. The tips of his ears turned red. "Instead of waiting until June to officially graduate, I was wondering if you were serious about me working for you. If so, I need to let my guidance counselor know, because I can early graduate the week after Thanksgiving, but I can still walk with my class in June."

His face now matched the color of his ears. I thought he might faint if he didn't exhale from his lengthy run-on sentence. He gave me a woeful look. "My grades are good enough, and I don't plan to start college until next fall anyhow. I-I could really use the money." His voice drifted off as he stared down at his tattered tennis shoes.

"Jeff, have you had breakfast?"

"Yes, ma'am. At school."

"Good. Now, here's the deal. If you work for me, it'll be full time, with overtime pay if I need you to stay late or come in on weekends. That means giving up your job at the Crispy Chicken."

I held up my hand when he opened his mouth to speak.

"Do you still plan to attend Enigma Community College?"

He nodded his answer.

"In the fall, if you can manage your class load and work too, we'll arrange it so you can continue working until you graduate with your two-year degree."

The grin on his face caused my heart to smile. "Here are my conditions—no falling behind in your grades. If necessary, bring class assignments to the office. Ella and I have been where you are. We understand the difficulties of juggling school and work." I stuck out my hand. "Deal?"

He pumped my hand up and down with vigor. "Yes, ma'am. Deal!"

The phone rang. Although he was grinning, he answered professionally, "Holliday Animal Clinic. How may I help you?"

I gave him a thumbs-up and walked outside to greet the truck pulling in with a horse trailer attached. My first patient had arrived.

As soon as I had a break from patients, I shot Ella a text informing her that Jeff Dempsey was soon to be our new full-time receptionist. She answered with smiley and thumbs-up emojis.

I was in the middle of performing a cesarean section on a Shih Tzu when Jeff tiptoed in and announced it was time for him to leave. "There's a message for you from a Mr. Arnie Lewis. Like it said in the instruction manual you and Doctor Sanders gave me, I explained that you were performing surgery and couldn't be disturbed. I hope that's okay. He left his phone number."

I assured the boy that he'd handled the situation perfectly. I wished him a good afternoon at school and said I'd see him on Wednesday.

By five, I was ready for the day to end. In addition to being awakened before the crack of dawn, dealing with an obnoxious reporter, gelding three stallions, delivering two puppies, and performing a C-section, I'd had a lightbulb moment and needed to contact my dad before I returned Arnie Lewis' call.

"Punkin, Andy told me you handled Bruce Webber with finesse and professionalism this morning. I'm proud of you for holding your temper."

I harrumphed. "Webber deserved a fat lip."

Dad guffawed.

I hesitated, then said, "During the autopsy, you said Doctor Sanders pulled Mrs. Gardner's fingerprints."

"That's right."

"Did she happen to pull prints from her body before she sanitized it for autopsy?"

"Tiny dusted all of the clothing for prints and came up with nothing. As for prints off the body, you'll need to explain."

I may be a veterinarian, but I'm still interested in human science. "In a recent conversation with Vaneeta, she said there is a study being done where latent fingerprints can be lifted from a cadaver's skin surface. As the head of the forensics department at the university, she stays up to date on the latest criminological techniques. She also said while little success has been seen in the US, there has been a level of success in other countries."

Dad cleared his throat. "Anything to catch this prick. I'll run it past Doctor Sanders. Do you have a list of chemicals needed for such an undertaking?"

"I don't, but since Vaneeta has willingly helped us with other cases, shall I send a text asking for a list and the formula for use?"

"We don't want to jump the gun. Hold off until I hear from Doctor Sanders."

As soon as we disconnected, I sent a text to Dr. Vaneeta Sunreet. I'd never defy my dad… However, it never hurt to be ahead of the game.

She answered within the hour with a list of chemicals, all new to me, and stating that if the cadaver had been washed in preparation for autopsy, any evidence on the epidermis might no longer exist.

I shot an immediate text to Dad: *Ask Dr. Sanders if the Gardner cadaver has been washed.* I gave him a short explanation for my question. All I could do now was sit back and wait.

It wasn't until I reached into my jeans pocket and removed a pink slip of paper with Arnie Lewis's name on it that I remembered his call. I wondered why he'd contacted me. He didn't own a pet.

I punched in his number. After several rings, his voice mail answered with a request to leave a message. Arnie was a virtual recluse. Except for lunch at Sweet's 'n' Eats, and church, his social life was practically nonexistent. The last time I spoke to him, he had stated that as soon as he was definitely cleared from Dad's suspect list, he would be selling the house he'd shared with his grandfather and leaving Enigma.

****

Something was off. I wasn't sure what. It was nearly seven, so I decided to treat myself to a plate of Uncle Charlie's BBQ, and then I'd check on Arnie if he hadn't returned my phone call by then.

I had stepped inside the truck and had reached for the ignition when my phone chirped. Dad's ID popped up. "That was fast. What did Doctor Sanders say?"

"Tullah…" He never called me by my name unless it was serious business. The hairs on the back of my neck prickled.

"What's wrong, Dad?"

"Arnie Lewis is in my office. He's an emotional mess and says he'll only talk to you. Can you come to town?"

"Sure. In fact, I was on my way to the Whitehorse when you called. Did Arnie say why he's upset?"

"All he would say is that he's afraid he'll be the killer's next victim."

I turned the ignition, put the truck in gear, and backed out of the carport. Arnie had to be mistaken. The raven hadn't made an appearance. "Did he say why?"

"I asked, and all he'd say is that only you will understand. Other than that, he's huddled in my office like the boogie man is after him, and he's holding a small white box like it's a valuable possession."

"What's in the box?"

"I don't know, and he won't say. He just repeated that you'd understand."

"I'll be there in twenty minutes. And Dad, I'm starved. Would you mind calling Uncle Charlie and ordering a burger, fried mushrooms, and a cola for me? I'll pick it up on my way."

"Sure thing, Punkin."

On the drive to town, I pushed Arnie's emergency aside and thought about the case. All killers made mistakes. If we could pull a print from the Gardner cadaver, then we could confirm the perpetrator's identity and nail him or her.

I was in deep thought, which is dangerous when driving, because I nearly drove past the saloon and had to do a quick wheelie into the drive-through lane. Vera was waiting for me. She opened the window and handed out a sack filled with aromas that set my stomach to growling.

She said, "Tullah, you are skin and bones. You need to stop skipping meals." And then she added, "Charlie added onion rings. He worries about you, you know."

I handed her a twenty. She held up her hand. "Compliments of your godfather."

After I pulled through the window, I grabbed a handful of hot onion rings and stuffed my mouth. I continued eating while I drove the short ten-minute distance to Dad's new office and jail. Before exiting my truck, I polished off the onion rings and consumed several bites of hamburger, then rewrapped it and folded the remains and the mushrooms in the sack. I'd finish the leftovers when I got home.

A gust of frigid air blasted me when I exited the truck. Shoving my hands into my coat pockets, I hustled through the double-paned office doors. The minute I walked inside, Tiny motioned me toward Dad's open door.

"Any clues to why Arnie wants to see me specifically?"

Tiny merely shook his head. "He hasn't said two words since Henry phoned you."

I shrugged out of my jacket and hung it on the coat rack, heaved a breath, and walked inside. Arnie sat huddled in a corner, his face a mask of fear. Dad greeted me with lifted eyebrows, and I dragged a chair to sit next to the frightened man. "What's got you so upset, Arnie?"

I'd never heard Arnie stutter until now. He explained that he'd gone to the funeral home this morning to clean out his and his grandfather's office in preparation to give complete control to Mr. Peebles, as per his grandfather's will. Arnie held a white gift box forward. "This was on my desk. Tullah, I tried to call you. I shouldn't have come here. What if the murderer sees me? I'm doomed!"

To say I was shocked when I removed the box lid is an understatement. On top of crushed red tissue paper lay the raven. My raven with the white cape behind its neck. I unfolded the note and read aloud, "I know you know. Don't tell, or I'll see you in hell."

Gingerly, I lifted the dead bird from its nest of red paper. The poor bird's neck dangled—limp. I glanced from Dad to Arnie as I laid the bird back inside the box, closed it, and set the box on Dad's desk. "Its neck is broken."

To give myself time to think, I walked to the

coffeepot and poured three cups. "Sugar and cream, Arnie?"

With his nod, I took my time preparing his coffee, Dad watching me. I handed Dad and Arnie their cups, then sat next to Arnie. "What is it that you're supposed to know, Arnie?"

His hands trembled when he lifted the cup to his lips, and a little coffee sloshed on his crisp white shirt. "If I knew, I'd tell you."

"Okay, let's try again. Since your grandfather died and Mr. Peebles inherited the business, has anything changed at the funeral home?"

He sipped his coffee. His face screwed into a frown. "Maybe with Anne—you know, the stylist we hired. You met her the day we found the…found the…head."

"What about Anne? What's different?

Arnie looked around the room. His voice dropped to a whisper as if he were afraid someone was eavesdropping. "She's always been a little strange, but lately she's been singing a song…'My Bonny Lies Over the Ocean.' She sings it over and over and over, until one day I couldn't stand it anymore and I actually yelled at her to stop. I mean, it was really getting on my nerves."

"And did she—stop?"

He shook his head. "She looked at me with those odd blue eyes. It scared me because they were filled with malice. And there's something else."

In the outer office, the ringing of the fax machine drew our attention. Whatever Arnie was about to say was temporarily forgotten.

Chapter Thirty-One

Tiny entered the office and handed the paperwork to my dad. "I think you'll find this interesting, Henry."

I, on the other hand, was more interested in what else Arnie had to say about Anne Brom. Much to our surprise, it seemed that chaos had been unleashed in the cyberworld. First, the broken fax machine suddenly began to work, spewing out paperwork, and then the office phone rang, and all the while poor Arnie huddled in the corner.

While Dad and Tiny mused over what the fax had spit out, I grabbed the phone and forced myself to answer calmly. "Sheriff's Office, Dr. Holliday speaking, how may I help you?"

"Tullah, this is Dr. Sanders—Sunny. Is Henry available?"

I said her name loud enough for Dad to hear. "Good evening, Dr. Sanders. Yes, he's here."

"I do wish you'd call me Sunny."

Even though she is Ella's mother, and a friend, I'm not sure why I hesitate to use her given name.

Dad motioned his hand to indicate that I should take the call. "He's not available at the moment. If this is in regard to his inquiry about Mrs. Gardner's body, perhaps I can help."

She sighed into the phone. "Sometimes I wish you were the medical examiner, and I say that with sincere honesty. It's all I can do to keep up with the latest surgical techniques and new pharmaceuticals."

With my own busy practice as well as being the medical director for Enigma's Animal Control services, I assured her I totally understood. "Were you able to pull a fingerprint from Gardner's epidermis?"

"Unfortunately, no. My denier had already prepped the cadaver for autopsy. However, I am curious to know more about fingerprint recovery from the skin."

Anxious to know what held Dad's and Tiny's interest, I said, "I'll have Dr. Vaneeta Sanreet send you all the up-to-date information." In the background I heard an intercom page for Dr. Sanders to come to the nurse's station. I could certainly empathize with her lament about busy schedules.

She said, "I'd love to chat, Tullah. Maybe when we both have some free time, we'll do lunch. And please, apologize to Henry about my not being able to pull the fingerprints."

Once I'd disconnected the call, I turned my attention to the photo that Dad held in my direction. He said, "This is Bonny Cowen. He's the patient that killed an orderly and then walked away from the Ohio Institute for the criminally insane." Dad handed me the stack of papers. "Cowen has a very interesting history."

Looking into the young man's eyes was like looking into liquid malice. I could almost feel the icy fingers of death squeezing my heart. I walked to Arnie and held the photo for him to see. He looked at it, and then at me. He covered his mouth, his eyes widened. "Except for the short hair and clothing, it looks like Anne."

Arnie's admission drew the attention of Dad and Tiny. Dad said, "Anne Brom, the cosmetologist that works for you?"

Arnie didn't so much as crack a smile. "Yeah, sure, Sheriff. But it can't be. Anne's a woman, and this is definitely a man. Maybe it's a doppelganger."

My gaze slid back to the photo. "Dad, with all that's been happening, I forgot to mention that I researched the source of the name Bonny. Its origin is both Irish and Scottish. For a girl it means 'pretty' or 'beautiful,' and for a man—attractive—as in 'a bonnie lad.' "

I held up the papers. "Do you mind if I make copies of these to study once I get home?"

Nothing against Dad's new secretary, Janice McElroy, but unlike Joyce, she didn't seem willing to put in extra hours. Instead of another deputy, Dad needed two secretaries, to include one for the night shift.

When I turned to leave the office, Arnie scooted to the edge of the chair, hysteria lacing his voice. "You're not leaving?"

I assured him I would return as soon as I ran copies of the report and photo. He mewled, "I can't go home, and I'm afraid to go to the hotel. Can I spend the night in one of the jail cells?"

I looked at my dad. He said, "This isn't a hotel, Arnie. Perhaps Mr. Peebles will put you up for the night."

"You don't understand, Sheriff. The note said I'd die if I told, and I did—I told. I-I don't want to die." His voice grew to a shriek. "I don't want to die. It's your sworn duty to protect me."

Dad looked perplexed. I came to his rescue. "Arnie—Arnie, calm down. Are you absolutely certain you don't know why the writer threatened you?"

The poor man wrung his hands together. "If I knew,

I'd tell you."

"Okay. Let's see if we can pull a print off the box." I'd already touched it. I looked at Dad's deputy.

Tiny nodded his understanding. He said, "Other than your prints and Arnie's, maybe the writer slipped up and forgot to wear gloves. Give me twenty-four hours to let you know."

Figuring out what to do about Arnie was a dilemma. I was on the verge of suggesting Dad accommodate the young mortician when Andy strolled into the office. It was if we were all of one mind when we greeted him with a smile.

The new deputy looked at us, his expression filled with skepticism. "What?"

Dad briefly explained the threat on Arnie's life. He said, "We're putting him in protective custody for twenty-four hours."

Tiny's grin widened. "As the new guy, you're elected to be his shadow."

If anyone of us thought to get a rise out of Andy, we were wrong. He shrugged and said, "It beats being huddled inside a cold patrol car with stale coffee, watching for speeders. I don't know about you, Mr. Lewis, but it's way past my supper time. C'mon, I'll buy you dinner." He looked at me and winked. "I understand the county is paying."

After he escorted Arnie from the office, Dad said, "That boy's all right."

And Tiny agreed.

While Tiny refilled the coffee machine, I ran a second copy of Bonny Cowen's photo. I sat at Joyce's desk with a felt tip pen poised. Tiny came to look over my shoulder. "What're you doing, Tullah?"

My art skills were limited to stick figures. I closed my eyes and recalled the image of Anne Brom, then bent to emulate her Dutch Boy hair style. After making a mess, I ripped the paper in half and tossed it in the trashcan. What I'd tried to create didn't match the image I had visualized inside my head.

"Dad, I'm going home." I held up the copies. "I'll read these tonight."

He looked concerned. "Punkin, it's late and snowing. Your animals are safe and they're warm. Humor your ol' man and spend the night. I'll get you up early enough to open the clinic." As an added incentive, he said, "Blueberry pancakes for breakfast; my treat."

I weighed the suggestion. A two-minute walk across the street to Dad's apartment or a twenty-minute drive on slick roads to my house? With Arnie in the safe company of Deputy Kemble, and Tiny pulling the night shift, I grinned. "Who in their right mind would turn down Patty's blueberry pancakes?"

"That's my girl. Grab your coat."

Outside, hunched against the cold, I unlocked my truck and grabbed the sack of leftover food. While we crossed the street to the former sheriff's building, Dad related his idea of purchasing the building and rehabbing it into apartments. "I'm waiting on Tanti and the city council to put their seal of approval on the idea."

"Knowing grandmother and her love of preserving all things historic, I don't think you have anything to worry about. I do have to ask, though—you're pretty much a solitary person, so how many apartments do you plan to build, and how will you like being a landlord?"

We stepped onto the sidewalk and to the door. Dad had installed a new keypad and punched in a code to open the outer door. I followed him up the stairs that led to his old office, and then on to the attic he had renovated into an apartment years ago.

Once inside, he said, "Those are good questions, Punkin. Right now, I'm too tired to think about the answers." He pointed toward the bedroom. "You know where your things are. I'll heat up a couple of cans of chili to go with whatever's in that sack you're holding."

I didn't often spend the night with my dad, but when I did it was a treat. In truth, I wasn't thrilled about his plans to renovate the building. I'd hoped that when he decided to retire he'd build a house on the property I'd inherited from my mother. I opened a drawer and pulled out a pair of flannel pjs. But who was I to tell him what to do with his life?

Over a bowl of chili, I finished off my half-eaten hamburger and mushrooms. Dad didn't own a television. He always said cop shows annoyed him because the writers rarely got it right, and he didn't want to get interested in a series when he'd have to miss several episodes, and for him game shows were boring. He settled in his recliner with his copy of the report on Bonny Cowen.

The easy silence between us was comforting. It's rare times like this that make me realize how lonely I am living in a big two-story house with a dog and a donkey as my sole companions.

I shook away my woes. "Dad, do you think Arnie knows who wrote the note, and if so, why didn't he tell us? I mean, the threat on his life was clear enough, especially if he had the courage to come to your office."

He thought for a moment. "You've worked enough cases with me to know that fear does crazy things to people's minds. My question is why does the note writer think Arnie knows his identity?"

"I guess we won't know the answer to that until we solve the crime." I turned my attention to reading the report. I used a red pen to underline information that stood out to me. I couldn't get the death of the raven out of my mind. Somehow the killer knew it would warn me. I hoped Andy would keep Arnie safe.

As much as I hated my empathic abilities, I needed to call them forth to solve this case. I finished scanning the first page of the report, set it aside, and on page two, in pure shock, my eyes homed in on a particular name. "Holy cow, Dad! Have you read page two of the investigative report?"

I glanced at him, he'd pulled a lap blanket over his feet, and his eyes were fluttering. I wondered how many hours he'd worked without adequate sleep. I hadn't meant to shout. He jerked alert. "Sorry, I must have drifted off." He yawned. "You read. I'll listen."

Chapter Thirty-Two

Dad wiped the sleep from his eyes and nodded for me to begin. I skipped over the routine information and dove into the investigative report that read like a plot for a mystery novel.

"Franklin County Investigation Report
Franklin County Sheriff's Office
Town Of Columbus, State Ohio

"On May 23 at approximately twenty-one hundred hours Sheriff Edward Baker and two deputies, Sgt Dwight Ham and rookie officer Terrell Sikes, from Columbus were dispatched to an area of the Bridgewater Mental Health Institute at Farmington Road on an alleged homicide. Sheriff Baker stated that photographs were taken of the scene and evidence collected.

"Reporting officers observed a male, white, approximate age in mid-forties. Victim was found in the exterior recreational area lying face down on a cemented floor of the volleyball court. The male victim was identified by the Institute's night supervisor as being the facility recreational director, Mathew Pilcher."

At the victim's name, Dad sat forward in his chair. He said, "Did I hear you say—Pilcher?"

"Yes, sir. I wonder if he is related to our victim number one—Nathaniel Pilcher?"

Dad let his recliner down. "Hang tight. Nature beckons." On the way out of the room he called over his shoulder, "Make a note to check the connection between the two men. I'm curious to know if they are related or if the names are purely coincidental."

"Way ahead of you, Dad." I held up my red pen and grinned.

He returned with two cups of coffee and a bag of ginger snaps. Ginger snaps dunked in hot coffee is one of life's little pleasures. After indulging in a few soggy cookies, I continued reading the report.

"The most significant evidence to be found was the blood distribution on the victim's face, arms, and upper body. It appeared the perpetrator used a long slender knife to execute stab wounds to the neck and left to right carotid arteries, and middle cerebral artery, causing death. A sack of donuts soaked with red substance that appeared to be blood lay next to the victim. A white substance thought to be powdered sugar coated the victim's upper lip and fingertips on the right hand. Pinned to the victim's white uniform shirt was a typed note with the words 'children playing at slaughter—oink…oink!' "

I emitted a disgusted groan. "You're not going to believe this."

Dad said, "That bad, huh?

"Worse." I read the last few lines of the report. "However, an FBI forensic report stated contamination of evidence: failing to wear evidence gloves, an officer touched the bag of donuts, then touched the suspect, then stepped in the pooled blood, leading to possible cross-contamination."

Dad emitted his own sound of disgust. "I've met Ed Baker. He's a strictly-by-the-book sheriff with a temper just as volatile. My guess, it was the rookie that messed up."

I'd met Sheriff Baker only once. It was enough. "If it was, I feel badly for him. What would you do in a case like that?"

Dad didn't have to think about his answer. "If it was a rookie, I'd send him back to the academy for more training. If it was a veteran cop, I'd put him on suspension with a warning that there'd be no second chances."

My dad is a cop's cop, and I knew he'd do exactly as he said. However, discussing rookie mistakes wasn't helping us solve our murders.

Dad said, "You're the expert on symbolism. Is this another one of the killer's references to a fairy tale?"

I grabbed my cellphone. "Give me a minute." And it took a few failed searches before I found the answer. "Here it is, Dad. The Grimm Brothers' story titled 'Children Played at Slaughtering' is gruesome." I raised my eyebrows as I read, "In this jolly game, one child plays a pig and the other a butcher. The butcher slits the pig's throat while another child catches the blood in a bowl and yells, 'Oink…oink!'

"In my opinion the symbolism of this tale is that the child playing the butcher is no longer a passive innocent child. He is now the punisher."

At first, Dad didn't say anything. He seemed to be sorting through his thoughts. Then he said, "With similar modus operandi, I'd say we're dealing with the same individual…or worse, a copycat."

I'm glad I was born with a strong constitution. Suddenly, the ginger snaps weren't sitting well in my stomach. "You know, Dad, this killer seems to have a very specific agenda."

He released a heavy sigh. "Yep, we've been at this for almost eight days, and we still don't have all the information we need. Does the report state a person of interest?"

I flipped to the last page of the report and finished reading, "A sketch was completed of the scene, including measurements. A search of individual client cells was conducted. All clients were accounted for except client Bonny Cowen, ward five, compartment twelve. The door was open. The lock did not appear tampered. At one o'clock in the a.m. we finished processing the scene."

Dad glanced at the clock. "Is the patient intake form attached to the investigative report?"

I held it forward. "It's late. Shall I read it?"

At his nod, I cleared my throat and began. "This is from the Bridgewater Mental Institute, Farmington Road, Columbus, Ohio. It states that Bonny Comhghan aka Cowen, age twenty-four, has been committed as an involuntary client. Mr. Cowen states he has no family and was placed in the social services system at the age of approximately six years. Mr. Cowen has been committed at the request of the Ohio State Court for psychiatric care. Mr. Cowen has a history of violence against animals, which often represents displaced hostility and aggression stemming from neglect or abuse from adult caretakers. Mr. Cowen has had previous run-ins with law enforcement which has resulted in multiple incarcerations in a juvenile detention center for numerous infractions to include cruelty to animals, running away from foster care, physical abuse toward a teacher and foster care parents, and habitual lying. As an adult, Mr. Cowen was incarcerated for substance abuse, shoplifting, and attacking an officer of the law with a knife. Numerous DUIs have resulted in the suspension of his driver's license. Having completed Ohio state requirements, Mr. Cowen is a licensed embalmer and a cosmetologist-esthetician. He is an extremely intelligent man with expertise in computer technology. He appeared to live a normal life with no prior history of mental health issues, as reported by his neighbors, until being orphaned, having witnessed the death of his identical twin sister and both parents, who perished in a house fire that may or may not have been accidently set by Mr. Cowen, then age five.

Mr. Cowen has no goals in counseling, as he believes nothing is wrong with him and is unaware of any underlying issues with his mental health. Evidence: Mr. Cowen has an obsession with fantasy and death, i.e., obsessive with Brothers Grimm macabre tales and Mother Goose nursery rhymes. Evidence: His fascination seems to stem from physical abuse, mental health neglect, and evidenced detachment from reality. Conclusion: Mr. Cowen presents with a varying range of mental health issues—dissociative identity disorder, antisocial personality disorder, difficulties with emotional reactions to regulations, inability to distinguish between right and wrong, hallucinations (states that his twin sister visits him). Final analysis: Mr. Cowen presents characteristics of a narcissist with malignant sociopathic and schizophrenic tendencies. Without care or treatment there is substantial likelihood that Mr. Cowen will cause serious bodily harm to self or others in the near future, as evidenced by recent behavior."

I looked up at my dad. "How horrible. I could almost feel sorry for Bonny Cowen." What fear, what dreadful experiences for a child, and no one to protect him. I found myself staring down at the sheaf of papers in my hand. I shook myself. I should be feeling sorry for the three corpses and the way they died. Lost in thought, I jumped when Dad's phone pinged.

He said, "Say that again, Tiny."

Evidently Dad's deputy repeated himself, because Dad agreed to meet him. When he disconnected, he said, "Tiny just found another page of the Cowen report. Apparently, it got jammed in that antiquated piece of junk, then spit it out when another fax came through. He says it's important. Stay here while I meet him outside."

Apparently, Dad thought the one-minute sprint between his apartment and his new office was quicker than fussing with the fax machine, scanning the document, and emailing it.

He assured me, "Be back in a minute."

I jumped to my feet and went into the kitchen to fix myself—something. Anything.

I settled for a spoonful of peanut butter, and had barely licked the spoon clean when Dad returned. The expression on his face told me the paper he held was a priceless piece of information.

Chapter Thirty-Three

Dad's top lip curled in anger. His expression was grim. "There has to be a special place in hell for degenerates that willfully and deliberately steal the innocence of children." He thrust the report toward me, then paced around the room before settling in his recliner. "Read it aloud. I want to make sure that, in my haste, and with the dim light from the street lamps, I didn't misconstrue the information."

I curled in my place on the sofa, and scanned the last page of the patient intake report. The cruelty of the three listed people was breathtaking; yet the horrendous way they had died was equally as awful.

Attached to the report was a copy of a newspaper article that was blurred to the point that the words were illegible. However, the headline was large enough to read: Three Dead in Canton House Fire.

The report stated the history of Bonny Cowen's ten years of foster care and named the foster parents as: Mr. and Mrs. Nathaniel Pilcher, Canton, Ohio; Mr. and Mrs. Lawrence (Larry) Parrish, Dayton, Ohio; and Mrs. Estelle Lewis Podarge Gardner, Beaver Creek, Ohio.

I was near tears when I'd finished reading. With all the shuffling from place to place, the poor kid had no security system. It took a moment to clear my head, but one name in particular had caught my attention—Lewis.

After reading the intake report, I asked Dad if he had

a magnifying glass. He searched around until he found one, and handed it to me. No matter how I tried, I could not bring the words in the news report into focus. "Dad, the only words I can make out in this article is 'twin' and possibly 'survivor.' I'm curious about the twin—and the cause of the fire. The intake report implied that it could have been arson."

Dad rubbed his eyes and yawned. "Call Tanti. As a former crime reporter, I believe she still has connections within the newspaper world. If anyone can get you a readable copy, it's your grandmother."

By now it was after eleven o'clock. While I sent a text to my grandmother, Dad punched the quick-dial button on his phone. He put the phone on speaker. Andy answered. "What's up, Sheriff?"

Dad said, "I need to speak to Arnie. And I need you to record the conversation as best you can, under the circumstances."

"Sure thing, Sheriff. We're playing a game of chess. Hold on."

Arnie answered. "Ah, Sheriff Holliday, is…is anything wrong?"

"I have a question for you."

"O-okay."

"Do you know someone named Estelle Lewis Podarge Gardner?"

Silence.

"It depends. Why?"

Dad rarely loses his patience. It was late, he was tired, and he was frustrated over the lack of clues that might lead us to a maniacal serial killer. "Just answer the damn question, Arnie!"

"Okay…okay, I didn't mean to upset you.

Grandfather removed all the pictures of her from the house and family albums. Her name was never mentioned and he never talked about her. I'm not exactly sure what she did to be banished from the family. She's my grandfather's youngest sister. I guess that makes her my great-aunt."

Dad said, "Did you know her personally?"

"Yes, in fact, I visited her a couple of times when I was a kid. My father wasn't as rigid as grandfather. She really wasn't a nice person. After my second visit, I asked my father why granddad hated her."

We waited for Arnie to continue. When he didn't, Dad practically growled Arnie's name.

Finally, Arnie answered, "Daddy said she had toxic behavior. He didn't elaborate. If you knew my daddy, he was like his father, asking detailed questions and expecting answers was prohibited."

Like me, Dad picked up on the hesitation in Arnie's voice. "Arnie, if you had to take a wild guess about a reason for the family's estrangement from your great-aunt, what would you say?"

Another hesitation before Arnie answered. "That she was a thief, a habitual liar, and that she forged her mother's name on a check and nearly bankrupted the business, then blamed it on granddaddy. The family never recouped their financial or social status because of her. And worse, she was responsible for her mother's suicide. Of course, this is all conjecture. I really can't swear to any of it."

"Was she a foster parent?"

Silence.

Dad's jaw was grinding.

I spoke succinctly. "Arnie, this is important. Quit

hem-hawing around and answer my dad's questions."

"Okay, but, Tullah, am I in trouble?"

I didn't want to frighten him more than he already was after receiving a threatening note and a dead bird. "No, Arnie. Dad's trying to find out who sent you the package, and who—"

I didn't get to finish my statement. Arnie blurted, "You think my great-aunt sent the package? Why would she do such a disgusting thing?"

"Calm down, Arnie."

Dad had asked Dr. Sanders to keep the third victim's murder and her identity confidential pending notification of next of kin. Now wasn't the time to tell Arnie that his great-aunt was our third casualty, or that we were no closer to solving the case than when the first murder was committed.

"I'll ask again, Arnie, was your great-aunt, Estelle Lewis Podarge Gardner, a foster parent?"

The regret in his voice was obvious. "Yes, she was. I'm ashamed to admit that she was mean to the kids."

Dad asked, "How so?"

"She'd make lavish meals, like fried chicken and mashed potatoes, or shrimp scampi, with chocolate cake or banana pudding for dessert, and then she'd sit in front of the kids gorging her fat face while the kids barely had enough potatoes or bread or meat in bowls of watered-down broth. If any of them complained, she'd whip them soundly and send them to bed. Sometimes she tied them to the bed to keep them from sneaking downstairs to the kitchen after she retired for the night."

Dad's voice quivered with outrage. "Arnie, this is important, so think before you answer. Do you remember a foster kid named Bonny Cowen?"

Arnie answered immediately. "Yes, sir."

"You're sure?"

"Yes, sir. I mean we weren't friends or anything like that. The other kids, especially the older boys, made fun of him because he had a girl's name, and…and, he was kinda, you know, pretty, and slight built, and…and…he had a nasty scar on his face. It was all wrinkled and ugly from where he'd been burned when he was a little kid… Oh! My! God!"

There was a loud crash. Dad said, "Andy, what happened?"

"He fainted, Henry. He turned white as a sheet, his eyes rolled back in his head, and he fell out of the chair in a dead faint. What's going on? Did I miss something?"

I clasped my hands to my chest. "I don't know when or how Bonny Cowen arrived in Enigma without any of us spotting him, but without saying it, Arnie has just confirmed that Cowen is very possibly the killer."

Dad said, "Andy, secure the house and douse the lights. Don't answer the door, and hang tight until I get there. We need to get Arnie to the jail for his own safety."

Dad pulled on his boots. He unlocked the gun drawer and strapped the Glock around his waist. I helped him heft into his heavy jacket. He said, "Stay here, Tullah. I'll meet you at Patty's in the morning."

He reached for the door knob. I said, "Dad, it's definitely Bonny Cowen. That's what the note meant when it said, 'I know you know.' He knew Arnie would recognize him. I'm wondering how he knew Arnie's aunt was in Enigma."

Dad gave me a brief hug. "We'll figure it out." He pointed to the knob. "Lock it, and don't open it unless I let you know it's me."

"Okay, Dad. I'll meet you in the morning at seven."
And then he was gone.

I snuggled under a quilt my mother had made, one of Dad's treasures. By the time I fell asleep, I'd come to the conclusion that I was wrong about Anne Brom. All evidence pointed to Bonny Cowen as Enigma's monster in the dark.

It was uncanny—and terrifying. I stood in front of a mirror. The girl—the same girl as in my first dream— stared back at me. One side of her face was flawless white porcelain with a slight blush to her cheeks, and then she shifted, causing me to shrink back—the other side had a horrific grin, with the flesh melting from her face. Her hands pressed against the mirror and her eyes pleaded with me as she mouthed, Help me!

I fought against the hands that shook my shoulders. I remembered yelling, "Who are you? Tell me your name!"

"Punkin, wake up…it's Dad. You're safe."

I sat up. My heart thrummed against my chest. Dad's voice cut through the vestiges of my dream. I reached out and grabbed his hand and clung to it. I had no idea what had frightened me. The dream. Something about the dream.

Dad sat on the bed and cradled me in his arms much the way he'd done when I was a child and thought a boogie man was hiding under my bed. His voice soothed me. "You were yelling, 'Tell me your name.' "

He released me, but I still clutched his hand. Silly me, almost thirty years old, and acting like a frightened mouse over a nightmare. I managed a smile. "I'm okay, Dad, really."

"Tell me about the dream."

I closed my eyes and allowed myself to drift, mentally summoning the vision of the young woman. My voice sounded distant and monotonic as I recounted both times the girl had visited me, each time asking for help.

"Dad, as preposterous as it sounds, I'm certain the girl is—" I was almost afraid to say her name.

"Who, Punkin?"

"Anne Brom."

He was quiet as if waiting for me to explain. "Dad, I know we have differing opinions about the killer."

He simply nodded.

I continued. "Remember when I told you that in Gaelic 'Brom' means 'raven'?"

Again, he nodded.

I pointed to my head and my heart. "Don't ask me how I know, but everything within me knows Anne Brom is the *real* monster in the dark. I've only seen her twice, but there's something sinister in her eyes. I also believe she's the one who sent the note to Arnie."

"If this is as you say, then why would she kill the raven and give it to Arnie?"

I gave the universal shrug for, "I don't know," but then launched into my theory. "I've given this a lot of thought. Think back to the day we found the horseman's missing head inside the embalming room; the day the raven was tapping at the window. In my mind's eye, I vaguely remember seeing a fluff of white. With the excitement of the moment, I dismissed it, thinking only of the raven's white cape."

I looked directly at Dad. "I'm now certain what I saw wasn't the band of white around the raven's neck. Rather, it was a wisp of snowy hair. Anne Brom has hair the color of pure white snow." I drew a breath and forged on. "At the Halloween dance, and just prior to the stallion rushing inside the barn, out of the corner of my eye I saw a person dressed as Little Red Riding Hood—and a fluff of white stood stark against the red hood. Her hands were clenched into fists, and she appeared angry. I'd forgotten about her until now."

Dad and I stared at one another. He said, "And in their statements, Hailey Becker and Mark DeLong said they thought they saw Little Red Riding Hood right after the wolfman was killed."

"Yes, they did. All we need to do is find Little Red Riding Hood's costume, and my guess is Anne Brom and Little Red Riding Hood are one and the same."

"Indulge me, Punkin. Why would Anne Brom write a threatening note, break the raven's neck, wrap it in a gift box, and send it to Arnie? What's the connection?"

I spread my hands, and shook my head. "That's the piece of the puzzle I can't seem to put together."

The thing I love most about my dad is that he's never judgmental about my empathic senses. He said, "Then we'll figure it out together." He motioned for me to get a move on. "It's breaking dawn. Patty's probably at the café whipping up pancake batter. We've both got a long day ahead of us." Before he left the room, he patted my shoulder and winked.

I swung my feet to floor. "Did Bonny Cowen show up last night?"

He said, "Nope. I'm beginning to feel like we're chasing ghosts."

"Did you tell Arnie about his aunt being the third victim?"

"I did, and he's an emotional mess. He fears he's the

next victim. He's assuming the killer, possibly Cowen, blames him for his aunt's sadistic treatment of the kids in her care."

"Well, I hope Arnie has the strength to get through this," I said.

He agreed. "Arnie said he'll claim his aunt's body today and have it sent to the funeral home. As a matter of precaution, I'll have Andy accompany him."

Chapter Thirty-Four

While Dad and I were enjoying our stacks of blueberry pancakes, the puzzle I had earlier mentioned took visual shape when Aaron and Ansley Ordwin strolled into the café. Ansley was the mirror image of her twin brother. In fact, I remember when Ansley would come to class dressed as Aaron to fool the teacher. We kids thought it was a great joke. The teacher, not so much.

Remembering the words *twin* and *survivor*, I didn't know which was worse, nearly choking on my coffee or surviving Dad's pummeling on my back to keep me from choking. I managed to gasp, "Dad, stop! I'm okay."

I waited a few minutes to catch my breath and to pull my thoughts together before speaking. "Dad, what if— what if—Bonny Cowen's twin didn't die in the fire?"

He arched an eyebrow. "What are you implying?"

"I know it sounds preposterous, and we won't know until Grandmother is able to get a copy of the newspaper report about the fire…" I stabbed another piece of pancake. "What if, somehow, his twin survived, and he never knew? I'm not sure how she fits into the scheme of murders, but I can't get it out of my mind that the girl in my dream is Bonny's twin, and possibly the killer."

His hand went up. "Whoa," he said. "Let's slow down here."

Not to be deterred, I almost pleaded, "Dad, let's at

least find out the name of Bonny's twin. What will it hurt?"

There was a long pause.

"All we have now is circumstantial evidence." He shot me one of his looks. "Okay, you win. We'll wait to see if Tanti comes up with the news article."

To change the subject, I said, "When are you going to hire another deputy?"

"Today. Tiny and I have narrowed it down to two candidates."

"Anyone I know?"

"Probably not. The rookie is a Kentuckian from Mayfield, and the veteran is from Chicago."

"Which are you leaning toward?"

"Not sure. The rookie is twenty-three, just out of the academy, and easily trained to our way of handling things, but also capable of making too many novice mistakes in a crisis situation, and after a while, he might find life in Enigma dull. On the other hand, the veteran is forty-three, knows about gangs, druggies, prostitution. He's been shot, knifed, beaten up. He has a wife and three children. He'd like to be around to see them grow up. I can't say that I blame him."

I licked syrup from my lips. "Without saying it, I think you've already made your decision.

Dad folded and refolded his napkin. "I guess a little birdie told you?"

"No, sir. You just did."

He furrowed his brow. "Me—how?"

I reached over and touched his hand. "Your eyes and the inflection in your voice. You were thinking of me—and Mother—when you were describing him."

He enfolded my hand and lifted it to his lips.

"Someday, we'll find out who killed her."

Patty came over to refill our mugs. I asked for a large to-go cup. My phone was ringing by the time Dad walked me to my truck.

It was Jeff, my student assistant. "Dr. Holliday, I came early to open up. I hope it's okay, because there's a lady here with a St. Bernard. It's bleeding from the nose, and I don't know what to do."

"I'm glad you're there, Jeff. Tell the lady I'm on my way. And, Jeff, don't try to move the dog. If it's in pain, it might bite you."

I kissed Dad on the cheek, and said, "As soon as I hear from Grandmother about the twin, I'll call you." I climbed inside and engaged the truck's ignition. "Catch ya later, Dad."

He waved and gave me his usual caution. "Don't speed."

As I drove, I mentally reviewed the investigative report and patient intake report. I knew the chances of Bonny's twin surviving the fire was a longshot. I focused on information from the final analysis of the intake report. The words that stuck out were: hallucinations, sociopath, schizophrenic tendencies, embalmer, and cosmetologist.

I actually didn't remember turning into my drive, but I'd arrived at my clinic in what seemed no time at all. Dad would have my hide if he knew I'd been speeding. By the time I shut off the engine, I'd convinced myself that I was completely off-base about the existence of a twin sibling. All evidence confirmed that Bonny Cowen was our prime suspect.

Jeff stood next to the client's SUV, huddled against the cold. When I instructed him to go inside and bring me a gurney, he didn't hesitate.

The dog's owner and I exchanged introductions, and I said, "What's the dog's name?"

I almost laughed out loud when Mrs. Miller said, "Tiny." Just like Deputy Tiny Goodbody, the name was an oxymoron.

As a precaution, I gently placed a muzzle on the dog. I pushed the gurney to the examination room, accompanied by Mrs. Miller's explanation that she lived in Dixie County but Dr. Redfern was overscheduled and had suggested she contact me. Rather than calling for an appointment, Mrs. Miller had decided that, in the best interest of her beloved pet, she'd arrive at my clinic before opening hours, and she understood there might be an extra charge.

Once I had the St. Bernard inside the examination room, I instructed Jeff to have Mrs. Miller fill out the patient forms and offer her a cup of coffee. I assured her I'd do my best for the dog. After administering a mild sedative, I cleansed the nostrils. An examination showed a large nodule inside the nose. With a signed consent, I prepped the animal and performed a complete excision. After the surgery, I explained to Mrs. Miller that "Tiny" suffered from nasal adenocarcinoma and she should immediately follow up with Dr. Redfern about radiation therapy. My next patient was a Congo Grey parrot with a severe case of bird mites.

The morning flew past. At noon, Jeff opened the door to the examination room to let me know it was time for him to return to school, and that he would see me on Friday. And so it went with kittens, cats, and dogs of every size, shape, and temperament, a Shetland pony, and a yellow boa constrictor. Was I missing Ella?

Absolutely! By the time the day was over, I was ready for a bath and planned to spend the rest of the evening in my recliner with a bag of chocolate chip cookies, a large cup of hot chocolate, and my newest mystery novel.

I had barely settled down when my phone chirped and showed me Grandmother's picture.

"Hello, Grandmother."

We spent a few moments chit-chatting and discussing whether I was willing to host Thanksgiving dinner. She said, "With the volume of business at the Whitehorse, Charlie's afraid if people see cars parked in front of the saloon they'll start banging on the doors for him to open." She pfft'd. "People these days have no respect." With a deep sigh, she added, "Check your email. I've attached a copy of the news article you wanted, and I sent a copy to Henry. This one is a legible copy. I hope it helps with the case."

I thanked her. Before disconnecting, she held me to the fire for an answer to her request. "Grandmother, you know my culinary skills are limited to heating up frozen dinners, with a possibility of making grilled cheese sandwiches and scrambled eggs."

Exasperation filled her voice. "Tullah, not even you can mess up a bowl of mashed potatoes. Patty will bake a sweet potato pie and a pecan pie, I'll do the cornbread dressing with gravy, and Charlie will cook the turkey and a ham. And Dr. Ritter, God bless him, will bring that disgusting canned cranberry sauce. Plan to make enough potatoes for ten."

I thought that if anyone suffered from a bad case of indigestion, at least they wouldn't be able to blame me. I reluctantly agreed. "Okay, I'll try not to make gloppy mashed potatoes."

I had one more thing to do before I called it quits for the night. I wanted to read the news article about the house fire. Perhaps I'd learn that Bonny Cowen was the villain in the story. I wanted all the facts at my fingertips the next time I met with my dad.

The article from the Starke County *Gazette* proved to be a so-so gift. I skipped over all the unnecessary words to get to the meat of the piece. It read:

"At approximately three in the morning, a paper carrier reported the fire. By the time the fire department arrived the house was engulfed in flames. The fire marshal stated in his report that the fire appeared to have been the result of a candle igniting a bedroom curtain. The sole survivor, a male child, approximately age five years old, wearing pajamas and clutching a book of Mother Goose nursery rhymes, was found standing in the front yard watching the flames. He suffered severe burns on the left side of his face and fingertips of both hands. Those perishing in the fire were the child's parents, Ian and Kathleen Cowen, and a twin sister. The surviving child was transported to the burn center and was unable to be questioned. His name was withheld pending notification of the next of kin."

From the grainy black-and-white photo, there was nothing left of the house except charred timbers. I wondered how the little boy had managed to save himself. Although the article filled in several gaps, it also left me with more questions than answers, like did the little boy accidently start the fire, and if so, why didn't he alert his parents, or instead of grabbing a book of nursery rhymes, why didn't he try to save his twin sister? Unfortunately, the article lacked an important piece of information—the twin sister's name.

River's wet nose startled me. He woofed. I patted his head. "Okay, I know it's past your bedtime." I stood and stretched the kinks from my tired body. River and Rascal followed me upstairs to the bedroom.

After my nightly toilette routine, I snuggled under the covers and prayed for a night's sleep without nightmares. Tomorrow was another appointment-filled day.

Chapter Thirty-Five

Being understaffed is grueling. My average of patients per day is between forty and sixty. Today, due to an emergency barn call, I had to rearrange appointments for ten patients, close the office, and hang out a sign stating to call my answering service to reschedule appointments, or to contact Dr. Redfern in Dixie County if it was an emergency.

I never refuse barn calls, especially if it's a mare or a heifer experiencing birthing difficulties, or if an animal is too badly injured to transport to the clinic. In today's case, I delivered a set of twin calves. The heifer's labor was long and difficult. Unfortunately, the heifer rejected the weakest twin. However, I brought the tiny calf home and put it with Roxie, my favorite Jersey milk cow. She took to the orphan right away and earned an extra pail of sweet feed.

My refrigerator was empty, and I was tired of peanut butter sandwiches. As much as I despise grocery shopping, it was time to make a trip to town. I phoned Dad and asked if he'd had supper. At his answer, I offered to stop by the Whitehorse and pick up enough BBQ sandwiches for all of us.

Dad said, "Good luck. He's out of pulled pork and ribs. He's also understaffed, and as irritable as a sore-tailed cat. I'll call the Crispy Chicken and have them deliver to the office."

After going through the refrigerator and pantry, I finished writing my grocery list. I double-filled River and Rascal's bowls with food and water. With November's unpredictable weather, I'd decided to err on the side of caution in case I needed to spend the night with Dad or Grandmother.

I resisted grinding my teeth when my phone indicated my answering service was calling. It was already after six o'clock. I kept my voice pleasant. "What's up, Julie?"

"I know it's after office hours, Tullah, sorry. A Mr. Dillard called. He was practicing casting with his new rod and reel and accidently hooked his dog in the ear. He wants to know if he can bring the dog to the office tonight."

I explained that I wasn't at the clinic, and asked for directions to Mr. Dillard's home. Conveniently, it was only five minutes out of my way. "Tell him I'm on my way to town." I checked the dashboard clock. "And I'll be there in a few minutes."

I arrived at the client's home, where I administered a mild anesthetic to calm the whimpering beagle. It took less than a minute to use a pair of snips to cut off the end of the barb and slide the rest through the dog's floppy ear, leaving a nearly invisible hole, which I dabbed with antiseptic cream.

I left the house, and as I pulled onto the main highway, a terrible surge of panic filled me. A thick dark cloud moved across the remaining bit of sun. To make it worse, the wind kicked up with the acrid smell of smoke. Part of me expected to see the raven land on the hood of my moving truck to issue its *"Nevermore"* warning. But the bird was dead. Hunger forgotten, I pressed the accelerator.

At the edge of town, black roiling smoke lined the horizon of an already pitch-black sky. Ahead, I spotted red rotating lights from emergency vehicles. My heartbeat ratcheted up a notch as I recalled the fire that had destroyed city hall and nearly took the life of my grandmother and Patty Sweet. Not caring about the speed limit, I pressed the gas pedal, and as I neared town, ashes peppered my truck's windshield.

A barricade blocked vehicles from entering the south end of town. I parked on the side of the road and, mindless of the cold, raced toward where orange tongues of fire reached up to lick the sky. Relief washed over me when I spotted my dad, Tiny, and Andy working to keep gawkers from getting too close to the fire. Arnie Lewis stood next to Mr. Peebles.

A loud explosion erupted. Glass and other debris spewed from the building's windows. Smoke and more debris spiraled into the air from a second explosion. Spectators ran for cover trying to avoid assault by bricks, boards, and shards of glass.

Mr. Peebles let out a squelchy sound. His knees buckled. Arnie put his arm around the elderly man's waist to keep him from collapsing. I rushed forward to help get the old man out of harm's way.

Mr. Peebles sobbed. "It's gone! All these years of being under that miser's stingy thumb, and finally when I'd earned my due, it's gone." He wailed louder, raising his fist in the air as he cried, "All gone!"

I'm not sure why I searched the crowd. Perhaps part of me was hoping to spot Little Red Riding Hood, or possibly Bonny Cowen. No such luck.

The crowd's voices had lessened to a low hum. Only

the drone of the fire engine, and Uncle Charlie barking orders to the fire crew and telling a reporter to get the hell out of his face, broke the silence. Now was not the time for me to bother him with questions.

I walked to where Arnie and Mr. Peebles sat and joined them on the sidewalk's curb. "Arnie," I asked, "Do you have any idea how or why the fire started?"

Before he could answer, someone came over and draped a blanket around Mr. Peebles' shaking shoulders and offered Arnie and me cups of coffee. Bless her heart, it was Patty and her crew of waitresses. Patty's face was a picture of fright, and I knew she was recalling her own narrow escape a year ago. She said to Arnie, "There's nothing you can do here. Why don't the three of you come to the café where it's warm?"

I assisted Arnie in helping Mr. Peebles to his feet. Somehow the eighty-year-old man suddenly looked older and frailer than a few days ago. After Arnie had assured me he didn't need help with the old man, I elbowed my way through the crowd to find my dad. With a large thermos and a sack of disposable cups in hand, Patty followed me.

"Patty, where's Grandmother?"

"Don't worry. She's at the café helping customers. Tullah, do you think the fire was accidental? The building was old, you know."

"I hesitate to speculate, Patty. We'll know when the fire marshal releases his report."

She nodded her understanding. As we approached the line Dad and his deputies were manning, Dad shouted through a bullhorn, "Go home, folks. Show's over. The fire's out, and there's nothing more to see."

Tiny took the bullhorn from Dad and added, "If

anyone is caught scavenging, you will be arrested. Do like Sheriff Holliday says and go home."

I'm not sure why I turned to look over my shoulder. Instinct? Or maybe it was my empathic spirit whispering to my psyche? The pale wash of her skin was red from standing close to the fire's heat. The first time we'd met, her feral eyes had clashed with mine.

Before Anne Brom whipped away, I read something altogether different in her eyes—distress, fear, anxiety. What had brought about this change from her earlier cold haughtiness?

Dad nudged me. "She's a cool one. You still think it's her?"

"I can't make up my mind." I shrugged. "In my opinion, she's a freaking ego with legs. My every instinct tells me she is narcissistic and mean-spirited."

He finished the remainder of his coffee. "I suspect you're right."

"Dad, don't you think the timing of the fire is a bit suspicious?"

"I'd thought that before you said it." His smile gave his face a completely different look. I sensed his weariness and frustration. "If we don't nail the monster in the dark soon, I'll need to call in the KFBI."

Dad was protective of his territory, and to him, calling in the Kentucky Federal Bureau of Investigation would be a sign of failure to do his job. "Don't worry, Dad. I have a feeling…trust me."

He flashed me a "yeah, right" smile and walked to where Uncle Charlie was talking with the fire marshal.

****

Sweet's 'n' Eats was packed with patrons. The overall buzz was speculation about how the fire had started. Some said the building was old and in dire need of new electrical work, while others hinted at arson.

I joined Arnie and Mr. Peebles and asked their opinions. Mr. Peebles said, "Those tongue-wagging fools don't know the money Arnold and I spent bringing the funeral parlor into the twenty-first century. It cost a fortune, and now it's all rubble and ashes." He cast a glare at Arnie. "Your grandfather would be highly incensed that you brought Estelle's remains to our place."

Arnie toyed with the food on his plate. His shoulders slumped. "We're the only parlor in town. Where else was I to take her?" Then, as an afterthought, and completely out of character for meek and mild Arnie, he added, "At least she got a free cremation."

He lifted puffy eyes to mine. "It was terrible what the murderer did to her. I didn't have the heart to ask Anne to fix Aunt Estelle's face." He shuddered. "Gross."

Out of the blue, I asked, "Arnie, where does Anne live?"

"I don't know, Tullah. The address was in her employment file, and now that's all gone. I'm sure Mary at the beauty shop has it, or you could ask Anne."

After leaving the café, I wended my way up and down the grocery aisles. On my drive home, I thought about Anne Brom. I was certain she had silently asked me for help. Considering my first unfriendly encounters with her, perhaps I was wrong.

On the drive home, the moon slipped behind the clouds and left me in darkness both literally and mentally.

Chapter Thirty-Six

Saturday arrived sunny and cold. After a brisk early morning ride on Gandalf, I unsaddled him, gave him a good brushing, and placed a warming blanket over his back. I raced to the house to shower and dress. Breakfast with Grandmother and Dad was always a treat.

I drove past the funeral home's charred ruins and farther down the street spotted Dad's 4Runner parked in front of his office. I parked next to an Enigma County deputy's car. At this time of the morning, the town was peaceful and serene.

Dad had agreed to meet me at Sweet's 'n' Eats. Disconcertingly, the moment I stepped out of my truck and onto the sidewalk, an overwhelming sadness struck me. I tried to shake it off. A little voice inside my head urged me to go inside the sheriff's office. As much as I wanted to ignore the feeling, I sensed my empathic instinct was speaking to me.

Once inside, Dad's new secretary looked up from a stack of paperwork. Janice said, "Terrible about the fire."

We chatted about the incident for a moment. "Is my dad busy?"

She nodded and thumbed toward the closed door. Through the soundproofed glass panes, I spotted him sitting at his desk with a man seated across from him. "Who's that, Janice?"

"Wayne Ramsey, the interviewee from Chicago."

The door opened and Dad motioned me in. He smiled. "Wayne Ramsey, I'd like you to meet my daughter. This is Dr. Tullah Holliday, veterinarian extraordinaire. Tullah, Officer Ramsey is our newest deputy."

I extended my hand. "Welcome to Enigma. It's a far cry from the big city."

"Yes, indeed, and a lot safer than the mean streets of Chicago." His grin deepened. "I promised my daughter a pony for her upcoming birthday. I hope you don't mind helping me with a selection. I'm absolutely clueless when it comes to horses. Oh, and you'd better add a dog to your list, too, because my son has been begging for a puppy."

Dad said, "Don't worry. Tullah is not only a great vet, she's an expert when it comes to all animals, especially dogs and horses."

I tried not to pay any attention to the compliments. A few more minutes of minor conversation and the newest deputy excused himself, saying it was a long drive to Lexington airport. Apparently, he thought I needed an explanation, because he volunteered that he was flying home to help his wife pack and get ready for the long drive from Illinois to Kentucky.

I wished him a safe trip and added, "When you get settled and ready to pet shop, give me a call."

We watched him depart. I was about to ask Dad if he was ready for breakfast when the dark part of my brain sent warning signals, forcing me to turn.

Anne Brom stood outside the glass entrance doors. I could almost read the thoughts on her face. She looked at me with wide blue eyes, and I motioned for her to come inside.

Dad stood next to me. "She looks like death warmed over. What are your thoughts, Tullah?"

The paleness of her skin, and the sad, sad sacs under her eyes reflected—guilt? Perhaps. "My instinct is telling me she's emotionally walking on fire."

I brushed away images of the headless body, a split skull, and the bloody mess hordes of rats had made of Estelle Gardner's face. Somehow, this girl was right in the middle of the three murders.

Anne stepped inside. She stood scrutinizing us, and she made no attempt to hide the fact that she was assessing us.

Dad said, "Miss Brom, can I help you?"

She walked to Dad's office as if assuming we would follow. And we did. Dad extended his hand toward a chair. At first, she declined, then changed her mind. I pulled a second chair to the corner of his new office. I needed to observe Anne's facial and bodily expressions.

She cut me a sour look, and said, "I know you're skeptical of my reasons for being here. Just keep your negative thoughts to yourself, please."

Score one for her. I *was* skeptical. Reading body language didn't take psychic ability. For at least three minutes, we sat in silence. She then reached inside her jacket pocket and withdrew a white sheet of folded paper.

"My brother has threatened to kill me." She made the statement matter-of-factly, no hint of panic.

Dad said, "Who is your brother, and what makes you think he wants to kill you?"

She handed the paper to Dad. He skimmed it, then looked at me. "It's a poem. What has this got to do with a threat to your life?"

In a soft voice, Anne said, "Read it, please."

I took the poem. And, like Dad, skimmed it. I leveled my gaze at Anne, then read aloud:

"Ladybird, ladybird,

Fly away home,

Your house is on fire

And your children all gone;

All except one

And that's little Ann,

And she has crept under

The warming pan.

"It's a Mother Goose nursery rhyme. I don't understand why you perceive this as a threat."

She looked at me; her voice laced with sarcasm. "Of course you wouldn't." She pointed toward the paper I held. "It was taped to my bathroom mirror when I got up this morning. I'm telling you, it's from my brother. You must believe me." Her voice had shifted from contempt to fear. "I don't know how he found me."

I sat back in my chair. "I'll ask again—what is your brother's name, and why do you think he wants to harm you?"

Her former animosity seemed to have faded. A gust of wind rattled the windows, and I felt a sudden chill slither down my spine when Anne said, "His name is Bonny Cowen, and when I was little, he set the house on fire. He'd locked the bedroom window and had placed a chair under the doorknob on the hallway side."

By this time, Anne was trembling. She wrung her hands together. "I was banging on the door and crying, "Bonny…Bonny…let me out. Please…please let me out."

She blinked away tears. "He didn't."

As I stared deeply into her eyes, I detected a shadow, a small hint of sinister darkness. I said, "Why is your last name—Brom?"

"It was my mother's other married name. I took it to keep Bonny from finding me."

My thoughts didn't make sense. Anne Brom was sitting in front of me. Her face was a cosmetologist's dream. There was no hint of skin grafts that would result in a puckering scar. And yet, like a misty fog, an aura of death surrounded her. But how was she behind these sick atrocities?

"Anne…" I hesitated, and struggled to formulate my jumbled thoughts. "The newspaper article said Bonny's twin sister died in the fire. Her body was found pressed against the bedroom door. Neither she nor your parents survived. Bonny was found outside the house. He was taken to a burn unit to treat his face and hands."

I mentally searched back for the words listed in the mental hospital's intake report. Was it possible that Anne was really Bonny? The report did state that Bonny presented with schizophrenic tendencies. Regretting that I hadn't paid more attention to the chapter about schizotypal personality in my psychology classes, I tried to think of a way to trigger an episode.

"Dad, do you have the photos that Deputy Goodbody took of Nathaniel Pilcher, Larry Parrish, and Estelle Gardner?"

He opened a desk drawer and withdrew a file folder. I opened the folder and carefully aligned the gruesome photographs in front of Anne. She leaned forward, and then, as if repulsed, jerked back. She glanced from me to my dad, her eyes dark and intense.

I knew I was venturing into dangerous territory.

Still, a little voice inside my head kept repeating—*It's her...It's her.* My breath hung in my throat when I asked, "Anne, are you Bonny Cowen, and did you kill these people?"

Dad looked aghast at the young woman sitting across from his desk. His expression told me I was treading on ground that could result in one helluva serious lawsuit. I mouthed, "Trust me."

Anne gasped and nearly screamed as she snatched the snow-white wig from her head and flung it at me. Fascinated, Dad and I watched as she clawed at her face, pulling hunks of rubberized flesh from hairline to chin and revealing hideous grafted skin.

Maniacal laughter erupted from her throat. I quickly stepped to the door and yelled, "Janice, call Dr. Sanders and Deputy Goodbody, stat!" And then I locked the door. Bonny Cowen was in full lunatic mode.

Like most sociopaths, Bonny gained quick control, and simply smiled, leaned back in the chair, and nonchalantly flicked a piece of rubber mask from his denims.

Taking this opportunity during his calm demeanor, Dad said, "Bonny, did you set fire to the funeral home?"

Bonny licked his lips, slightly. "Jack be nimble, Jack be quick, Jack jumped over the candlestick." He cooed, "Maybe yes... Maybe no."

I asked, "Why did you kill the raven?"

He huffed an impatient sigh. "Four-and-twenty blackbirds baked in a pie. Don't ask questions when you already know why."

Dad peppered him with another question: "How did you know Nathaniel Pilcher, Larry Parrish, and Estelle Gardner were in Enigma?"

Bonny snorted. "Stupid is as stupid does. I was kidnapped and held against my will." He tapped the side of his head. "I was too smart for them. One of my guards was named Pilcher. As soon as he told me his brother was Nathaniel and that he lived in this little Kentucky berg…well, you know the rest. I almost peed my bloomers when the headless horseman fell off the stallion. Great costume, don't you think?"

I asked, "Was that you dressed as Little Red Riding Hood?"

"Um, yes. I knew you'd seen me."

Nonchalantly, Bonny asked for a cup of coffee. Dad picked up the desk phone and punched the intercom button. "Janice, would you bring three cups of coffee."

Bonny stood and leaned over the desk. "Make mine with three sugars and lots of cream, Miss Janice dear."

While we waited, Dad said, "Okay, what about Parrish?"

"You know, dear sheriff, you are as dreary as the Sheriff of Nottingham." He heaved a sigh. "Where is Robin Hood when you need him?"

I had an urge to slap the smug smile off Cowen's face. "Cut the crap, Bonny, and answer the question."

He pointed a perfectly manicured fingernail at me. "Tullah…Tullah…you are no fun. But to answer your silly questions…"

There was malice in his voice. His eyes narrowed to mean slits. "Pilcher and Parrish were perverts. We played dress-up—Alice in Wonderland, Sleeping Beauty, Little Miss Muffet—and after the tea parties, they told me I had to pay them back by playing…ride the ponies." His lip twisted into a snarl. "Get my drift?"

It was a question that didn't need an answer. He

continued, "I ran away, and those horrid State people brought me back."

Bonny left his chair and stood propped against a wall. He didn't miss a beat. "Tullah, you're an intelligent woman. You tell me—what is the symbolism of 'The Legend of Sleepy Hollow' and 'Little Red Riding Hood'?" He cocked an eyebrow and stared at me.

"Briefly, not to trust strangers."

He snapped his fingers. "Exactly!"

His demeanor changed from guarded anger to relaxed. "I really hated splitting the wolf's head with an axe. It took me hours to apply all that fake hair." He guffawed. "It took hours of practice before I could hit the bull's-eye target. I didn't want to miss. Pilcher and Parrish got what they deserved."

Janice knocked on the door, and Bonny made a mad dash, except I was quicker. Dad rounded his desk and grabbed Bonny. The struggle didn't last long. Dad plopped Bonny into a chair, and said, "Try anything more and I'll put you in a cell."

I accepted the tray from Janice. She whispered, "I did as you said. They should be on their way."

I was almost afraid to trust Bonny with a hot cup of coffee. He fooled me by sitting in the chair and crossing his legs. Between sips, he sang—"My Bonny lies over the ocean…" In the middle of his third refrain, he suddenly stopped. "You haven't asked about dear old Estelle. Don't you want to know how I knew she was here?"

Dad and I sat quiet. Our silence seemed to unhinge Bonny. He slung the remains of his coffee in an arc, sending liquid across the room as he stood and yelled, "The fat bitch came to the beauty shop to get her hair and nails done every Thursday! Stupid fat cow, always stuffing her face in front of us kids…" He slammed his fist against a glass pane, breaking the skin. Blood peppered his knuckles. "Do you know what it's like to be so hungry your stomach feels like it's glued to your backbone, and you can't sleep at night, and the younger ones are crying because their little tummies hurt?"

Bonny tossed the chair across the office. Janice raced to the window. Dad waved her back. Bonny lunged at me. I held my hand up to motion Dad to stay. My heart beat against my chest. I had awakened the monster.

Chapter Thirty-Seven

Every muscle in my body froze. I'd worked with enough abused animals to know that showing fear only escalated their emotions. I also knew that sociopaths aren't motivated by love but by power. I needed to hold my ground and show Bonny that he had no power over me.

His saccharine-blue eyes darkened as he assessed me. Before I could jerk aside, he reached out and grabbed the pigtail that draped over my shoulder. I beckoned Dad to stand back.

Bonny used his thumb to fluff through the ends of my hair. As if nothing at all had happened, he smiled at me, and said, "Tullah, you really should do something about these split ends."

His own hair, white as the wig he'd ripped off, stood wildly on end as he suddenly moved unexpectedly. Dad couldn't react fast enough.

Bonny had pulled a long slender blade from his jacket pocket and, with lightning speed, raised his arm and flung the knife.

I screamed, "Dad!" as the blade found its mark in his sternum. I prayed it had missed his heart. Blood stained his shirt, and I watched as he wrapped his hands around the knife's hilt.

"No, Dad! Leave it!"

His face turned ashen as he wilted into his chair.

With a cruel, determined smile, Bonny stepped forward. His eyes burned with insanity. His face was taut with anticipation. "We all know what happened to the wicked Sheriff of Nottingham." He made a kiss sound. "He died."

"Cut the crap, Bonny. This is Enigma, Kentucky, not fantasy land." I knew if I made a wrong move Dad and I might both die. I, however, had the advantage. Out of the corner of my eye, I spotted Tiny and Dr. Sanders entering the reception area. I needed to keep Bonny's back to the glass pane. I just didn't give a damn about anything except ending this fiasco and getting my dad to the hospital.

"Bonny, don't give me any more crap about how abused and mistreated you were as a kid. Plenty of children have gone through much worse than you, and they haven't become sociopaths. You're insane. If it's the last thing I do, I'll see you locked away forever."

I could almost see the wheels whirring inside his brain. I goaded him further. "You are a sick bastard, a roach that needs to be squashed."

I watched the doorknob turn.

Bonny snarled and reached out to grab me.

Thwaaack!

Tiny slammed his huge fist against the back of Bonny's head. He staggered, fell forward, and crumpled against me. I shuddered in revulsion as Tiny hauled Bonny's body off me. Dr. Sanders immediately shoved up the sleeve of Bonny's jacket. She held the needle upward, thumped it, and then injected serum into his arm that would slow down his brain and calm his nervous system.

While she and I ministered to my dad, Tiny put in a

call to Bubba and Rita to get to the office with the ambulance, asap.

Chapter Thirty-Eight

A small cavalry of goosebumps marched up and down my arms as I bumped up the thermostat. It was perfect weather for a Thanksgiving bash. The pastures were coated with frost, and a tundra of white fluff occupied rows of fence posts.

Dad was home from the hospital. The mortality rate of stab wounds is about eighty-five percent. Due to the location of his wound, Dr. Sanders said, if he had removed the knife, he would have bled out in about five minutes. I thank my lucky stars she was there to stanch the bleeding until the ambulance arrived and for the short drive to the hospital.

Today was a special day to be thankful. A maniacal serial killer was behind bars, and my father was alive. I was determined to put the case aside and enjoy Thanksgiving with family and friends.

I had dressed in a new pair of black jeans and an elegant blue velour blouse. I rarely used the dining room for anything more than a substitute office. Today, the dining table gleamed with silver candles. I'd set out my mother's chinaware, linen napkins, and leaded crystal. I stood back to admire the table. Everything was perfect. I raised my glass of merlot and saluted the masterpiece I had created.

River and Rascal set up a fuss. I knew by River's wagging tail that company had landed. In a moment, the doorbell rang, and Dad, aided by Dr. Sanders on one side and Tiny on the other, walked in, behind him a parade of guests that included Ella, home for Thanksgiving break.

The women gathered around the kitchen table, and the men occupied themselves in front of the television, with conversations that ranged from sports to politics.

I was in the midst of whipping the butter-and-cream-saturated hot potatoes with my brand-new hand mixer. I had barely begun mixing when the electricity blipped off.

Uncle Charlie shouted, "I'll take care of it."

We heard his heavy footsteps on the stairs that led to the basement. While we waited, Ella continued to gush and admonish her mother and uncle for deceiving her about purchasing Old Man Pickett's property to give her as a graduation gift.

In moments, Uncle Charlie raced up the stairs, out of breath. He entered the kitchen and announced he'd had to flip the switch on the breaker box. "Everything working okay in here?"

Propped against the kitchen counter, I had been holding the mixer like a pistol, and as he spoke it shot mashed potato bullets all over the kitchen. Globs of spuds decorated Grandmother's hair and Patty's glasses, and a large splat landed in the middle of Uncle Charlie's forehead.

Frustrated, I couldn't figure out how to turn the darned thing off. Dr. Sanders rushed to my aid. Laughter erupted when Uncle Charlie swiped the dab of potato from his forehead and plopped it into his mouth. He grinned and said, "Yummy!"

Aided by Tiny and Andy, Dad hobbled to the kitchen. "What's all the commotion?"

Patty removed her glasses to clean them with a paper towel. She proclaimed, "Arrest this woman for assault with a deadly hand mixer!"

The expression on her face and her silly demand resulted in more raucous laughter. We had temporarily forgotten about the monster in the dark.

With the last touch of holiday meal rescued, we adjourned to the dining room. With Tiny's help, Dad pulled out a chair to seat Grandmother. And as was our custom, we clasped hands and went around the table sharing our reasons for being thankful.

As I glanced around, my gaze settling on my grandmother and my dad, the memory of my mother and other Thanksgivings was so real it nearly took my breath away.

Traditions can mimic the past, but they can't make it real. I hadn't realized it was my turn to speak, and everyone was looking at me.

I dropped hands with Tiny and Dr. Ritter, lifted my glass of wine, and said, "I'm thankful that all of you are an important part of my life."

I settled in my seat and simply enjoyed the friendly chatter, and the clatter of dishes being passed around the table.

Epilogue

Ironically, on Halloween Eve, exactly one year after the first murder, the sentencing hearing occurred. I sat between my dad and Tiny. Joining us was Grandmother, Dr. Sanders, and Deputy Andrew Kemble. I can truthfully say we all feared that, due to his mental instability, Bonny might receive a light sentence and possibly be released back into society.

The bailiff called, "All rise, Judge Eileen Landers, presiding."

Dressed in an orange jumpsuit, with shackles around his ankles and wrists and attached around his waist, our monster in the dark stood next to his defense attorney.

The judge said, "Bonny Brom Cowen, evidence supports that you are a sociopath with paranoid tendencies and show no remorse for the three murders in the state of Kentucky and the one murder in the state of Ohio. It is determined that you are a permanent danger to yourself and to society. I therefore sentence you to life in solitary confinement at Hill Crest Institute for the Criminally Insane."

Once the judge had passed sentence and motioned for the guards to remove him from the courtroom, Bonny lifted his head and emitted a guttural noise that was a cross between laughter and howling—a maniacal sound that raised the hairs on my arms.

He shouted, "That's right, Judge, I'm as mad as the

Hatter, and late for a very important date."

Bonny turned. Our eyes met. He winked and said, "Snip. Snap. Snout. This tale is all told out."

Dad had fully recovered from the knife wound. Although he insisted on driving us home, Tiny pulled rank on him and drove us to Sweet's 'n' Eats for a late afternoon lunch. I'd been filled with adrenaline in the courtroom, but now I felt as though a plug in my body had been pulled and every ounce of energy had drained from it.

I didn't want to talk to anyone. I really wanted to go home and have a large glass of red wine. Dad interrupted my thoughts. "Punkin, what nursery rhyme was Bonny quoting from when he said, 'Snip...snap...snout'?"

" 'Three Billy Goats Gruff.' It's where three goats need to outwit a voracious troll to cross over a bridge without being eaten. And the Troll meets a deadly end."

Uncle Charlie pulled a snifter from his pocket. "I think we all need a little snort of rum, no pun intended. Patty, bring on the glasses of cola. I'm buying."

Everyone around the table laughed. It was good to feel safe again.

Turn the page for an
excerpt from
the next exciting Doc
Holliday Mystery
by Loretta C. Rogers:

8 SECONDS
TO DIE!

Chapter One

There's nothing like springtime in Kentucky, and especially in Enigma. The landscape was alive with showy flowers, and the land in the front pasture rolled away with rich green grass. After a difficult winter, the near-fatal injury to my dad, and the trial that sent a psychotic killer to an asylum for the criminally insane, I sat, relaxed, in my front porch swing, enjoying a cup of hot chai tea.

I'm not generally given to nostalgia, especially those memories that involve my high school years. Most times, being half Cherokee and half Irish had caused me emotional grief, which often led to bullies meeting the happy end of my fist. I was fourteen when Dad became sheriff of Enigma. He taught me to solve my own problems and to never tattle, but he also reminded me I was his daughter and I could come to him, anytime. I tried hard never to hide behind the protection of his badge. Sometimes he had to remove his father's hat and be the lawman that he was—daughter or not.

Looking at a particular picture in my high school album resurrected a flood of hurtful memories. I closed the book, not wanting to revisit a particular not-so-funny practical joke.

My name is Dr. Tullah Crow Holliday, veterinarian. I live with a black Labrador Retriever named River and his sidekick, a gray teacup donkey named Rascal. My father, John Henry Holliday, is Sheriff of Enigma County. When he's serious, he calls me by my given name or "Dr. Holliday." However, most times he calls me—Punkin.

Although I am a veterinarian and lead a fairly sane life, I was born with the innate gift of being contacted by spirit animals that lead me to crimes that have happened or are about to happen. While I wouldn't wish this curse on anyone, it does help me assist my dad in solving difficult cases.

The closed Enigma County High School yearbook sat idle in my lap as I let my tea wash away thoughts of the past. I looked across the yard to where my friend and partner, Dr. Ella Sanders, resides in her newly constructed ranch house. Her yard is rife with azaleas. The sweet fragrance of purple wisteria drifts across the yard to tickle my nose. It's a great day to be alive.

River lifted his head from the porch step and woofed. He and Rascal scampered down the steps to meet the vehicle barreling down the driveway toward my house—Dad's 4Runner. Dad parked under the sprawling oak tree and hurried to the passenger door to assist my grandmother, Mayor Tanti Crow, to the ground.

My grin widened when I spotted the box from Sweet's 'n' Eats in her hands. I held the door wide and invited them into the kitchen. Grandmother set the coffeepot up in record time, while Dad looked pensive as he straddled a chair, opened the box, and helped himself to a lemon curd donut.

While the coffee brewed, I mulled my selection and settled for a Boston cream donut. Grandmother filled our mugs with aromatic hazelnut coffee, and we settled around the kitchen table. Dad spotted the album I had put on the table as we came in. He opened it and flipped through a few pages before settling on the page showcasing a few photos of Enigma High School's rodeo events.

I watched him sit back and square his shoulders, his finger marking a page. A deep dread settled over me as I looked into his craggy, tanned face. He was a very handsome man, especially when dressed in his tan uniform, with his badge pinned to the shirt pocket. My instinct said his visit was more than Sunday donuts with his daughter and mother-in-law.

I didn't need a sixth sense to tell me I didn't want to hear whatever it was he was about to spring on me, and I decided to beat him to the punch. "Dad, you're always telling me to relax, unwind, that stress is a killer. Whatever it is, the answer is no! I'm on vacation from crime."

"Yep," he spoke blithely, and smiled. "I didn't say a word."

Grandmother picked at the flakes on her glazed donut. Her gaze traveled between Dad and me. We sat in silence, savoring our sweet treats and coffee. Dad's finger still held a place between the pages.

"Okay, Dad, I give. Why are you finger-marking the page filled with shots of my high school rodeo blurbs and bloopers?"

He was thoughtful for a moment. "Does the name Caleb Calloway ring a bell?"

Righteous anger iced my heart as I grabbed the album and pointed to a picture of my gray mare standing in the middle of the football field. "If you mean the Caleb Calloway who painted black zebra stripes all over Venus's body and then hung 'that' sign around her neck…" By now my insides trembled. "Yes, I remember him. And if you also mean the Caleb Calloway who purposely buried a stone beneath the underside of her frog, causing a painful bruise that lamed her so badly she stumbled and fell—she was in so much pain she limped when I led her from the arena, costing us the barrel-racing championship—then, oh, yeah, I remember him."

My fury demanded another donut. This time, I chose a chocolate-covered glazed one and chomped into it.

Dad waited. He's all too familiar with the Irish side of my temper. To fuel my fire, Grandmother swiveled the album to look at a picture of my beautiful zebra-striped gray mare standing in the middle of the football field during half-time, with a large cardboard sign hanging around her neck. Emblazed in dripping red paint were the words "Squaw Horse."

Indignation filled her ebony eyes. "That was a sorry day. Especially when we found you tied up in the girl's locker room with your face painted and your long hair butchered."

She arched her eyebrows. "Those boys should have been horsewhipped."

The fact that the principal and the football coach had acted quickly to lead Venus off the field and Dad had sentenced Caleb and his buddies to several hours of mucking out stalls at the various horse farms didn't erase the humiliation I'd suffered for the remainder of our senior year.

The words I spoke didn't seem to come from my voice. "You're here because he's in trouble." Not tasting the sugary sweetness, I finished off the donut, and, shaking my head, said, "No, Dad. Just plain, no!"

His voice was gentle. "It was twelve years ago,

Punkin. You're a good detective. He needs your help." Dad glanced at his watch. "Tanti, if you're ready, I've got to get back to the office."

My head itched with anger as I walked them to the porch. Before climbing into his vehicle, Dad said, "I told Caleb to call you. Listen to him, Punkin. Think about his dilemma before refusing to help."

As an afterthought, he turned back and said, "You've always loved the rodeo."

I planted myself in the porch swing and used my feet to furiously push myself back and forth. Day was slipping into dusk. I thought about Dad's last words. I also wondered how bad Caleb's problem could be. After all, no spirit animals had appeared—no owl, raven, buzzards, or cardinals to warn of an impending death. I sat, thinking about…nothing.

The melodious chime of my cellphone interrupted my reverie. Without looking at the caller ID I knew it was Caleb Calloway calling. This was not going to be a fun conversation.

I didn't bother to hide the terseness in my voice. "What do you want, Caleb?"

"Ah, I see you've spoken to Henry."

"Sheriff Holliday, to you. Just because you're all grown up doesn't mean you can get all palsy-walsy with him."

"Sorry, Tullah. Really, I'm sorry."

"Just cut to the chase, Caleb. I'm busy."

Silence.

He whispered. "Maybe this was a bad idea."

The line went dead.

I experienced thirty seconds of regret. As if it had happened yesterday, I clearly saw my raggedy hair that had been hacked off in haste by Caleb, while three of his buddies held me down, and the zebra stripes painted on my gentle mare.

I walked inside to the kitchen and turned on the faucet to splash cold water over my face. A loud bellow and River's frantic barking drew my attention. I leaned against the sink for a better look. A Brahma bull was chasing my little donkey around the yard. I owned only black angus and some belted Galloways, better known as Oreo cows, so where did this guy come from? I grabbed my broom and raced outside to open a corral gate. To escape injury, Rascal dashed through the gate, followed by the bull, and I held the snorting bovine at bay until the little donkey had raced to safety, and by the skin of my teeth I escaped being hooked by the bull's horn. I recognized the broken triangle brand, and once inside the house, called the owner to come get his wayward bull.

My heart was still racing when my cellphone pinged. I didn't recognize the number. My finger hovered over the answer key. "Okay, okay," I said aloud. "The bull must be the omen."

"Dr. Tullah Holliday, how may I help you?"

"Tullah, please don't hang up. It's Caroline Tupper. I hope you remember me. We were on the cheerleading squad together." She hastened on. "I'm Mrs. Calloway now. Please, Tullah, Caleb is in big trouble. What he did in high school was stupid and wrong, but please…"

I relented. The pleading in her voice sounded genuine. "What kind of trouble, Caroline?"

"Caleb is outside with our son and daughter. They're nine and six years old and the delight of our lives." I heard her draw a breath, and waited. "Tullah, Caleb and I own Triple C Ranch in Oklahoma. We breed some of the finest bucking bulls in the nation."

I had stopped following rodeo news years ago and had not heard of or thought about Caleb or Caroline in years. "Why do you need my help?"

Her voice dropped to a whisper. From the hush, I knew she had placed her hand over the phone's mouthpiece, and I wondered who it was she didn't want hearing our conversation. She said, "Someone is juicing up our bulls, making them extra mean. Two top riders have been seriously injured."

"Caroline, call your local vet to do a serum sample, then trace it to the source."

"No, you don't understand. We can't trust anyone. Last night, someone poisoned the children's pet goat. Caleb called the sheriff, who said he'd investigate. Here's the thing—he's been known to consort with a few shady characters."

"Caroline, I live in Kentucky. There's nothing I can do from here."

"Hold on, Tullah, Caleb wants to speak to you. Don't hang up, please...please."

"Tullah," Caleb's voice held the same note of fright that had filled his wife's. "We have a rodeo in Austin, Texas, in May. From there it's on to the Cheyenne Frontier Days in Wyoming. I know it's unreasonable to ask you to work under cover. I've followed you and Henry...uhmm...Sheriff Holliday in the news and know you're a good detective. I'm not a man to beg, Tullah, but whoever killed my kid's pet goat and cut off its head is sending a serious warning. Understand?"

I did. All abused or suffering creatures, big or small, human or animal, always touch my heart. I heaved a deep sigh. This was a dilemma. "Caleb, I have a busy career.

I can't just walk off and leave my clinic for goodness knows how long. Plus the moment anyone saw me with my medical bag would know I'm a veterinarian and the reason I'm examining your bulls."

"You could go under cover. You were once an accomplished barrel racer, Tullah. In fact, you would've won the championship, if I hadn't…" His voice trailed off. "We were stupid teenage football jocks and full of ourselves. No amount of apologizing can excuse the hurt we caused you."

He continued, "I'll supply the horses, the equipment, whatever you need. I'll even pay your airfare, hotel expenses, entry fees, and make sure you get on the competitor's docket. I'm a wealthy man. If it's money that's holding you up, then name your price."

Outside my kitchen window, I spotted the Brahma bull trying to climb over the corral fence. Brahmas are mean and dangerous by nature. I envisioned a rider being gored to death by a bull that had been injected with a serum to drive it mad.

"Caleb, I'll need to make arrangements with my business partner to see if she can handle the extra workload. I'll also bone up on rodeo protocol, and I'll even try to fit a little barrel practice in. Tell me when to meet you in Austin. I don't think coming to your ranch is a good idea."

"I'm beholden to you, Tullah. What name should I register you under—not Holliday?"

To honor my mother and to have her spirit with me on this dangerous journey, I said, "Josie Waya Crow."

A word about the author…

When not writing, Loretta enjoys traveling and working crossword puzzles. She likes hearing from readers. Posting a review of her books is greatly appreciated.

Visit her at:

https://amzn.to/2GBb0iI

Thank you for purchasing
this publication of The Wild Rose Press, Inc.

For questions or more information
contact us at
info@thewildrosepress.com.

The Wild Rose Press, Inc.